A Sister's Power

NO LONGER PROPERTY OF
ANYTHINK LIBRARIES/
RANGEVIEW LIBRARY DISTRICT

Also by Cydney Rax

A Sister's Secret
A Sister's Survival

The Love & Revenge Series
If Your Wife Only Knew
My Married Boyfriend
Revenge of the Mistress
My Daughter's Boyfriend
My Husband's Girlfriend
Scandalous Betrayal
My Sister's Ex
Brothers & Wives

Reckless (with Niobia Bryant and Grace Octavia)
Crush (with Michele Grant and Lutishia Lovely)

Published by Dafina Books

A Sister's Power

CYDNEY RAX

KENSINGTON PUBLISHING CORP.
www.kensingtonbooks.com

DAFINA BOOKS are published by

Kensington Publishing Corp.
119 West 40th Street
New York, NY 10018

All Kensington titles, imprints, and distributed lines are available at special quantity discounts for bulk purchases for sales promotion, premiums, fund-raising, and educational or institutional use.

Special book excerpts or customized printings can also be created to fit specific needs. For details, write or phone the office of the Kensington Sales Manager: Kensington Publishing Corp., 119 West 40th Street, New York, NY 10018. Attn. Sales Department. Phone: 1-800-221-2647.

ISBN-13: 978-1-4967-1541-8
ISBN-10: 1-4967-1541-1
First Kensington Trade Paperback Printing: November 2019

ISBN-13: 978-1-4967-1547-0 (ebook)
ISBN-10: 1-4967-1547-0 (ebook)
First Kensington Electronic Edition: November 2019

10 9 8 7 6 5 4 3 2 1

Printed in the United States of America

This novel is dedicated to the memory of a ten-year-old
Michigan girl named London Eisenbeis.
She died and was laid to rest on March 3, 2018—
the same day she was expected to attend a
daddy-daughter dance.
Rest in peace baby girl.

"A woman is like a tea bag—you never know how strong she is until she gets in hot water."

—Eleanor Roosevelt

"Nothing external to you has any power over you."

—Ralph Waldo Emerson

Chapter 1

My Sister's Husband

The Reeves family was still mourning the loss of Nathaniel Taylor. Six weeks ago, he was found unconscious in a bedroom of his house. Coco was one of the last people to see him alive. When he first died, the police conducted a probe to determine what happened. Coco voluntarily gave the police a brief statement, however, the results of Nate's autopsy had just come in. And things weren't looking good at all.

It was the first Friday in October. The day sizzled with a combination of intense heat and unbearable humidity.

Coco was at home trying to stay cool. Wearing two house slippers that slapped against the dusty floor, she walked from one end of the tiny dining room to the other; her glassy brown eyes took in everything, yet saw nothing.

Elyse stood nearby and watched.

"I don't know why you're doing all that walking, Coco. And you've been praying like crazy . . . nonstop crying and praying for the past hour. Seems like you're very worried."

"I can't help but worry. The results of Nate's autopsy got mentioned on the fucking Internet. Can you believe that shit would make the news?"

"And so? Worrying won't solve anything. And crying like a crazy woman is a waste of time too."

"But what else can I do?"

"Try sitting down. All that pacing makes me feel dizzy."

"Don't look."

"And all that crying makes you sound weak."

"Cover your ears then."

"You don't have to be rude," Elyse gently told her. "I'm concerned about you. I don't want you to give yourself a heart attack."

Coco sped up even more; her feet slapped the floor hard and furious.

"Chill out, Coco."

"I can't." Coco coiled her thick fingers tightly around her neck as if in deep thought. "I have rehearsed this thing over and over in my head. Ever since I found out Nate died, I knew that everyone would somehow twist it around and point their finger at me. And only because I happened to be in my sister's house the day her husband died. But you were there too, Elyse."

"I know that, but—"

"But what?" Feeling like a caged animal, Coco needed someone to pounce on. She was twenty-nine years old and had made many mistakes in her life, but none as severe as those involving Nathaniel Taylor.

"I don't know why you'd bring up my name," Elyse told her.

"In my opinion, if the police try and get me to answer more questions about what happened, then you should be on that list of people too—"

"I don't think so," Elyse stubbornly told her. "You know way more about what happened than me. We left the house and went outside to sit in the car. Me and Natalia waited on you to come out of there. We waited a real long time. And because you were there in that house, only you know what happened to him, not me!"

The fact that twenty-year old Elyse, who was normally calm and composed, was now speaking up for herself with dignity and force, made Coco want to lash out even more.

In a bout of nervousness, Coco yanked at her thick mass of hair which was in her usual style: a long part that went straight down the middle of her snarled and knotted strands. Her two big Afro puffs were stuffed in ponytail holders. She smelled of hairspray and cocoa butter, and her exotic-looking eyes threatened to fill with tears.

"Why are so many bad things happening to me?" Coco muttered in a hoarse voice.

"I dunno," Elyse replied. "I think I'm the last person who would know why bad things happen." The past seven years of Elyse's life had also been troubled. Elyse hated how Nate molested her since she was fourteen, yet she had mixed feelings about his death.

Coco understood where Elyse was coming from. Yet she felt inconsolable. "I've made a few mistakes here and there. We all do. But why do I get sucked into the most miserable shit anyone can ever imagine? Look at me. Four kids. No man. No prospects. I'm struggling to pay these bills all by myself."

"Calhoun helps you out with the kids. That counts for something."

"Oh really? I see you're trying to be helpful by giving my baby daddy some credit."

"That's because you act like he does nothing for his kids, and you know that's a lie."

"He may be a good daddy, but he was a fucked up fiancé. I swear, I still don't know why he dumped me at the altar after eight years of being together. I wasn't the type of woman that he'd live with off and on. That man was in my bed every night."

"Every night?" Elyse asked.

"Okay, he was there just about every night. And one thing I know is that Calhoun promised to marry me. We both went to that courthouse to apply for that marriage certificate. Yet he flaked out on me, then up and married that African bitch."

"Samira Humphries is her official name," Elyse calmly reminded her.

"She's that *African* bitch to me."

"Oh, Coco, I know you're still hurt, but you can't blame Samira for what happened."

"I sure as hell can. As far as I'm concerned, she schemed and plotted to take Calhoun. I have a mind to pay back that African bitch for what she did to me. Stole all my dreams, my whole life, and now look at me." Coco continued to weave a foot-stomping path throughout the dining room. "In fact, I can blame both her and Calhoun. Because if his bitch ass hadn't done what he did to me that night, before—"

Coco's voice fell silent. She glanced warily at Elyse, a young woman who was petite, yet shapely. Elyse was stunning in appearance, and fiery in nature.

"Wait, what did you say, Coco?"

"Nothing."

"You're lying. You said Calhoun did something to you that night. What did he do?"

"N-nothing. I meant to say that *Nate* did something to me, not Calhoun. That's what I meant."

"Okay, so you're saying that Nate did do something. And I can believe that. Because of all the abuse I took off of him. I hope he's rotting in hell." Elyse gasped as if surprised by her own admission. "Is it wrong to say things like that, Coco? If a man abuses a woman and then he dies, and you feel happy about it, does that make you a bad person?"

"Good question," Coco said. She decided to stop focusing on her own hurt and offer to Elyse what she wished she could have.

"Considering the circumstances, in a way, Nate got what he deserved. He hurt you when he was alive, and I can never be down with that."

"You're right. I can't ever forget what he did to me."

"I'm just happy that you're safe now, Elyse. You don't have to go through all that abuse anymore. And it's okay to feel good about that, even if that sick ass man had to die."

Coco pulled Elyse into her arms and hugged her until she herself began to relax.

"Thanks," Elyse whispered, grateful for her support.

"Maybe it is wrong to be happy that someone is dead," Coco continued, "But there's no telling what Nate would have done to you if he was still alive."

"I know," Elyse replied. "Sometimes I wish I didn't know so much. Knowing a lot can get you in trouble."

"Ha, you don't have to worry about the police questioning you. But what *I* know might get *me* in trouble." Coco had to laugh at the absurdity of the entire situation. Because Coco knew that's how deep, dark, family secrets worked. They had just found out that Elyse, raised to be their sister, was actually Alita's daughter.

Alita Washington was her oldest, divorced sister. Second in line was Burgundy Taylor, the entrepreneurial sibling, and the one people turned to when they were in trouble. The next sister was Drucilla, the intelligent, level-headed one who seemed to dodge trouble if she could have her own way. Then there was Coco, the wild and wayward one of the bunch, who often wore her heart on her sleeve and who made impulsive decisions which caused her to unearth great feelings of regret.

"Coco, you could be right though. I might have to start thinking like you and being ready to give my statement just in case. For all I know, I'm next on the list," Elyse muttered. "I just want to be left alone. I just want to be with my man and enjoy true love for the first time in my life."

Gamba Okore had become Elyse's knight in shining armor. He was a strong, dedicated, knowledgeable man who had won Elyse's heart.

"What should I do, Coco? Please tell me what to do if they contact me. What should I say?"

"Don't worry yourself out, Sis." Coco laughed at her mistake. "I'm sorry. I keep forgetting you're my niece. Not my real sister. It feels so strange. I got to get used to this."

"It's alright. We all have to get used to me not being Baby Sis anymore."

"Except Burgundy still doesn't know about you being Alita's daughter, and she still doesn't know about me and her husband, and that's what scaring me to death," Coco admitted.

"When you think you gonna tell B about you and Nate?"

"Girl, please. I have worse things to think about than that."

"But you can't keep this a secret forever, Coco."

"Why can't I?"

"Because," Elyse said in a stubborn tone. "It wouldn't be right."

"I'm sorry. I just can't tell her. I just can't. It would kill her. Burgundy would hate me even though it was just one little stupid mistake. Plus, I'm still on her payroll. She would probably fire me. Then what would I do for extra money? Noooo, Elyse. I want to take this secret to my grave." Coco walked over to Elyse and pointed a stiff finger. "And I'm telling you right now, you'd better not say anything to B, either. Ever! If I find out she knows something, I'm blaming you. And it's going to be ugly from then on," Coco resumed her pace. "I've let you come live with me. And it's been cool so far and I want things to stay that way. And I let your little military man come over here and chill with you all the time. I know how much you love Gamba and he ain't in no position to take you in since he's usually on some government assignment; and Alita is still down to one job after losing two damned jobs in the past year. And you forget about Dru. So, looks like you're stuck with me, Elyse. Stuck with me and my rules, you hear what I'm saying?"

"I hear you."

"You promise me you won't tell B anything about me and Nate?"

"I promise."

"Pinky swear." Elyse walked over to Coco. She lifted her delicate slender finger and wrapped it around Coco's thick one. But Coco was a bigger woman and doing a pinky swear with her was a struggle. Elyse tried but her skinny finger kept slipping off.

Frustrated, Coco took her other hand and smashed Elyse's finger hand against hers.

"Now it's official. You just gave me your word. I now feel that I won't have to worry about you or this topic ever again. Right Elyse?"

The only thing Elyse could do was nod and quickly back away from her Aunt Coco.

"Now that I've sworn to be loyal, does that mean I can trust you to fix me something good to eat?"

For the first time that day, Coco let out a hearty chuckle. And it was true that under normal circumstances, the woman would have prepared a tasty lunch or supper by then. It was one o'clock in the afternoon. Her daughters, Cadee and Chloe were in class, attending the local elementary school. Cypress, her youngest child, at twenty-eight weeks, was peacefully resting in one of her three bedrooms.

Three-year-old Chance was hanging out with Q, one of Coco's past lovers. He also was a former friend of Calhoun. At one time, Coco lied and told Q that he was Chance's father. Even after he bonded with the little boy just to find out that Chance did not share his DNA, he wanted to be a father figure to Chance. Coco was fine with it.

"It's time that I relax and stop worrying so much," Coco said. "And the one thing that gives me peace is doing the things that I know how to do best."

Coco sashayed to her kitchen. In no time at all, the woman was defrosting steaks, slicing up potatoes and onions, and preparing to cook a pot of holiday rice. After they ate a hearty meal, Coco appeared somewhat like her normal self: the joking, happy-go-lucky woman who tried not to let things bother her as long as her man was by her side. But as the giggles subsided and reality settled in, Coco knew she'd have to think like a man. Or at the minimum, she'd be forced to pretend like a man was by her side and that everything would turn out fine concerning all of her latest problems.

A couple of days had passed and now it was early Sunday morning right after the sun had risen.

Coco had been out in the front yard trying her best to pick up the toys that her kids had forsaken in the driveway. She was squatting and trying to collect all the toys when she heard a car enter her driveway. Coco looked up. It was Burgundy's big, luxury SUV. The headlights were on and Coco froze solid as she peered into the blinding lights. The car slowly inched forward heading directly at Coco.

Does my sister even care that she's about to run over me?

With the car only inches away, Coco hastily scooted to her feet. Burgundy glanced up, honked, then waved. Coco frowned.

I know that heifer saw me. But what else does she know?

Burgundy rolled down her window.

"Sorry, Coco. I got distracted. I didn't see you."

"I hope you won't make a habit of popping by here on Sunday mornings. You being a faithful church member and all."

"Coco, look, I'm sorry. I know I should have called first. But I've been having a tough morning. Natalia and Sidnee have been up since five. They were crawling up the walls, and barely wanted to eat breakfast. And we got dressed and started going for a drive. We took a nice little joy ride and before I knew it, we ended up here."

"Oh, I see." Coco's face was emotionless. Then she watched the rear window roll all the way down.

"Hey Auntie Coco." That was Natalia. At eight years old, she was the oldest. Sid was six.

Coco waved at both of her nieces.

Burgundy continued. "I promise this won't become a habit. But is it okay if I leave my girls right now so they may hang out with their auntie and favorite cousins?"

"How long we talking?"

"A couple hours maybe. Three or so?"

"I guess it'll be okay. I have nothing special planned. I was just going to cook dinner and—"

"Yayyy." Before she knew it, Natalia had popped the locks and was at Coco's side, and squeezing her hand real tight. "I want some cookies. Remember how you promised me the day my daddy died that you were going to bake me some cookies? But you didn't. You lied to me. And—"

Coco yanked her hand from Natalia's grip.

"What did you say, Natalia?" Burgundy asked.

"I was saying—abet Co-cooo, whadda u-doing. Dob it."

By then Coco had clamped her hands over her niece's lips. That's because Coco knew that Natalia was there in her parents' house the night before Nate died. Even though Nate wasn't around to tell his side of the story, in Coco's mind it seemed like one person's death could cause more deaths. Hers, or anybody else's. And she did not want that.

Burgundy gazed at Coco in wide-eyed confusion. Her daughter was still mumbling and trying to yell through Coco's hands.

Natalia's screams sent tingly vibrations against Coco's palm.

"Why are you covering my daughter's mouth? Can't she talk?"

"Of course, she can," Coco told Burgundy. But her hand remained flatly pressed against Natalia's moving lips.

"I'm just playing with her. She talks so much. Always yapping nonstop."

"Let me go," is what Natalia tried to scream, but Coco prevented her from speaking.

"Sis, you're too old to be acting like a kid. What's wrong with you," Burgundy asked. "Why won't you let my daughter talk? You trying to hide something?"

Tears sprang to Coco's eyes.

"Um, you know that girl has tons of energy. She's probably 'bout to talk my ears off. And my babies are still asleep and I want it to stay that way for as long as possible. But anyway, looks like you're in a hurry, so yeah, I will gladly take the kids." Coco removed her hand from Natalia and smiled at her.

"Don't be mad, niece. It was just a little game I wanted to play."

"I don't like those kinds of games," Natalia said.

"I don't either," Burgundy replied.

"No problem. I won't do it again. Game over," Coco promised.

After Burgundy was assured that the children would be safe, Coco waved goodbye and let Natalia and Sidnee inside of her house.

"I don't mind y'all being over here but you're going to have to mind me. If you push me over the edge, I will have to make you behave just like I do with my own kids when they act up. You got that?"

Natalia nodded then ran off.

Coco headed to the kitchen to get started on her Sunday dinner. As soon as she placed a pot of chicken in the oven, she went to search for Natalia.

She found the girls in the backyard. Natalia and Sid were seated on a metal swing set that Calhoun had purchased and assembled several years ago.

"Oh, this is where I find you girls. Why am I not surprised?" Three seats made up the swing set; plus there was a sliding board along with a hanging trapeze. Coco decided to sit on the other empty chair.

"It's been a while since I've done this type of thing. It's kind of fun," she said, as she gripped the grass with the tip of toes. She stepped backward as far as she could go, then allowed her feet to let go of the ground. Coco felt the chair move forward and she got lifted up in the air, clumsily at first due to her weight.

"You're too big for that swing, get off," Natalia told her.

"And you're too young to be in grown folks' business. Stay out," Coco retorted. She was self-conscious about her size and felt insulted. "Don't think I won't spank you for being bad."

"I never get spanked. I'm too old for that. Plus, I don't do anything wrong."

"Oh really? You mean to tell me that your daddy never

took a belt to your behind? Because as quiet as it's kept, we know you like to act like you all perfect and goodie-goodie, but Natalia, nobody is that good. Not you. Not me, and not your creepy daddy. Get what I'm saying?"

Sidnee gasped then suddenly took off running.

"I don't know what you're talking about," Natalia finally answered. She kept swinging higher and higher as if she did not have a care in the world. The birds were singing and fluttering nearby, but a group of dark clouds started to loom above them and caused the large backyard to look gray and lifeless.

"Let me tell you what I'm talking about. You're my niece and I love you. But there's something going on. It has to do with your daddy and the night that he died. And see, it's like this. The police might want me to answer a lot of questions about what happened to your daddy. And I'm supposed to tell them everything I know—"

"I don't want to hear you talk. I just want to swing. Will you go and finish cooking my food so I may play by myself?"

Coco knew she was pressuring her niece, but she didn't know what Natalia knew about her father's death and the way he died.

"Wow, I can't believe you. That smart little mouth of yours is gonna get you in trouble one day."

"I'm not getting smart. I don't want to play with you right now."

"First of all, if you'd stop being so rude and obnoxious."

"Spell obnoxious."

Coco hopped off of her swing and sharply grabbed Natalia by the arm. She twisted it hard enough for Natalia to yelp. "Stop it. You're hurting me."

Coco covered the girl's mouth until she quieted down. Then she let go.

"You promised my mommy that you wouldn't put your hands on my mouth. But you just did. And it hurt. And I'm going to tell her."

"The only reason I did that is because of your sassy attitude. Who do you think you are asking me to spell a word? Why don't *you* spell obnoxious?"

"O-B-N—"

"Hush up, Natalia."

Natalia burst into tears and nursed her arm.

"Look, don't cry, please. I didn't mean it." Coco hated to see the girl cry. And she realized that the stress of the entire ordeal was causing her to act out of character.

"I'm sorry for twisting your arm and for putting my hand over your mouth. I could have handled that better because I am the grownup. You may not believe this, but I got smacked quite a few times when I was young. I would imitate Alita. She was always mouthing off. And I wanted to be like her so bad."

A nervous smile formed on Natalia's face.

"Long story short, trying to be like someone else who is doing wrong will get us in trouble. It would be a tragic situation. For both you and me."

"I don't know what you're talking about, Auntie Coco."

Coco stared at the girl. "I know you don't. And I apologize for even expecting you to understand. You're a kid. And I need to remember that. I'll try to do better. That sound alright?"

Natalia nodded.

"Do you still want to swing by yourself?"

She nodded again.

"Oh well. I guess I deserve that," Coco said. "And I will leave you alone, but first I want a hug."

Coco got off the swing and held out her arms.

"Can I get some love?"

Natalia stared at the sky. She gazed at it so long that both of them ended up laughing.

And this time when Coco spread out her arms, Natalia bounced off the swing and flew into her aunt's bosom.

"Love you, niece."

"Love you back, Auntie. But you better not put your hands on me again. They taste like chicken."

The two burst into soft giggles, and Coco promised to keep her adult hands to her adult self.

Chapter 2

Racing Toward Freedom

Burgundy picked up her daughters from Coco's, then decided to make a stop at Super Target. Her destination was the lingerie section.

When they reached the aisle where the intimate apparel was located, Natalia loudly asked, "What size bra are you looking for?"

"Um, what?" Burgundy said.

"I heard you talking to Dru on the phone yesterday. And you said you needed some new bras. I want to help you find some. What size?"

"Um, I wear a thirty-six, B cup."

"Ok, you want black or white? Or you like pink or blue?"

"Uh, um. Black will do. Other colors are fine too. T-thanks, Nat."

Natalia spun around to begin her search. She gazed at each rack that was low enough for her to view. She groped through a wide selection: pushup bras, sports, bustiers, and more. She mostly play-guessed at which ones to pick. And she instantly rejected those she thought her mother wouldn't like.

Burgundy stood frozen in the aisle, startled with disbelief. In that moment, she felt like the kid and Natalia was the mother. "This is unreal," she said out loud. "Things shouldn't be this way. How'd they get this way?"

Natalia had always been the type of child who seemed wise beyond her years. At times she'd be silly and infantile, but other times she could grow keenly observant, outspoken, and developed an ability to repeat phrases that she'd often heard from adults. She could even mimic them as children were prone to do. Her behavior had become more noticeable ever since her father passed away.

Right then, as Burgundy debated if she should tell her daughter to knock it off and let her find her own bras, she felt a hard tap on her shoulder. Burgundy slowly turned around.

"Hey Sis," Alita told her. "Let's talk."

She steered Burgundy further down the aisle.

"I heard what Natalia just said. She talks so loud I heard her before I saw her. And I know that child's voice. And I—"

"Lita, please don't start." Burgundy tried to glance behind her but Alita cornered her. When she found Natalia gaping at them, Alita lead Burgundy a few feet down until they were safely tucked away from her daughter's itching ears yet they were still within sight of Natalia.

"I know what you're about to say," Burgundy remarked. "But this Natalia thing that you heard or saw, well, let me tell you something. It's been happening all week. Like, every single day. She blurts out whatever's on her mind. A lot. And I'd rather she speak up and shock the hell out of me than to suppress everything she's feeling."

"But her talking to you like she's on your level, it's so odd."

Burgundy sighed. "Yeah, it's *different*. I don't know what to make of my daughter sometimes but no matter what she does, I love her to death."

"I know you love her, but you need to make sure that she doesn't skip her childhood. And from what I just saw, she's acting too grown, and I don't like it."

"I know, Sis. I think it's because she's still grieving. Natalia was her father's little princess. She wants to have her say, and continue playing the role of the Queen of the Universe."

Alita wanted to angrily scoff at Burgundy's declaration, but she thought twice.

"Yeah, I know Nate loved her and spoiled her like she was that Meghan Markle chick or something. But," Alita said and glanced behind her back, "This is the real world, not a movie. She's not an adult. Please, B, don't let Natalia get away with that. And if you can't find the strength to do it just say the word and I will—"

"No, Lita. She's my child and I'm the one who decides how to handle Natalia. Case closed."

Seconds later Natalia fled to her mother's side. "I heard you talking. You sounded upset. You good?"

"Natalia, how long have you been standing there?"

"I wasn't snooping, Mommy. I was having fun shopping. But I heard my name. Is everything all right?"

"Everything's fine, sweetheart."

"Am I in trouble?"

"No, Nat! Go and run along, just a few more minutes okay?"

"Okay." She abruptly raced into Burgundy's arms. "I love you, Mommy. I just want to see you smile. I want to do a good job." She held up one of the bras that she'd found.

"Um, no wire bras, sweetie. I hate those. Find push-up if you can."

"Ok, I'll do better, Mommy."

"You're doing a great job, little lady. Keep it up."

At the surprise compliment that made her little heart feel empowered, Natalia took her sweet time walking away, looking back at Alita as if to mock her.

"That one there . . . is a piece of work," Alita told Burgundy.

"And that 'piece of work' is my baby girl. Don't you see that she's trying her best to show me love?"

"I don't know about all that."

"Alita, I'm done with this conversation. No matter how much you disagree with how Natalia's acting, she's my business way more than yours."

Alita quieted down for a minute. Since her own mother, Greta Reeves, was the one who raised Elyse, she honestly had no clue of how it felt to parent a little girl. Maybe she could listen more and talk less.

Burgundy spoke up. "Lita, I'm not trying to be hard on you. I'm glad you're concerned. We just need to give it some time. The psychiatrist said that—"

"Wait, hold up. Are *you* going to a shrink or are you sending Natalia?"

"Not a shrink. He's a grief counselor. We both go. It feels good to talk to someone who understands."

"Oh yeah?"

"I-I can't always talk to family. Sometimes I can. But other times, it feels safer to admit all these weird, awful emotions that I have to a complete stranger. Someone who won't judge me as harshly as family. Not you, of course, Alita. You know I'm not talking about you."

"Hey, I caught that. And I apologize for sounding too harsh. But if you believe that Natalia is just trying to love you and help you in her own way, then hear me out and trust that I want to do the same thing. I care about y'all even if I have a hard time showing it."

Burgundy gave a tired smile that allowed her to overlook her sister's plainspoken nature. "I know what you say comes from a good place, Lita. But what you've got to remember is that we're treading on unfamiliar territory. You have no idea how I suffer from guilt, so much guilt, on some days."

"I heard that. I guess I should believe you, seeing as though I never had a spouse die on me, even though Leonard's wack ass should have croaked a long time ago."

"Please, Sis. Don't even joke like that. Being suddenly single when you never planned for it is nothing to laugh about. Things aren't always as they seem."

"School me on it then."

"Alita Washington. You're divorced. You've bumped heads with your ex. But you've met a great new guy since the divorce from Leonard. It's apparent that Shade Wilkins is good for you, good to you, and I'm glad you all are hitting it off. And although you think Leonard is 'wack,' it seems like you're finally getting over him. Nothing's perfect. But life is much better than it was. Do you agree?"

"You pretty much nailed it, B."

"Good. You're transitioning."

"Hold up! What a minute."

"Stop playing. I'm trying to say that you're transitioning from what used to be to what's going to be. You've survived the worst parts of your life of trying to be the best single mom to your son. And I think you've done a good job."

"Why thank you, Sis." Alita was startled by Burgundy's compliment.

"But it didn't happen overnight, right?"

"Right."

"It took you time to get to this new place in life."

"True that."

"So if it took you some time to make these important changes, you need to cut my child some slack, and let us take time to get to our new place in life."

For a rare, humble moment, Alita was speechless. Burgundy was right and arguing seemed pointless.

"I think you're enjoying your new happiness so much, Lita, that you've forgotten how it feels for a woman to suddenly face new, frightening challenges that she never ever expected to experience. And trust me, I haven't read a handbook on how to deal with every miserable thing I've personally gone through the past six months."

Burgundy then noticed a man walk nearby. His facial features and body type reminded her of Nate. With one arm he pushed the shopping cart. The other arm was wrapped around a woman who probably was his wife. They looked comfortable and happy. And suddenly, Burgundy's bottom lip began to tremble. She and Nate used to shop together when they had free time. And now she knew that simple human experience that she frequently took for granted when Nate was alive would never happen between them again.

"Lita, my having to become a mother and a father to two children and handle every responsibility by myself is a real adjustment. I can't bounce ideas off their father anymore. I *am* their father. It feels like a bad dream. And every night when I go to bed, I wish I can wake up and none of this be true."

"Oh, B. I'm so sorry. I'm an asshole."

"You can be, but I understand. You don't mean any harm, Lita."

"Girl, you know I don't. I-I've always had a mouth on me. You know that."

"Hold up, Sis, because I want to share something else with you. You're not the only one who has strong opinions."

"Okay. Who else out here acts like me?"

"Nobody!" Burgundy had to laugh. "But anyway, you

know how I attend Solomon's Temple? I've taught classes there for many years. Some of the members look up to me. But not long ago, when the rumors spread and the word got out about Nate being accused of sexual assault, some people looked at me as if I had Hep C. They whispered behind my back. Some didn't even want me working in the bookstore anymore. They acted like I was responsible for Nate's actions."

"Well, if they did that, then they're simple ass church folk."

"I wouldn't say all that, Lita. It's just that, and here is the tough part. I got mad at *them* for getting mad at *me*. And I know that in the beginning I defended my husband because I couldn't imagine him sexually assaulting anybody. And so I believed him."

"Humph, and that was crazy."

"Lita, I was just trying to be the best wife and mother that I could possibly be. But the people kept gossiping. Things got worse. And a couple of members confronted me in the church hallway. It got ugly."

"Who did it? Who was it?"

"It doesn't matter, Lita. But back then, I hated how they made me feel that what Nate did was all my fault. Like I should have known better and I should have controlled him."

"People are stupid."

"These people's stupid, hateful ways got under my skin. And one night, I pretty much attacked Nate."

"What?" Alita laughed. "You did? How? How'd you do it?"

"I rushed at him when he was in the kitchen and I beat him across his chest. I balled up my fist and punched him in his forehead as hard as I could."

"Wow. What else? Did you kick him in his nuts?"

"No, Lita. I wanted to though. But the things I did do

made me look nothing like a woman who goes to church every other Sunday."

"You were mad, B. Your own husband did shady shit behind your back. He was acting like a perv and you got sick of it. God can't blame you for that."

"I wasn't worried about God being mad at me. I was worried about why I kept defending someone who shouldn't have been defended. I thought I was going crazy."

"B, you weren't crazy. You were facing a tough reality."

"There you go, Lita. I had to stop burying family secrets under a rug. And I finally got to the point, thank God, where I couldn't make any more excuses for Nate. And so yeah. I cursed him out and hit him across his face; they were hard punches, Sis. I only got in four or five hits before he stopped me. You know Nate is strong and his arms are muscular."

"I hope he didn't hit you back."

"No. He knew better." Burgundy's eyes moistened and it felt quite liberating to be upfront with her sister . . . to admit the truth and not sugarcoat her seemingly perfect life anymore.

"Anyway, our fight ended. I calmed down. He could have had me arrested for assault and battery but he didn't. We ignored each other for a couple of days. And then we talked. We made up. This happened right before I went out of town to that restaurant convention in Seattle. I don't think I told you but back when our legal problems intensified, I begged my husband to get a room at a motel so he could be there instead of at the house. At first, he fought me on it but then he agreed it was the best decision. He moved out," Burgundy sighed. "Things got better. I felt more peaceful. But sometimes I let Nate come home so he could see the girls and help me with certain tasks around the house. I was mad at him but I still let him be

Mr. Taylor, be a good daddy to his girls and still act like a husband to his angry, disgusted wife."

"Ha. You're a better woman than I am. I don't know if I should admire you or call you the words I usually call you. But I don't want to insult you in Target so I will leave that one alone,"

"Thanks, Lita. You're so kind," she said jokingly. "I'm saying all this to say that all of us are just flawed human beings. I've done a few things I'm not proud of. And my kids might be guilty of the same. Stop being so hard on them, please. Because nothing's normal right now. And there's no telling when they will get back to normal. And that's just Act I of my story right now, Ms. Alita Washington."

"Reeves, baby girl. I'm always a Reeves."

Burgundy allowed herself to show a genuine smile. "Geez, Ms. Reeves, I've talked so much that my daughter has probably placed fifteen bras in the shopping cart by now."

"She's so grown you'd better hope she's not trying to find bras that will fit her own chest."

"Ha. That would be funny. Thank God she doesn't have to wear a training bra yet. But Natalia has definitely acted more grownish. I think she feels like she needs to mother . . . her mother." Burgundy gave a wry smile. "It's shocking, but at the same time Natalia's behavior is admirable. I like that she's concerned. It proves that my daughter isn't as narcissistic as I feared."

"Mmm hmmm," Alita murmured. She heard what Burgundy told her but she only believed half of it. She truly adored both of her nieces but didn't have patience when kids acted like 'entitled people-in-training.'

"Anyway," Burgundy said. "Change of subject. What are you doing in Super Target? Aren't you more of a Walmart type of chick?"

"Ha-ha, I know right. I don't know, girl. I needed something that my neighborhood store didn't have, and since I was in your area, I decided to take a chance and come here. And look who I run into."

"You were in *my* neighborhood? Really?"

Alita had briefly moved in with Shade but recently he helped her get her own place on the southwest side of town. An affordable efficiency that was good enough for the moment; and he also financially helped her with a few of her utility bills.

"Alita, you don't stay anywhere near here. And if I didn't know any better, I'd swear you were going out of your way to check up on me."

"Yeah, and so what? I can't check on my sister?"

"Of course, you can. To know that you care, that Natalia cares, that anybody out here cares about me, well, I'm all for it. I need it."

Right then Natalia cautiously approached her mother, breaking apart the nearness that Burgundy and Alita shared as they quietly talked in the lingerie aisle.

"Mommy, I'm sorry to interrupt. But I found six different bras you can try on. Two black, two white, a lavender one, and a red sports bra. They didn't have blue."

"Why thank you so much for finding these for me," Burgundy said. She winked at Alita. "You're such a big girl. Your daddy would be so proud of you."

Natalia acted like she didn't hear her mother's reference to Nate. She stared at the panties that her mother had found earlier which were now sitting in her shopping cart.

Natalia frowned as she delicately picked up one pair of 'barely there' bikinis.

"Mommy, I don't like these at all. You'd better put this back. I'll do it for you." Natalia grimaced and proceeded to slide the sexy underwear back onto the clothing rack.

Stunned, Burgundy could only shake her head.

Things had certainly changed for her and her family. It

was humbling to admit that life was not in her control. That even though she was a meticulous planner who knew what she wanted from life and had an idea of when she wanted those things to happen, she felt resentful when she realized that she had no power over any of her plans.

Thirty-three-year-old Burgundy Reeves Taylor had been married a little more than one decade when she became a widow.

She never could have imagined that twelve years after she walked down the church aisle to marry her best friend, that she'd be back in church with him for a different reason: Standing in front of the altar, surrounded by family members and friends, staring at the taut, plastic, macabre face of Nate while he rested in a pine box.

Last fall, during his funeral, she shook countless hands and accepted hug after sympathetic hug from all kinds of people. It seemed like the procession of mourners would never end. When she had a moment to take a break, she noticed two women standing around who she did not recognize. The younger woman's leg kept jerking. She frequently gave Burgundy the once-over, then looked away. The lady next to her wore a pinched face, no smile. She seemed both hostile and annoyed. Finally the nervous woman approached Burgundy.

"Hi," she said.

"Hello."

"I wasn't sure if I should come up to you or not but I just wanted to tell you that I'm so sorry about what happened."

"Thank you." Burgundy paused as she gazed at the woman. She had almond shaped eyes, sensual lips, a decent figure that included wide hips, and large, rounded breasts that were the first thing one would notice when they saw her. She looked to be thirty-one.

"You have my deepest sympathies, ma'am."

"I appreciate that. But we've never met. Who are you and how did you know my husband?"

"Well, you know, I just knew him that's all. We were cool like that."

"What do you mean?"

The Annoyed Lady came over and tugged on the other woman's arm. Nervous Chick pulled away and continued babbling. "I was shocked when he died. And to be honest, when it comes to me and Natey—"

"Natey?"

"Yeah," she said with a shrug. "That's what I liked to call him. I don't know if he liked it or not, but I did it anyway every time I saw him."

Peeved, Burgundy told her, "Go on."

"We were pretty tight. He'd see me eating alone at one of the restaurants that you all owned. And he'd be very nice, a perfect gentleman. And he'd asked me how I liked the food and a few times he let me have a meal on the house. We'd talk every time I came in and eventually Natey tried to get things on and popping between us. And even though I thought he was sexy as hell, I knew that would not be cool in any type of way because he was already in a relationship, you know. I pushed back on Natey and we kept being cool with each other. I thought he was cute and smart and everything. But when I found out he passed away, I had to come here to this church and let you and God know that nothing ever happened between us. I mean *nothing*." The woman stared straight ahead and refused to look Burgundy in the eyes during her confession.

"Good God, Torrie," Annoyed Lady finally blurted. "You are so damned stupid. Did you really have to go to this woman and open up your damned mouth and tell her all that unnecessary shit? I told your ass not to come here.

You should never go out your way to tell wives shit like this. Remember what happened last time? Use your brains. Let's go."

And just like that the two strangers left the building. Left Burgundy alone with a red-hot face. And that's the moment when Burgundy realized that *The Bridges of Madison County* wasn't just a popular movie. Many times it's only after someone dies that their truth really gets revealed.

And as she watched the women flee from her presence and out of the church, Burgundy walked over to Alita and looked her square in the eye.

"That's it."

"What? You mean the funeral?"

"No. the marriage. When Nate died, my marriage died too."

"No shit."

"But it seems like our marriage gave out long before he died. I'm just now realizing it."

"You feel like me, huh?" Alita asked. "Like you're going through a divorce?"

"You stated it perfectly. I feel divorced. I know one thing. I was depressed the moment he died. But I will try my best not to let that sorrow to take over my heart anymore."

"Wait a second. You're a widow. Aren't you supposed to stay depressed for like a year? Don't date or make any big decisions?"

"Alita, after what I've been through and what I'm still finding out, I refuse to be bound anymore. Bound to a concept, or a fantasy that has made an utter fool out of me. God knows what else he was doing behind my back."

"I know you're angry but give it some time, B. I saw what happened. Why let these women come in here and get you shook? You don't know them from Adam. They're weak. You see how they said what they had to say and then sneaked off like two rats hotfooting down a dark alley."

Maybe Alita had a good point.

"I guess I need to find out what to pay attention to," Burgundy replied, "and what to ignore."

"Ease up, Sis. Like the advice you gave me, allow yourself time to heal."

"You're right."

"Even though he wasn't perfect," Alita continued, "Nate wasn't the best husband in the world but he was still your husband. You have to respect what good things he did do without letting the bad things make you feel worse about yourself. Nobody deserves that. Especially after everything he took you through."

Burgundy heard what Alita was saying but she felt like she'd been suddenly handcuffed and tossed into jail. Learning about the existence of Torrie was something Burgundy never would have predicted. The new knowledge felt like prison. Like something she could do nothing about. But it also felt like it was nearly time for her prison sentence to end. And Burgundy was counting down the days, the hours, the minutes until she could be free.

At that point, all Burgundy yearned to do was unshackle all the invisible chains from around her ankles; to turn around and run.

Run for her life.

Race toward her freedom.

Chapter 3

Sex Has Everything to Do with It

After their trip to Super Target, Burgundy had been home for thirty minutes when she heard a noise coming from out front. An engine shut off. A heavy door slammed. She logged into her home security app and viewed the live footage of what was happening outside her front door.

She programmed the alarm system to shut off and then hurried down the hallway before the bell could ring.

When she opened the door, Burgundy couldn't help but laugh.

Edmund Langston Murray looked like he was about to knock. He nearly fell on the floor right inside the doorway. But she caught him by the arm and managed to keep him from falling and making a fool of himself.

"Elm," Burgundy told him. Elm was Edmund's initials and her nickname for him. "You're too funny."

"I'm glad you see the humor and I hope your security camera did not tape that."

They both laughed. She allowed him in the house and he followed her in the hallway. She stopped walking. His eyes met hers, then softened. She let him embrace her. Edmund held Burgundy with a strength that made her feel safe and cherished. His scruffy beard caressed her soft cheek and he started to nibble on her earlobe.

She and Edmund had known each other for years on friendly terms. He owned a successful fried catfish chain. Burgundy and Nate owned a brunch business called Morning Glory. She and her husband also owned some barber shops named Baller Cutz.

Because they ran in the same circles, she and Edmund would cross each other's paths at various civic events. They'd meet for lunch and discussed the highs and lows of restaurant ownership. But, last summer, he confided in her about the recent divorce that he had endured. She and Edmund were the same age. Ambitious and attractive, they shared easy-going, frank conversations and found themselves becoming close friends as well as business associates.

Since Nate died, they'd become even closer.

With him now in her house giving her a much-needed hug, Burgundy shut both her eyes and felt herself relax. It felt wonderful yet strange to be locked in an embrace with another man.

She enjoyed the feeling of skin touching skin. His body felt tight and solid, comforting and oddly delicious.

"This feels good," she finally allowed herself to murmur. Edmunds's lips brushed against the top of her wayward-looking hair. That's one of the qualities she appreciated about him. No matter how imperfect she looked, he still treated her with utmost kindness and respect.

"It does feel good, and you look good too, Burg."

"Please don't call me that."

Burg was the nickname that Nate had given her.

"Okay, sorry about that. You look damned good, Burgundy. That better?"

"Much better."

Burgundy allowed her eyes to close as she leaned into

Edmund for a friendly, much-needed kiss. She pressed her body into his. The heat from his chest made her moan. She felt herself weakening.

"Mommy!"

Burgundy's eyes flew open.

Natalia gave Burgundy a vicious look.

"Mommy, what are you doing? Who is this man? Why is he always at our house?"

"Natalia Anne Taylor!" Burgundy stared apologetically at Edmund.

"Hey, no problem," he said. He relinquished his protective hold of Burgundy and tried to offer Natalia a friendly smile.

"Natalia, is it?"

For the past few months since they'd been hanging out, Burgundy had talked to Edmund about her daughters on numerous occasions. Friendly chatter about her girls' activities but nothing too personal. Then Nate had died unexpectedly. It was a shock to Burgundy's system and shattered her entire world. Edmund quickly comforted her in private and was there for her as long as she needed him. Lately, he'd just begun to pay a few visits to her house in a suburban area called The Woodlands, Texas. Burgundy made sure the girls were tucked in bed long before Edmund came by, but somehow Natalia always knew when he visited her mom. Usually it would be late at night. When she'd hear Edmund's voice, she'd sneak out of her bedroom and quietly tiptoe halfway down the staircase. Natalia would sit on the steps, lean in and listen, her mind wildly racing in multiple directions as she assessed the situation. One time, Natalia even boldly came all the way down to the first floor and nearly bumped into Edmund when he rounded the corner as he exited the powder room. He gave her an awkward stare, said hello, and dashed away.

Since then, Natalia had seen him come to the house to

check on Burgundy. Of course, many relatives, friends and associates had also come by the house to help out, but Natalia perceived there was something different about this man.

But on this particular day, when everything came to a head as she saw her mom embrace Edmund, Natalia was ready to stand her ground and not just look, wonder, and quietly walk away.

When the girl responded to Edmund, she bore the demeanor of an aristocrat.

"Yes, I am Natalia Taylor," she finally said. "I'm named after my father Nathaniel Taylor. He died. Did you know he was dead?" Anguish was written firmly across her childlike face.

"My father was supposed to take me to the daddy-daughter dance and teach me a lot of important things about life, but he can't now. But I still wish that he could."

"I'm sorry to hear about your father."

"Thank you."

"He would be proud of you if he could see you right now."

"Hmm," she said in a curious voice. "Did you ever know my daddy?"

Edmund discreetly backed away from Natalia.

Burgundy felt bad. She'd found out the hard way you can't child-proof this child.

"Did you know Daddy died when mommy wasn't even at home? She was out of town when he died. Did you know that?"

When Edmund failed to answer her question, she continued with her probe.

"Why are you always here?"

"Natalia?" Burgundy said, this time feeling very irritated. "Please. This is our company."

"He's not my company. If he was my company you would have come and told me."

"He just got here," Burgundy explained.

"But what about the other times when he'd be here a long, long time and you never told me that we had company? It's because he's not real company."

"Natalia, don't be rude."

Natalia stubbornly crossed her bony hands across her flat chest. For some reason it seemed like the girl had sprouted another inch or two. Not just in height but also in knowingness.

The air was wrought with tension as mother and daughter continued to stare each other down.

"Natalia Anne Taylor, did you hear me ask you a question? Are you going to tell your mother where you heard that mess from?"

"I heard it from TV."

"What?"

"Cable TV."

"How can you do that when I have child-proofed the channels?"

"I learned how to unlock it."

"What? You'd better not be messing around with those parental controls."

Natalia looked frightened. "I'm sorry, Mommy. Am I in trouble?"

"It depends. Who taught you how to do that?"

"Daddy did. He snuck and did it and he didn't want you to know."

Burgundy sighed. "Why would that man do something that doesn't even make any sense?"

Natalia asked again. "Am I going to get put in time out?"

"I don't want you to mess around with the TV like that anymore. And I won't tolerate you speaking to my guest like you're grown. You heard me, Natalia?"

"Yes, ma'am." She hesitated. "I don't want to be in time out. I wanted to play with you, Mommy. But I can't because you have company."

Burgundy gawked at Natalia in dismay, not certain if she should believe her or question if her quick-witted daughter was testing her.

"Whoa," Edmund said. "It sounds like I'm interfering with some mommy-daughter time. It sounds like she's unhappy because I'm stealing you away from her. I'm sorry, Burgundy."

"Look, you don't have to apologize," she replied.

"Oh, but I do."

"No, you don't."

"Yes, he does," Natalia replied.

Burgundy had had enough. She yanked Natalia by the elbow and thrust her directly in front of her so that the girl had to look up into her mother's fiery eyes. Burgundy wanted to box the child across her sassy mouth but she knew that the girl would call 911 quicker than she could scream for help.

"If you really think you're grown, Natalia, I will do something to prove that you're not."

"W-what did you say, Mommy?"

"If you're so grown, I'd love to see you prove it. If you're that much of an adult, you can move out this house, be a grownup and live in your own place instead of being here."

Edmund shook his head. "Burgundy, no, please don't say things like that—"

"No, I'm sorry but she's gone too far."

"Sounds like you're going too far too, sweetie," he gently told her.

"Stay out of it, Edmund, please. Let me handle this my way." Burgundy was so frustrated. Everything solid thing in her life seemed to be crumbling apart, but one thing she would not allow was her daughter to control her life and disrespect her very good friend, a supportive man whom she did not want to scare away.

"Natalia, if you think you know so much, find your own place to live so you won't have to see who I invite to the house that I maintain. A lovely home that me and your daddy provided so you can have a roof over your head, food to eat, the comforts of a good life, and all those pretty clothes you like to wear. You talk a lot of stuff, but when you're grown, really grown, you have to figure out everything all by yourself. How to solve your own problems. How to do it all by your damned self."

For once Natalia lacked a comeback. It appeared that what Burgundy was saying didn't completely register in her mind. The girl remained in quiet contemplation and Burgundy was pleased to sense that her authority was no longer being challenged.

"So, Nat, what's it going to be? Are you smart enough to make it on your own, find your own place to stay, get a job, and take yourself to school? Huh?"

Edmund again shook his head at Burgundy.

"Burgundy, um, I may be overstepping my boundaries, but I really don't think you should be saying things like that to a child."

"I don't think you should be saying that to me seeing that you've never been a father to any child."

Edmund flashed a look of anger. "Burgundy. Let's go somewhere private. We should talk."

Burgundy released her firm grip from Natalia's elbow. She was still steaming mad at the girl even though it seemed like Natalia had shrunken right in front of her. Burgundy wasn't only mad at her daughter. She was disappointed in herself.

But as she thought things through, when it came to Edmund and his sudden frequent presence at a recently widowed woman's house, maybe Natalia was right—once again.

Natalia finally escaped up the stairs. Burgundy heard

the door of her bedroom slam shut. It made her feel even worse . . . about everything.

"Edmund, sweetie . . . I-I'm sorry for that low-blow comment."

"No problem."

"And I do want to be sensitive to my daughter's feelings. Maybe we can see each other during business hours only. Not after work. Not until I figure out how to handle my kids and make sure their emotional and physical needs are met."

"Hey, you don't have to explain. I may not be a father, but I understand."

Edmund leaned in for an innocent goodbye peck to show that he wasn't holding any type of grudge, but Burgundy turned him down.

"Let's connect later . . . when the time is right, okay, Edmund?"

He told her he'd check on her in a few hours then he turned around and left.

That evening everything between Burgundy and the girls went well.

She had reestablished the routine that she and Nate had created years before he died. Natalia did her homework while Sidnee pretended like she was reading. Sid grabbed the book *Big Hair Don't Care* and quietly pored over the striking images. Then they were called to the dining room table to eat dinner. The girls took their bath, and Burgundy played with them, gave them loads of kisses and hugs, then sweetly tucked them into bed before settling down for the evening.

This nightly pattern continued for the next few days.

But by Thursday, she received an unexpected telephone call.

"Hello, Mrs. Taylor?"

"Yes. This is she."

"This is the American Inn Hotel on Woodlands Parkway Drive. I'm calling from the front desk."

"Oh. Hi. How may I help you?"

"Yeah, um, just wanted you to know that a large delivery has arrived for Nathaniel Taylor. I know that he's no longer staying here but I thought you'd want to know that we'll hold the package for him till you are available to come pick it up."

"Hmm, okay. No problem. Thanks." Burgundy hung up the phone.

She went on about her business and on Saturday, she decided to take the brief drive over to the hotel. Liz the nanny was at the house attending to the girls. Alita happened to be visiting Burgundy to help out with some household issues. The two sisters rode together in Burgundy's SUV and shortly thereafter they arrived at the inn.

"I'll be right back, Lita. He probably had some things shipped here instead of to the house."

Burgundy got out the car and went inside.

The front desk clerk asked her to sign and date a delivery slip and told her that he'd be right back. He returned huffing and puffing as he carried a big box. It was so large that he was hiding behind it as he cradled it.

"What is this?" she asked.

"I have no idea, ma'am."

"Hmm. I'll be right back. I need my sister to help me. She's in the car."

Alita's eyes bulged when she saw the box.

"What the hell is this, Sis?"

Burgundy ignored her sister's mutterings and made room in the back of the SUV to carefully load the box.

When they got home, Burgundy got a pocket knife and slit the tape. Alita sifted through mountains of bubble wrap, looked at the boxed item, then shrieked so loud the noise resounded through the house. She began dancing around the kitchen, hopping about like she was deliriously happy.

"This is not funny," Burgundy told her as she took a peek inside the box.

"B, your husband was a straight up freak." Alita pulled out a life-sized doll. "Well, I'll be damned. Nate got his own Becky."

Burgundy stared at the silicone doll. Pale skin, balloon-sized tits. Tits so plump they were way more gigantic than her own little thirty-six Bs. The doll had long blonde hair, a plump ass, and what appeared to be a lifelike vagina.

Becky was cute but she had an odor. She smelled like burnt plastic mixed with rubber. Burgundy's legs trembled as she sat down on a chair.

"Damn, B. This is messed up. Did you know Nate was into sex dolls?"

"No."

"And he probably didn't know you had your own dildo too."

Alita smirked like something was funny. But Burgundy was in no mood to laugh. She felt confused, then angry.

Natalia walked into the kitchen.

"Oooh, that looks real. Is it a baby alive doll? I've never seen one that big. It must be for Sid 'cause I'm too big for dolls." Natalia reached over to caress the hair.

"Ugh, what's that smell?"

Alita covered Natalia's eyes.

"Niece, you need to find your way back upstairs. This doll ain't for you or your sister."

"Then who is it for?"

Alita and Burgundy locked eyes.

"Why are you always in grown folk's business? Go on upstairs till we tell you to come back down."

Because Natalia refused to obey Alita's orders, she had

to physically lead her by the arm all the way up the back staircase. Burgundy stuffed the doll deep inside the box and pulled it into her bedroom.

She stiffly sat on the edge of her bed and stared into space for several minutes.

She leaped up and removed the doll to examine it. She retrieved the packing slip wondering if there'd been some type of mistake. But the item was addressed to Nathaniel Taylor. Ordered on August twenty-fourth. It originated from somewhere in China which might explain why the delivery took so long to reach the States.

"Was this Nate's first time ordering this type of thing?" she said out loud. "Did our lack of a regular sex life force him to go this route?"

Alita walked in while Burgundy was talking to herself.

"Girl, stop tripping. Your husband was a freak, point-blank period. This Becky would probably let him do all the sexual things that you were so against. Some men are like that, if they can't get it from one woman, they'll get it from another. Whatever works as long as he gets it in."

Burgundy let out a loud hiss and tossed the plastic lover on the bed. It buckled up and folded like it was hopelessly intoxicated.

"Damn him. Is this what our marriage ended up being? Something that started out real and authentic, full of love and passion and hope and dreams, Alita, all kinds of dreams. We, Nate and I, wanted to conquer the world. Yet it seems like the world did us in."

"I know the feeling, Sis. It starts out great, just about everything starts out great. Like a new man or a new job. You feel so pumped. So lit at how everything seemed to be falling in place. But then it goes backwards. It shifts. And the relationship starts to trip, and you don't want to fall down but you do. I don't want that anymore, B. I'm walking on pins and needles so that me and Shade stay good. I never want my man to be fucking around with another woman, or even a plastic doll."

Burgundy screamed at the ceiling. She snatched Becky off the bed and stuffed her head first inside the box. Her long legs stuck out of the top.

"I'm taking this ridiculous piece of shit to the dumpster. How can she compare to me? How?"

"She was going to give it up to him with no excuses, B."

"Alita, please be quiet."

"Truth hurts."

"Truth is a lie, that's what it is. Ha!" Burgundy banged her fist on top of Becky's legs and tried to stuff the doll further into the box. She closed the top, found some tape, and secured the opening.

"You can help me take this out to that garbage bin in the garage. I don't want to see this in my house. I can't believe him."

'You're in denial, sis. That's your problem."

"I don't recall asking you what problem I had," Burgundy snapped.

"Even so, you have trouble facing reality. Everything has to be so perfect and so planned out in your world. Life ain't like that, B. It's just not. This man craved pussy and it seemed he did almost anything to get it. Messing around with Elyse, messing around with that strange chick at the funeral, and now this."

Burgundy covered her ears.

Alita removed her hands.

"Denying shit won't solve a thing. Most people can't deal with the truth. That's what's wrong with the world. We want things the way we believe them to be instead of how they really are."

"But this doesn't make sense. He never told me anything like this."

"That's because your husband knew you better than

anybody else. He knew you wouldn't go for it. Ha, B. You threw the man out of the house, y'all became one of those LAT couples."

"Basically. We barely had started living apart though."

"You kicked him out!"

"Alita, no, I did not. I suggested that he leave. At first he resisted but then he was open to it. He moved into the hotel and, after a while, Nate started thinking that the living arrangement would work out better for both of us. It's not like we were separated or hated each other. And so, we'd meet for a late dinner here and there and discuss our relationship and our legal issues, the kids and so on. And before everything blew up, he even considered getting his own condo, somewhere in mid-town."

"Yet but long before any of that happened, I remember you telling me that you'd stopped having sex with him. And he loves having sex. What else was he supposed to do? Become a priest? But hell, even some of 'em can find a way to get laid just like any other man."

"My goodness, Alita. You're so vulgar."

"Truth is offensive, B. It just is."

"I see. I'm listening to you as difficult as that may be, and it seems like you're suggesting that I drove him into this? Like really? All of who Nate was, every single disgusting trait, was my fault? Even the Elyse thing?" Burgundy frowned. "No, I refuse to believe it. Because when Nate supposedly first started touching Elyse, that was at least five years ago. And I know we were still making love back then. Nope, no, these events are not my fault. I won't believe it. I won't. There has to be some other explanation."

"Ain't no other explanation. If one woman won't do what a man wants, another one will. Even a stinky silicone woman whose tits are bigger than yours and mine put together. Now, on the other hand, that isn't a good excuse for Nate to do what he did to Elyse. But in his mind, he wasn't at fault. That's how a lot of abusers feel, that they've done nothing wrong. And that is so wrong."

"The worst part is I can't ask him what he was thinking." Burgundy felt she was fighting an uphill battle. "A dead man can't talk. All we have are the things Nate left behind. Like this ugly sex doll. And some ugly memories."

"Oh, but you're forgetting two other important things."

"What's that, Lita?"

"He left you with those two beautiful girls. And as far as I'm concerned, that's the best thing he's ever done."

"Coming from you, that's a miracle." Burgundy let out a laugh. "And a miracle is exactly what we need right about now."

Hours after Burgundy discovered Nate's doll, she was at home dealing with household issues when she pondered a sudden idea. She made a quick phone call and then went into the family room where the girls were playing and being watched by Liz.

"Liz," Burgundy said. "Something critical has come up at the last minute. I need to handle it. This situation might even take all night." Burgundy attempted to look the woman in her eyes. "That means that I will need your help, need you to stay here with the girls tonight. Can you manage that? Of course, you'll be generously compensated for your efforts."

"It's fine, Mrs. Taylor," Liz told her. "I don't mind watching the girls."

"Can I trust you?" Burgundy's voice trembled.

When Nate passed away, Burgundy was tempted to fire Liz. Her commitment back then was sketchy at best, but at the same time, Liz had grown to become like a second mom. She, in fact, proved to be one of the most stabilizing forces in Burgundy's life after her husband died.

"Liz, you know I'm trusting you to watch my babies closely. We don't need a repeat of what happened last time. In fact, instead of sleeping in the downstairs guest room, you should use the upstairs one."

Liz nodded.

"Yes, ma'am. You can trust me. I won't let you down." Liz felt awful about what happened to Nate and since then had shown great remorse and increased responsibility regarding the girls.

Once Burgundy felt secure that Liz knew what she expected from her, she sneaked her overnight bag into the garage and then laid it on the floor behind the driver's seat. It was eight o'clock that Saturday night in mid-October. It was pitch black outside.

She was about to back out of the garage when she remembered to cover her weekender bag with a quilt that she always left in the vehicle in case of an emergency.

Just as Burgundy was about to back down the driveway, the front door opened. Natalia raced out of the house with no shoes on.

She waved at her mother who sighed and then rolled down her window.

"Y-you leaving us? W-where are you going?"

"Um, Natalia get back in the house. You're barefoot and it's freezing cold out tonight."

"I asked you where are you going?" The girl rose up on her toes. She stared into the SUV.

"Nat, I don't feel well and I need to make sure I get better."

"You're going to the ER?"

"Not quite. It's called Urgent Care. It's kind of similar but doesn't nearly cost as much . . . And the lines aren't as long."

"Are you going to get sick and die like Daddy?"

"Oh my God, sweetie. No. It's not that serious. Just

something I need to take care of. I'll be back before you know it."

"No, Mommy don't go. Let me go with you. Please."

"Oh God," Burgundy cried out. Ever since Nate died, neither girl liked for Burgundy to be out of their sight for long. She got out of the car and gave Natalia a nice, long hug, and kissed her several times. Then she got back in the car and started the engine.

"I swear nothing is going to happen to me, or to you, or your sister. Stay away from that stove and do as Liz tells you. Go back in the house. I'll call you as soon as I can. Love you."

Natalia stood there as her mother slowly drove off.

Burgundy fought back tears all the way to urgent care.

She parked outside Edmund's house and called Natalia. "I made it to Urgent Care."

She hung up, sat for a while and got her head together, and shortly thereafter Edmund welcomed her inside.

A warm bath awaited Burgundy as well as a glass of Cabernet Sauvignon. The flame from the apple spice candles flickered around the whirlpool tub. Edmund was a jazz enthusiast with an appreciation for good music. When Burgundy entered the bathroom, smooth jazz could be heard. Lush, lovely, melodies made the ambiance pleasant and romantic.

"Wow, all this for me?" she cooed.

"Why of course."

"I'm impressed."

"I actually had to let the water out and run another tub full. But you finally made it." Edmund grabbed Burgundy around the waist. He kissed her lips, hungrily devoured her, as he'd been wanting to touch her and be with her all day long.

"I'm sorry, Elm. I-I had to handle some things first." Her mom guilt was trying to take over. "You know how it is."

"It's fine. You're here now. Make yourself at home."

First Burgundy called Liz to see how the girls were doing.

"They are totally into this movie," she said in her Caribbean accent. "They aren't paying any attention to me."

Burgundy laughed. "Sounds good."

Liz whispered to her, "Enjoy your night. We're all right over here."

After she hung up, Burgundy joined Edmund. She threw her arms around his neck. Upon smelling him she felt she'd made the right decision. He smelled good. He had an earthy, petrichor scent that made her feel womanly and sensual.

"Let's get you more comfy," he told her. She was wearing a black, double-breasted coat dress that clung to her wide hips.

Edmund sat on the bed and reached out to grab her. He pulled her close as she stood in front of him. He squeezed her around her ass which was as smooth as a baby's bottom. She smiled and looked down at him. Staring at Burgundy in admiration, he slowly undid each button. He unlatched her bra and tossed it to the floor.

When her round, plump breasts were exposed, he couldn't help himself. They stood at attention, not sagging at all, and the mere vision of her body made Edmund hunger for her even more.

"May I have some?" he asked.

She nodded.

He took one nipple into his mouth and sucked it softly at first and then more firmly. He flicked his tongue across the nipple and felt it hardening as he licked it repeatedly.

Warm sensations flowed through her. She closed her eyes and felt herself grow weak.

"Mmmm, Edmund."

He moaned too. They moaned together as he proceeded to go from her breasts to her flat belly, then from her thighs to the taut skin underneath her bosom. He made a soft trail of tender kisses all across her body.

When he finally mustered up the strength to undo the last button, he slipped his fingers on the sides of her bikini and slowly pulled them down past her knees until they dropped around her ankles.

She laughed, stepped out of them, and kicked them out the way. When she looked up, Edmund, who had been wearing a wifebeater T-shirt and some boxers, was completely nude.

"When did that happen?"

"I'm fast, baby. Very fast."

"Oh, I'm sure but right now I need you to go nice . . . and slow."

Soon they both stepped into the tub filled with a mountain of bubbles. She sat behind him with her legs clasped around his waist. She kissed his back then washed it. He turned around to face her. He took a sponge, dipped it into the warm sudsy water, and rubbed it across her breasts that were glistening in the dimly lit room.

He got up and sat behind her. Edmund kissed her bare shoulder, something that felt extraordinarily electrifying to her tired, aching, love-starved body.

Once the bath was over, they dried each other off with huge bath towels. Then took their glasses of wine to his bedroom.

He pulled back the covers, let her climb in bed and he joined her.

"Your hair looks beautiful, Burgundy."

"Thanks. I got it done a couple of days ago. I was at the salon for four, almost five hours. It was very crowded and Destiny, she's my hairdresser, she's always in demand. The wait is awful but I love the results."

"You look very pretty, my dear."

She smiled at Edmund from ear to ear. Being with him

took away some of the hollowness that had settled inside of her since Nate passed.

"Your support means everything to me, Elm. I don't know how I'd make it without you."

"It's always my pleasure to please you, Burgundy."

He scooted down the bed until he was at the foot of it and was on his knees.

Burgundy gazed at this man, just taking him all in and brimmed with joy.

"You know what?" she said. "When you wear boxers, I can't see what I normally see."

"And what do you normally see?"

"Your big dick. I mean, I know you're packing but when a man wears boxers, unless he's King Kong, you can't really see his size."

"Don't worry. You'll be seeing my big dick in no time."

He sniffed her feet.

"I love how you smell. Clean, sweet, fresh, and eatable."

He kissed her toes.

"You like that?"

She pretended like she didn't hear him and kept talking. "I love how you've decorated your house. And I think it was a good idea to change things around and make it reflect your own tastes." She knew he was divorced and she never really wanted to mention his ex-wife. Her name was Kyra. She was an attractive woman who also worked in the restaurant industry and she'd be photographed at various shindigs and would be mentioned in the Houston society newspapers. Thankfully, Burgundy had never met Kyra. She didn't want to meet her. And she never wanted to directly mention the woman either. At least not while she was in bed with Kyra's ex-husband.

Edmund nibbled on Burgundy while she rambled away. He knew exactly what she was doing. Talking a few minutes before they made love helped her deal with what she was doing. For although she told herself that allowing him to make her feel sexy and wanted, sometimes she did struggle with what they'd started. This was their third time having sex since Nate died. She would have fun with him but felt guilty afterwards. Edmund did not agree with her opinion but went along with it.

"I think I did alright," he replied. "Rather my interior decorator did a great job. She gets all the credit."

"Her name?"

He stopped nibbling on her feet.

"Why do you ask?"

"Just in case I need her to do the same for me," she explained. "I think my house needs a do over."

"Ahh, I see," he shrugged. "Look her up. Jennifer Mosley. A sixty-five-year-old white woman who wears bifocals and lives with twenty cats."

"Oh okay. Thanks for that *very* unnecessary detail."

Edmund laughed and resumed his nibble fest that included placing his entire mouth over her big toe and sucking on it until Burgundy started her little squirm dance. That's when her hips and legs would rotate and twist and turn around on the sheets as she enjoyed the good feelings Edmund gave to her. If Burgundy squirmed, he knew he was doing a good job. And that's all he wanted. To please this woman and help make her life easier.

As the music continued to play Burgundy allowed her mind to be whisked away. His ardent attention to her made her feel very special.

"What have I done to deserve you?" she asked.

"Just be yourself, my dear. And if you can find it within yourself to do it, love me back."

"That's definitely a good plan." His words and his actions made Burgundy feel very good.

Once he was done working on her feet, Edmund flipped her over.

"Get on your hands and knees," he ordered.

She obeyed.

"Today was kind of challenging," she told him.

"Mmm hmmm," he said as he positioned himself behind her.

"But I won't dwell on the particulars. Some things are just life. You just have to get through them."

"A lot like I'm trying to get through you."

She felt him insert his tongue in the crack of her behind. He wiggled it around touching all her hot spots. Goosebumps raced through her.

He moved his tongue back and forth and dug in and out until he found a nice rhythm.

She shivered and tried to hold onto the pleasure he was giving her without screaming. "This feels sooo good, Edmund. Keep going."

"Don't worry," he said.

He dug deeper like he was trying to become one with her. She loved how he made her feel and was somewhat regretful that in their earlier years, she and Nate did not always share this type of sexual intimacy. But the more she thought about Nate, the more she thought about Becky. And the more she thought about Becky, the colder the room felt.

Burgundy decided to shift gears.

"Edmund, you have no idea, oooh, what this means to me. My God!" She loved the intricate way his tongue probed nearly every sensitive part of her.

"I need this," she murmured.

She wanted to say 'I need you too' but stopped short of doing so.

"You like it?" he asked.

"More than you can know. Can't you tell?"

When he sucked her vagina, Burgundy's eyes fluttered out of sight.

"I think I'm just about ready," she murmured. His fingers rubbed across her clitoris. He rubbed her over and over until she almost shrieked.

"Oh Edmund."

"Yep, you're good and ready," he assured her. "But I have a little bit more to go."

"Please, baby. I can't wait any longer."

He licked her from behind and drove her nearly insane. He found her erogenous zone and caused the most thrilling sensations to zoom through her. The erogenous zone was that mystical sexual island that few men were lucky enough to locate in a woman. And if a woman came across a man who could find it, she tried her best to hold on to him as long as possible.

Burgundy let Edmund do his thing. Wave after wave of pleasure seemed to roll over, then up and down her body, coursing through her until she could barely stand it.

Each erotic touch from her lover made her forget everything that had been going on.

Life was strange and unpredictable and many eligible women lacked a sexy, understanding, intuitive man who knew how to bring everything he had to the table. Edmund Langston Murray was that type of guy.

He flipped her over and sucked on her vagina like it was a treasure, and kept doing it till she was dripping wet. Edmund loved how Burgundy stroked his penis between her fingers until it grew rock hard. She rolled a condom on his erect penis then let him ravish her. He pounded against her over and over again, slapping her thigh with his thigh and making her loins sore. And when he hit her spot with one good hard thrust, she screamed and clawed his back with her pointed nails. Scratches ignited him. He pumped wildly into her like a crazy man. Burgundy shuddered and screamed, releasing all her anxiety into one long, soothing, jerky climax that renewed her.

"My God," she said gasping for breath. "That was . . . that was wonderful."

"That wasn't shit."

"Huh?"

Just when she thought it was all over, Edmund thrust hard against her one last time. He was like a woodpecker, he kept going and going. With widened eyes, she sharply inhaled then bore the pain of his penis and let pleasure invade her body once more.

"Ohh, baby you got some good pussy."

"Do I?"

"Yeah, oh shit, here it comes."

He howled and whimpered as satisfaction began to take over. Burgundy lifted her neck and bit his shoulder. Unbelievably, he caused her to come again and she screeched against his arm and let him plunge into her.

"Oh, daddy, that's never happened to me before." She laughed. "This is just how I like it. Do it harder again but even harder. Slap my ass or something. Hell, I need this, I deserve it."

After he climaxed, she pushed him off of her, then fell back, spreading out on her stomach; she looked like a drunkard after a long night of drinking.

"Uh, umm," she panted and tried to catch her breath.

"You alright?"

"I'm wonder-wonder-wonderful, baby. Just lovely. But sleepy as hell." She pretended like she was snoring.

Edmund could only laugh. He was becoming more acquainted with her. He felt like he knew her like a book. He'd let her get some rest, then he'd wake her up, nibble on her breasts and her toes, then they'd start all over again.

* * *

Exhausted from their sexy liaison, they promptly fell asleep in each other's arms. And later on, when she had to use the restroom, she couldn't go back to sleep just yet. Making love again was the last thing on her mind. Since he woke up too, she decided to say what was on her mind.

"Elm, do you think I handled things all wrong with Natalia? Go on. Tell me."

"I think you thought you made the best decision at the time."

"Yeah. But—"

"But if you had to do it all over again . . . ?"

"I'd choose better words and I'd look at things from her perspective. I'd try to understand that she acted that way because basically, you're like a stranger. My hooking up with you feels too much, too soon."

When she realized how deeply she could have hurt her child, she placed her hands over her face and burst into tears. Edmund stroked her hair and let her get it all out.

"Baby, if you think we should slow things down a bit, I can pull back. But truthfully, I don't want to."

"I want to do the right thing. Yet at the same time, if I am honest, I don't want you to pull back either. No, don't do that. Don't even think about doing it."

"But I don't want to make things any worse for you. I care about you too much to let that happen . . ."

It touched her deeply to see that Edmund didn't see her as just a bed buddy that he could easily discard.

"Edmund, sweetie, if you don't mind, I'd like for us to find a way to make all of this work. I will tread carefully when it comes to Natalia. Make her feel loved and secure. And make you feel just as loved and desired. But family comes first. Alright, baby?"

"I'm here for you, Burgundy. In whatever way you need me, for as long as you need me."

The next evening, Alita found her way back at Burgundy's

house. The two sisters had gathered in the kitchen sipping from cups of hot coffee and chatting. That's when Burgundy, still on her sexy buzz, let it slip that she spent the night with Edmund.

"Really, B? You fucking Edmund Murray now? I've heard of him. He owns those catfish restaurants around town. What are you now? A food chain groupie?"

"Lita, my friends are none of your business."

"Your Daddy Warbucks ain't been in the ground a minute and you already slobbing on his knob like some corn on the cob?"

"Alita!"

"It's true, though right? You've been letting him get it only two weeks after your hubby croaked?"

"Not that it's any of your business but it's been longer than two weeks."

"Okay then, excuse me for getting it wrong. You shed your wifely tears then started dating after six *long* weeks."

"Having a friend, meeting up with a friend, or even kicking it with a friend at his house is not dating."

"I doubt that since you spent the night, that all you did was kick it at his house. Sounds like you've been *kissing it* if you know what I mean."

"Lita, I have no intention of justifying my behavior to you."

"Don't get defensive. I'm trying to look out for you. The streets aren't kind. They'll add extra info to the rumors to what might be the truth and damage your cred even more, you know what I mean?"

Burgundy knew she couldn't pull one over on Alita and pretend as if things were different than what they really were. "Okay, Lita, I'll level with you. In the beginning, right after I lost Nate, my friend was very sympathetic."

"I'll bet he was."

"Alita, seriously. When Nate died I was in shock. I felt

paranoid and insecure. And I just wanted Edmund to be physically near me. His presence comforted me. He started out holding my hand which I did not mind. Then he would put his arms around me and that felt even better. Eventually, I could literally cry on his shoulder. I could tell him how I felt no matter how silly it sounded. He listened. I believe he cared. And after long, I started to ask Edmund if he wouldn't mind holding me while I laid in bed. He didn't mind."

"I'll bet he didn't."

"And slowly but surely, one thing lead to another. It just sort of happened. But it was all innocent."

"Innocent, my ass. But I get it. A pretty young woman like you has needs. But all this closeness and comfort that you're enjoying with Edmund, don't you think you're being disrespectful to the memory of your dead husband, asshole that he was?"

"In what way?"

"You got yourself boo'd up pretty fast, B. And it's not because I give a damn about Nate with his sex doll having ass, but I'm just saying."

"Trust me, Alita, I have grieved Nate in my own way. Grieving doesn't always have to be done publicly to satisfy all those folks who pull out a rating card in order to judge how I'm grieving and whether or not I look remorseful enough about his death." Burgundy felt with all the other things she had going on that stressed her out, people would be more kind and understanding and not give her the business over her newfound friendship with Edmund.

"In my opinion, B, you ought to try having a couple of public meltdowns here and there. Act more sad and lost. I mean, shit, he *just* died, girl."

"I-I know that. You think I don't know that?" Her voice quivered as she sought to adequately express her feelings. Burgundy was growing weary of the conversation and lack of understanding for her feelings. "Tell me. Am I supposed to sit around being lonely and bored out my mind with a coochie that's drying out just because I'm scared of what other people think?"

"Oooh, then you just admitted it. You two *are* fucking."

"No, we are not."

"Do you let him kiss you, B? Because that's where it all starts. If he kisses you right, he can get it."

Alita stared at her sister for all the telltale clues that a woman is in a sexual relationship with a man. The woman seems happy for no apparent reason and there is a spirited strut in her walk.

"Do me a favor. Stand up, B, and walk across the room. I'm asking for a friend."

"No, you are not, silly woman. You are being too damned nosy and reading too much into things," Burgundy gently told her. "Forget about Edmund, Lita. This really isn't about him. It's about me trying to go on with my life. Because whether I grieve for two months, or two years, Nate is gone," she said in a wistful tone. "I miss him for our girls' sake. But I can't stay hurt and miserable forever."

"Forever, B? Hell, it's only been thirty seconds."

"No, it has not, Alita, now stop playing around. Because believe it or not, it's hard to totally shake off the bad feelings. Yet I have a right to be happy, to grab myself a little happiness. And the people who look at me and twist their lips and who don't like what I'm doing and think it's a disgrace, unless they're walking in my shoes, there's no way that they, or even you, can understand how I feel. I don't have to defend myself to you, or Judge Judy, or my entire church."

"Ok, B. I was just—"

"You were just giving me your unwanted opinion that rarely ever helps me."

"Well, damn I was just—"

"Think about this for a second. You finally moved on from Leonard and you're living your life. Dru moved on as well. Even nutty ass Coco is trying to go on after all she's been through. So don't think for one second that Burgundy Reeves won't be trying to get a fresh start in life either."

"Burgundy Taylor. Your name is Burgundy Taylor you little slut."

"Lita, you need to stay out of my bed. And maybe even out of my life. But I know at least one of the two will be impossible."

"You got that right. You need me. I need you. We're stuck together like superglue. Tootle-loo."

And just like that, Alita waved her slender hand, took a last sip of her coffee, and decided to leave while the leaving was good. She could always tell when Burgundy had had enough.

When Burgundy was a little girl growing up in Houston, she was completely enchanted by women like Diana Ross. Even though she wasn't born when Ms. Ross found success with the Supremes, Burgundy learned about Motown, Diana, and her hit songs because their mother, Greta Reeves, always played the most popular 60's soul songs around their house. And early on, Burgundy would read books and magazine articles about how Miss Ross went from growing up in the Detroit Brewster projects to blazing the trail as an international superstar. Diana was a singer, an actress, and ultimately, a business woman. She'd have troubles and drama but seemed to always bounce back.

And learning from her caused Burgundy to make a decision: she wanted to be a successful, powerful black woman who ran her own businesses. She wanted a husband, a family, to create generational wealth, and make good decisions and learn from the bad ones, just like Diana. And just like Ms. Ross, Burgundy's responsibilities meant she had to get focused and be about her business.

The very next morning, she woke up, got showered and dressed, and then greeted Liz who had just arrived at her house.

The two women usually worked together to prepare the girls for school. Cooking breakfast, packing lunches, and organizing backpacks. Liz did most of the work, but Burgundy would also pitch in if time allowed.

And on that particular Tuesday morning, she ran the girls' bathwater while Liz got started scrambling eggs, slicing oranges, and getting the cereal bowls ready.

When Burgundy got an unexpected call from one of her employees, everything changed. She let Liz take over from there.

"Hi, Jordan. What's up?" Jordan Andrews had been Nate's right hand man. And these days he was practically running their Morning Glory restaurant.

"Mrs. Taylor, I just wanted you to know there was a security incident at the midtown restaurant. I'm here right now. No one has been hurt. But there is helluva lot of damage."

"What happened?"

"I got a security text and phone call about the alarm going off. This was about an hour ago. I didn't think it would be anything major since sometimes the alarm goes off for no good reason. But this time, there was a burglary. I hate to say it, but the robbers made off with all the cash that was left in the register."

"I'm not worried about that. It's just money. What was damaged?"

"The front door and a few windows. The police are

here and I've given a statement. I was thinking you're up and probably on your way. I just wanted to give you a heads up."

"Did you view the camera footage?"

"Yes. Two males. Slender. Medium height. Wearing black hoodies and masks."

"Great. That's all I need. We open in what, less than an hour. We may have to temporarily close the restaurant, Jordan."

"I will wait for you to get here to decide what to do."

"Thanks. I'm on my way."

Burgundy tried to remain calm so as not to upset her children. She placed a quick call to Edmund who told her he'd stop by the restaurant as soon as he could.

"Edmund, I appreciate that, but I'm not sure if it's a good idea."

"What? Why would you say that? You need my help and I want to be there for you, Burgundy, please don't be silly about this."

"I'm not being silly."

"Oh, but you are. You're worried about how it will look if I show up at your restaurant this early in the morning," he told her. "People will put two and two together and you're scared of what they think. They can go to hell. You're my woman and I am going to come see about you."

"Edmund, I don't know about that."

"You need to think about how you want me in your life. Because this compartmentalizing my love isn't going to work for me. I'm either all the way in or I'm all the way out. I love you and I'll be driving over to the restaurant to check on things."

"Okay, come on through," Burgundy said, and took a deep breath. Not knowing what else to do, she quickly threw on some casual clothes, ran a comb through her hair, and grabbed her purse, keys and cell phone. By then it was six-fifteen. She dialed Alita and hoped that her sister was up.

"Hey B, what you doing calling me at this time of the day? You know I don't get up till seven."

"I know. I'm sorry. But there's been an emergency."

"What happened?" Alita sounded more alert. "Is everything okay?"

"I'm on my way to Morning Glory. We got robbed last night, or rather early this morning. Jordan Andrews told me they made off with all the cash. Usually we don't deposit our Sunday earnings until Monday and the cash is left there overnight."

"Oh wow, B." Alita's heart rate increased. She felt very uneasy. She knew that she had received a few threatening text messages on Sunday morning. But she ignored them. They were from Jerrod Dawson, Dru's ex-boyfriend. And he was the son of a man that Alita had sex with twenty years ago.

She recalled the last phone conversation she'd had with Jerrod.

"Time's up," he told her. Alita knew exactly what he meant. "You need to pay up, Alita."

"I lost my second job, Jerrod."

"Stop lying and making up excuses. I want my money."

"I don't have any money and I am sick of you trying to shake me down for a dollar. I don't care about you threatening me anymore. Elyse knows she's my daughter. Ain't no reason for you to be blackmailing me 'cause my family knows too and don't care. Get a fucking life and leave me the hell alone."

Jerrod was stunned. What used to work, him threatening her to pay him hundreds of dollars for keeping her secret, wasn't working anymore.

And it made him angry.

"I don't believe you."

"Well, I don't care what you believe, Jerrod. It's all the truth."

"I will go to that restaurant and tell Elyse everything."

"Leave my daughter alone. I mean that. Stay away from my family."

"I'll bet your son doesn't even know he has a sister."

"He does too know. I already told him. Go and blackmail someone else, or better yet, get a better job so you can stop using me for money. I hate your stupid ass. And you're about to get blocked." Alita trembled as she hung up and blocked Jerrod from calling her.

Her eyes welled with tears. She didn't want to think about Jerrod and his threats. She just wanted peace and tranquility. And she wanted to hurry up and do what she should have done a long time ago. Tell her son Leno that Elyse was his sister and not his aunt, and stop the nightmare that began so long ago.

But considering the threatening texts that Alita received last night from an unrecognizable number, it seemed the nightmare was flaring up again.

Chapter 4

Every Woman for Herself

Alita decided to go to Morning Glory. She offered to take Elyse since she had to be at work by eight o'clock. Elyse currently worked as a hostess but Burgundy was fast-tracking her to become an assistant manager.

"Thanks for the ride," Elyse told Alita as they traveled along the freeway. "But Gamba could have taken me like he always does."

"Elyse, I wanted to take you to work and let you know how proud I am of you. You have done well at your psychotherapy sessions, and now it looks like you could get a promotion and a raise at your job."

"Thanks, I want to do better and hopefully one day I won't even have to go to therapy."

"Right," Alita coughed and cleared her throat. "Which brings me to this. One thing I plan to do, starting today, is tell the rest of the family about us."

"That I'm your child?"

"Yes. Is that fine by you? You've been doing so well. I don't want to stress you out and cause you to have a relapse."

"I think I can handle it. Who do you plan to tell first?"

They had arrived at Morning Glory. Alita parked her vehicle. A police car was stationed outside.

"You're about to find out, Elyse. That's all I can say."

They went inside the restaurant and it looked like the front entrance would be temporarily fixed so the business could remain open.

"Let's go to the business office."

Elyse meekly followed Alita until they found Burgundy who was just hanging up the phone.

"Hey, B. I'm here. I got Elyse with me. I'm sorry about the robbery and if I could pay you back every dime, I would. But you know me, I'm still struggling financially. I have been looking for a new job, a better paying one, so that Elyse won't have to live with Coco anymore. Once I get my stuff together, I wouldn't mind getting a bigger place and let her live with me again. I want to nurture her, take care of her, because she is . . ." Alita sighed. "She's um."

"What's wrong?" Burgundy asked.

"Look B, there's something I've been meaning to tell you for a long time. Real long time. But—"

Burgundy's eyes widened. "Does this have anything to do with my dead husband?"

"No, B. Thank the Lord." Alita wanted to laugh. Maybe this would be easier than she thought. "It has to do with me and Greta Reeves, our dear mother."

"What about her?"

Alita went on to explain how when she was barely sixteen, she got pregnant. And how the father was the man who lived across the street from them, Mr. Dawson. His wife, their son, Jerrod, and the three daughters were in disbelief and devastated by the whole thing.

"I was young. Naïve. Taken advantage of. And pregnant."

"But hold up," Burgundy said. "Wasn't mama pregnant at the same time as you?"

"Yep. But she faked her pregnancy, B. Mine was real but hidden. And one day I gave birth to my first born . . . this beautiful young woman," Alita hugged Elyse and kissed the top of her forehead.

There. She spoke her truth. At last Alita felt free.

Burgundy was stunned. "If I am hearing you correctly, Elyse is your natural born child?"

"Yeah, B. She's my daughter. Mine. The other sisters already knew. I've been wanting to tell you for the longest."

Burgundy had to let the truth sink in before she could respond. "Okay, fine. She's your daughter. But why was I the last to know? Do you think I'm that emotionally fragile that I wouldn't be able to handle it? As much as I want to hold up our family and make it strong as possible, you went around hiding this news from me as if I'm the enemy. I feel so confused."

"Sis, you've been through so much as it is. I didn't want to add to it. I didn't know how it would make you feel, knowing that your husband did what he did, to my daughter. I just couldn't predict how you'd react, B."

Burgundy nodded. But her initial state of calm started to boil over. "Damn it. All of it makes me so angry. Because I still don't get it. I don't understand Nate. Why did he do what he did to Elyse? Did he ever tell you?" Elyse could only shrug.

"I'm sorry that I believed him. A wife wants to believe the best about her man. And it's maybe the reason why so many people did not believe Dr. Christine Ford. She told her truth and got raked over the coals. Even so, Brett Kavanaugh's wife stood by him. And Camille Cosby has always stood by her husband no matter what. That's what us wives think we're supposed to do."

"But not all wives are the same. Some may be disgusted but they stay just for the money or the fame."

"And some stay because it's all they know to do. Maybe

that's why I did it," Burgundy replied. "It's no excuse. Because the bottom line is whether I believed in my spouse or not, if he did those dirty deeds, I am not the one that he must answer to. I'm amazed by your confession, but oddly enough, I feel better now. About everything. No longer will I beat myself up for another adult's behavior. My husband made his choices. I'm about to make mine."

She quieted down and heard Edmund's voice. It sounded like he was talking to a policeman in the front lobby. She decided not to make a deal about it and felt very happy that her man had shown up during a critical moment of her life.

"You're about to make some choices, B? I don't know if I like how that sounds," Alita said.

"That's because you don't know how it feels to be me, right now, Lita."

"That's true."

"You don't know how it feels to think you're an intelligent, perceptive woman just to find out you were duped by someone you knew. Hell, I cross paths with all kinds of people on a daily basis. Being in the restaurant business makes you a people-watcher in some ways. And yet I still could not pick up on all these secrets that surrounded me." Burgundy shuddered. "Being the last to know really sucks."

"B, don't get yourself all worked up."

"All of you knew?" she asked.

"Dru and Coco found out in August," Elyse replied. "They learned after Nate died. They were shocked but they got over it. And I'm hoping you can do the same."

Alita reached over and hugged Elyse. "Don't blame my daughter. It ain't her fault. And don't you dare be mad at me either. You may not have been able to sense what was going on but at least I finally told you."

"Better late than never, I guess," Burgundy murmured.

So much had happened in such a brief time she wanted to brace herself for any other earth-shattering announcements.

"Elyse, it must have rocked your world to learn Alita is your mom. How do you feel about this?" Burgundy asked.

"Like I finally know who I am and I can move forward. Because now I have the truth. That's what you tell us all the time at our Sister Day meetings. You once said that the truth may take a long time to come out but that shouldn't matter."

"Well, I guess if everyone else is alright with this then I won't be any different. It's all just so sudden and so shocking. But why did you finally tell me, and at this time of the morning?"

"Girl, you haven't heard the worst." Alita went on to explain the extortion threats she'd been getting and how she felt that the restaurant was targeted because she didn't take Jerrod seriously.

"And you told me all this to explain the robbery?"

"Yeah. Jerrod was getting what little money I had so he wouldn't expose me which is dumb because his father was the rapist. Like a fool, I fell for it. But when I got mad enough to realize I had nothing to be ashamed of, I shut it down cold. No more cash from Alita! But Jerrod thought he'd take it to the next level. He heard about you, B, and it was like 'cha-ching'. And now he's after your money too. The bastard."

At hearing Alita's extended confession, Burgundy's whole body shook uncontrollably. She felt caged in, paranoid, and like she had no escape. Her sister's ex-boyfriend wanted to harm her, to take something from her he didn't deserve. For a moment she wasn't able to think.

Sometimes, that's how bitter truth hits you. It stops you dead in your tracks before you're able to move again.

Once she organized her thoughts, Burgundy asked a

staff member to bring her a fresh cup of coffee with plenty of cream and sugar.

"I've got to pull myself together. Too much is going on. And I, I just don't know what to say, Lita."

"Say that you forgive me for putting you in this mess. If I stood my ground with Jerrod in the first place, I doubt this would have happened."

"And you really believe, you're totally sure, that he robbed Morning Glory?"

"B, I can't prove it but I know this dude. The timing is too suspicious. Anyway, how much he get y'all for?"

"Jordan told me that we lost only four grand. Because yesterday the restaurant was closed. Thank God for that! It could have been a lot worse."

"Only four thousand? That prick. I'll let the cops know what I think about him being a possible suspect. In my head no one else would want to do that except Jerrod Dawson."

Right then Coco burst through the office door, out of breath and looking wild-eyed.

"I heard that there was a break-in earlier today. What the hell is going on?"

"What's going on," Burgundy said, "Is that I am just now learning some family stuff that no one bothered to tell me before now."

Coco looked mortified. What family stuff had they been talking about? When Coco noticed that Burgundy appeared to be eyeing her with disdain, she felt guilty and remorseful. This wasn't how she wanted her sister to find out about her and Nate.

"Aw shit," Coco said. "B, I'm so sorry—"

"And what I'm wondering is why was it such a big deal that no one cared enough to just let me know way before now?"

"Um, that's because we thought you'd be upset with

our mother for pretending like Elyse was her child." Alita hoped Coco caught on that her secret was still safe.

"Oh right. That," Coco said. "You just now finding out about Elyse."

"Yeah, because some family like to hold secrets around here," Burgundy told them. "But it's not like I could do anything about that. I'm a grown ass woman. I can take more than you think."

"Yeah, you're proving that to be true." Alita winked at Coco then nodded but Coco shook her head. Now was not the best time to tell Burgundy her own news.

Burgundy walked over to Elyse.

"Baby girl, if I never told you before, I'm telling you now. I feel so very bad about everything that happened to you. The fact that you are just recently learning about your real mom and for what Nate did to you and how I treated you when I found out."

"It's okay, B," Elyse said.

"No, it's not okay. I should have listened but it was so, so hard. He was my husband." She talked in a hushed tone, like she was finally recognizing that the ability to accept things as they were was the best course of action. "Even though he was my spouse, if he hurt someone, especially my family, I should have sided with you and given you lots of support. I should have gotten him some help too, of course. Again, please forgive me, Elyse. And you too, Lita."

"Girl, you know I forgive your big old head. Hey, you are B. And B stands for 'Bank'. So I gots to stay in good with you."

They all laughed at Alita's outrageous remark. Even Coco felt warm and fuzzy inside. Seeing Burgundy so willing to accept her other sister's secrets filled her with hope. And she prayed that on the day she finally got to tell the truth about Chance and Nate, that Burgundy would have enough forgiveness to pardon her as well.

Chapter 5

Making It out Alive

Elyse asked Gamba to pick her up from work that afternoon once her shift had ended. He agreed to come and get her.

"What do you want to do?" he asked once they were seated in his pickup.

"I don't want to go home. I want to hang out at your spot. Let's go."

In no time at all they arrived at Gamba's quaint one-bedroom apartment. He used the key to let her inside. They settled in the living room which was filled with black leather sofas, bulky armchairs and multiple tables that displayed carved ivory sculptures.

"I'm glad you wanted to come here. We can finally get to talk." Gamba patted an empty space next to him on the sofa.

Elyse sat down then shuddered as if she were freezing. He hurried to adjust the thermostat then found his soccer jacket and carefully arranged it over her shoulders.

Gamba was from Zimbabwe and he was the true definition of a good man. Assertive, strong, kind, comforting, and a perfect gentleman.

Gamba offered Elyse a large, cold bottle of sparkling water, her favorite drink.

"Thanks," she said in a hushed tone. "There was a lot of family drama at work. I just had to get away. This feels way better than being at Coco's."

"I'm sure it does. How are you doing, Elyse? You've been quiet lately. I can tell when something is bothering you."

"I know. I'm sorry about that, Gamba. I think I'm doing better but sometimes I feel like I'm still trying to find myself." When Nate began abusing her at the age of fourteen, the experience caused her to grow distrustful of the opposite sex.

"Sometimes I have troubling expressing how I feel," she continued. "But maybe the best thing to do is be honest."

"There you go. I agree." Gamba offered Elyse a sweet kiss on the lips. When he released her, she felt herself begin to relax.

"Alright, Gamba. What do you want to know?"

"When you texted me about what happened at Morning Glory, you told me that you found out more info. About the identity of your real dad. And you told me that Burgundy now knows the truth about you and Alita. That's a lot to handle."

"Yes, it is."

"I just wanted to know, if you don't mind telling me, how you feel about it all. Like, your dad."

Elyse shrugged. "I don't know him. I just know his name is Jack Dawson. Alita never really talked much about him. I'm doing good just to find out about her being my mom."

"I see. But do you think you'll ever want to meet your father and make up for lost time?"

"How can you miss something you never really knew? I just found out about him. He feels like a stranger who leaves me with no feelings at all."

"But you must be curious about that side of the family, right?"

"I guess one day I will want to see him face to face. But

Lita said he's in jail. And I doubt I'm going to visit him. Jerrod is his son; I know I've seen him in Morning Glory a few times. I've caught Jerrod staring at me. And I wondered who he was . . . what he wanted. But he was using me to get himself some money. And if father is anything like son, I don't want to meet Jack at all." She smiled at Gamba. "The only man, the most important man that I want in my life, is sitting right next to me."

"Elyse, thank you for saying that. You are as important to me as you say I am to you."

"I'm not just *saying* it though," she said in a stubborn voice. "I meant every word. You are my world, Gamba."

He relished her lovely sentiments, but Gamba had more probing questions.

"Elyse, I hope you don't mind me asking about Nathaniel Taylor."

"What about him?"

"He's been dead for some time now and I hope you're ready to open up. I want to know everything that happened between you and that guy. I want to call him a son-of-a-bitch but I was taught to never disrespect the dead."

"Gamba, I already told you what he did to me."

"I know and I feel like some of what happened is my fault."

"No, it's not. You had nothing to do with it. It all started before I even met you."

"I know. But I'm talking about the things that happened after we met. The tragic thing that happened when I left town."

"Him dying?"

"Yeah, I wished I had been around that day. Maybe if I had been there, he wouldn't have died. Things would have gone differently."

"Gamba, please, there's nothing you could have done about it."

"But I should have been here in Houston to protect you, instead of being out in California trying to help the residents bounce back from those wildfires that broke out in that state."

"You're in the military. You were just doing your job."

"But as your man, my job is to also protect and love you to the best of my ability."

His words warmed her heart. And a warm heart wasn't something Elyse was accustomed to feeling. When she lived with Nate and Burgundy, she would often feel tense. Then she'd grow nonchalant, and finally she learned to muffle her feelings. Every time Nate even looked at Elyse, her tender heart would turn to stone, like freshly poured cement.

Gamba continued. "Now that it's all over, where is your mind at these days?"

"These days, I want to be able to feel again, let myself feel whatever is in my heart, good or bad. I don't want to be what Dru told me one time. She said I'd been, 'emotionally locked up'. And I asked her what that meant. And she told me that it's like being shut up in a prison cell. Like when you're in that cell, your heart can't feel anything but anger, hatred, resentment."

"That's all over and done with."

"Yep, it is. Hold my hand," she commanded.

Gamba quickly grabbed it. His hands were warm, oversized, and slightly rugged. "I like how it feels when we do this. And, I-I am sorry for acting like I don't have any experience. But the truth is I don't have any experience," she said in a soft voice.

"You mean in making love with a man who really loves you? Is that what you're saying Elyse?"

"Yeah. When I work at Morning Glory, I hear all the other girls, girls younger than me, and they talk about how they had sex with this man and that man. They know all the tricks, the moves, how to wear the Victoria's Secret, how to give—"

"Give head."

"Yes, give head, and every other thing they can give." She forced herself to look her man in his eyes.

"Is giving head what you want to do to me, Elyse?"

"Yeah, of course."

"And are you trying to prove something to someone? To your co-workers? To yourself? By making love to a man?"

"What do you mean by 'a man'?"

"I was just asking—"

"Look," she said with impatience. "There is no other man. Has never been. And I swear to you I never enjoyed Nate being on top of me. I hated it. People lie about rape victims and say they seduced the man—"

"Is that what you did to Nate, Elyse? Be honest. Because I heard something—"

"What? What did you hear?"

"That *you* seduced *him*. You did it on purpose. Is it true, Elyse?"

His eyes flickered like he was bracing himself, in case the rumor was true.

"Who told you that? Did Coco tell you that?"

"She told me some things."

"She has some nerve."

Elyse dropped Gamba's hand and stood up. She removed his jacket and flung it to the floor. As an afterthought, she stomped on it and left an imprint of dirt on the sleeves.

When Gamba did not respond, she picked up the jacket and threw it at him. It landed on his head and partially covered one eye. As he slowly pulled it off of him, Gamba's eyes did not reveal a single negative emotion.

He quietly watched Elyse storm across his living room floor.

"Coco had no right to tell you that," she continued.

"That is my story, my life. She's always trying to throw someone under a bus. Coco know she's wrong but that's only because she feels guilty about what *she* did, but I don't." Elyse thought about their pinky swear and how loyalties must work both ways.

"What don't you feel guilty about?" Gamba asked.

"Don't you know that already? Didn't Coco tell you?"

"I want to hear it from you, my love. Coco will have her own opinion about what went on in that house the day before Nate passed away. And you have yours. And your side is the one that I really care about."

"I don't believe you. You're saying it, but I don't believe it."

"Why not?"

"Gamba, you believed *Coco*, not me. You doubted me. You questioned me like you don't trust me."

"I do trust you. I just want to find out more—"

"Gamba, I'm not sure if I should be telling you anything. If you believe everyone else but me, what good will it do to tell you more?"

Gamba's eyes grew dark with frustration. Within seconds he jumped up, clutched her scrawny shoulders, and leered into her fiery eyes. Their noses almost touched and he could hear the rapid, tiny gasps that escaped her mouth.

"Look at me, Elyse."

"No." She jerked away from him.

"I said look at me."

She'd escaped his grip and refused to face him. When he tried to stand in front of her, she whirled back around in an angry twist.

"Elyse, c'mon, don't act like this."

"No, Gamba. I don't want to look at you or anybody else right now."

The energy in the room changed. Gamba felt Elyse disappearing. He wanted to reconnect and get her to trust him again. Dammit! He hated Nate for he knew that his foul actions toward this young woman had obviously scarred her. In truth, Elyse was still trying to heal. And Gamba blamed himself right then for possibly wounding her even more.

"Whoa, whoa, whoa. I don't like how all this is going," he told her.

"You started it though. You attacked me and I don't deserve it. I don't."

Again, her words surprised him into a reality that he needed to face. "Elyse, baby, I'm sorry for offending you. For acting like I don't trust you. I fucked up. Forgive me?"

"I dunno, I'll have to think about it."

Feeling as though that answer was better than the alternative, he decided to switch things up.

"Okay, that's fair. Meanwhile, I think we both should take five and calm down," he told her in a gentle voice. "We don't have to talk about that anymore."

"Good. Because right now I could eat."

"I'll go get you another drink and while I'm doing it, I have some leftover sadza and peanut butter stew in the fridge. Does that sound like a plan?"

Elyse did not respond, but she followed him to his kitchen. She sat at the table and cautiously watched Gamba's every move as he retrieved large porcelain bowls from the cupboard and then warmed up their food.

All that arguing sapped her energy. She knew Gamba was a skilled cook. And she knew that sadza was a chewy and salty porridge. The peanut stew was a thick and flavorful dish. It consisted of spinach, okra, sautéed onions, carrots, with a sweet tomato sauce and peanut butter all simmering together.

Eating the food reminded him of Zimbabwe and of family, love, and togetherness. And right then he knew he needed to restore the previous bond that existed between himself and his lady.

He set the meal before them and had Elyse sit down.

He fixed their bowls. "Let's pray first."

"Okay," she said in an effort to be peaceable. Elyse was learning to be independent but she knew she needed to consider the good insight of those who knew about life.

They began to eat.

"How's the food? You like it?"

"It's different from what Coco cooks. But yeah, I like it. You did good." They continued engaging in small talk, but Gamba knew that speaking about anything that bothered him was essential to restoring good communication.

"Elyse, my dear, I-I wasn't trying to accuse you of anything a little while ago. But I just wanted you to know that in my country—"

"What do you mean your country? You're American."

"I'm African!"

"And American!"

He paused. "I meant to say from a man's perspective, if a woman throws herself at him—"

"But I *didn't* throw myself at Nate."

"Let me finish, sweetie. We're just talking in general. This isn't about you."

"Yeah, right."

"Elyse, if a woman shows great sexual initiative, it may cause the man to think she is interested in him, that she finds him very desirable." He droned on and on. And for a few minutes, Elyse listened to him as he gently chided her for the info that Coco gave him.

"Gamba, ever since I've known you, you've taught me a lot of different things: how to swim, how to change a flat, how to escape from a house that has a locked garage door. Things like that."

"That's true. But what does this have to do with seducing Nate?"

"You never told me how to survive a man who breaks

into a woman's room, and who starts touching her body while she's asleep, and who makes her kiss him and suck his dick even when she doesn't want to." Elyse felt dirty and violated all over again by the mere memories of what happened.

"Gamba, I told you how he was, and you knew I had to go back and live in that house with him and B, but I don't remember you teaching me how to make it out alive. I had to teach myself how to do that."

"I can't argue with that logic. I guess I messed up."

"How?"

"I told you too much of some things, and not enough of others. Not enough of the survival skills that could really matter. I think I was too afraid and I was hoping that Nate had stopped being an asshole but I should have known better. But you knew that Nate was still like that even though I wasn't sure."

"My point is, Gamba, even if you didn't understand me, I did what I had to do. And I'm the one who's still alive."

"Physically, sure you are. But emotionally? I don't totally know where your head is."

"Does that make you nervous, Gamba? That you don't know all of my thoughts all day long?" Elyse wanted to laugh at the irony. What she thought she wanted, right then, she somewhat had. She always wanted a good man who was intrigued by her. But it did not feel how she thought it would feel.

"Gamba, everything I did that day in my room when Nate had me locked up and not wanting me to get out, well, it made me want to live long enough to escape from the room, to get out of that house for good. Just like when you are overseas fighting against the enemies. You fought with one picture in your mind—getting back home to America and not arriving in a wooden box. Gamba, I swear to you, it sounds like you blame me for being strong and for fighting."

"What?"

"Yes. You've punished me. That's what it feels like you're doing. Like I'm on trial." Suddenly she wasn't hungry anymore. "You say that you care about my progress. But I don't want to talk about this. Because you make me relive the nightmare. I already do that in psychotherapy. I don't want to do it with you. I want to be free."

"And I want you to be free. Go ahead, Elyse. Be free." His voice was choked with emotion. "Be free!"

His words sent a shock through her system.

"I don't know what you mean by you want me to be free," she angrily responded. "But it sounds like you don't want me anymore. And I won't have that."

"Elyse—"

"Gamba, since you gave so much advice on how to be as a strong woman guess what? I'm strong right now. Congratulations. You did your job." The tables had been turned, something Gamba did not expect.

"You did a great job, so pat yourself on the back, you asshole."

What type of woman have I created, he asked himself.

"Elyse, I'll pretend like I didn't hear that. But we need to—"

"I'm serious, Gamba. I don't want to talk. Already talked enough. Again, what good has it done except push me and you further apart?" She folded her arms clumsily across her chest.

"Elyse?"

Silence.

He tapped her on the arm. "C'mon, don't shut down like this. Talk to me."

She said nothing.

"Elyse, you've come so far. I hope you aren't thinking

about going back to the way you used to be. Barely saying a word. You can't regress. Not after you've made so much good progress. Elyse! Elyse!"

He had no clue what she was thinking.

Fear of the unknown can paralyze a person and make them assume their worst fears.

Does she hate me now? If she sleeps on it will we wake up tomorrow not caring about each other? I don't know what I'd do if I lost her.

Gamba wanted to kiss her and rub his hands all over her body.

"C'mon, baby, don't be this way."

She opened up her phone and paid his begging no attention. The more she ignored him, the hotter he got.

He knew that many guys were so hungry for sex they will get it any way that they can. The man shuts out the fact that the woman wasn't having it. That's how Gamba felt right then. He wanted Elyse more than he ever wanted anything in his life.

"Is it okay if I steal a kiss? Please?"

She finally couldn't hold it in any longer. "Who are you now, Gamba? Are you another Nate Taylor? You want to force me to kiss you? You want me even when I've shown you that I don't want you?"

Elyse showed Gamba her phone and let him see that she'd requested an Uber ride. She was ready to leave. Gamba knew he'd hurt her and he felt torn. She looked so tiny and vulnerable. So sweet yet so coldhearted.

"Don't leave me like this," he said in a desperate voice.

"I can't stay here. I've got to get away."

She waited for her ride. When it arrived, she left the apartment and walked toward the car without telling Gamba goodbye.

Chapter 6

Black Sheep

Elyse's driver dropped her off at Dru's. She walked up to the townhouse and rang the bell. Dru answered and did a double take. "I don't believe what I'm seeing. I hope everything is okay."

"It is. Yet it isn't. May I hang out here for a minute?"

Dru welcomed her inside.

It was after seven and the night was brutally cold. Elyse appreciated having somewhere else to go. She hated feeling disoriented.

"You look worried, Elyse."

"We just had our first fight. I'm so confused."

"Just an argument, right? Not a fist fight."

"Yes. A real bad argument."

"Whatever it was about," Dru advised her, "try to straighten it out. Apologize or forgive him. As long as he did not abuse you in any way, make peace with your guy."

Elyse took a seat on the edge of the sofa. Dru's home felt comfortable and filled with warmth and serenity. Its loveliness actually made Elyse feel better and painted a simple picture of how her own life could be.

"You know what," Elyse said. "I'm sorry for showing up like this, but I really needed to talk to somebody."

"I'm glad you feel you can come to me."

Elyse's phone screen lit up.

"Is it him?" Dru asked.

Elyse nodded.

"Go on and answer."

"I was so pissed at him that I didn't want to be around him anymore. And now I feel stupid for leaving. I could have stayed instead of running away. What if he thinks I'm weak?"

"You're still learning how to give love and how to receive it. If Gamba cares for you like I think he does, he'll understand."

"I hope so."

"Has he ever hit you, Elyse?"

"No!"

"Cursed you out or even threatened to hurt you?"

"No, not even close. He loves and respects his mother and even when we argued, he did his best to respect me. I'm glad about that, but sometimes I don't think he understands me."

"Then try and help him to understand you. You two are in a serious relationship. You owe him that, Elyse."

By then the ringing had stopped.

Elyse waited for her phone to ring again but the screen remained dark.

"Give it a couple of minutes then call him back. One thing you never do is go to bed mad. Misunderstandings are just something that you must learn to nip in the bud."

Dru came and sat beside her niece. The young girl was so incredibly beautiful and she still had so much innocence. But the lessons she'd gained about the challenges and unpredictability of life were evident as well.

In many ways, Dru could relate. She knew how it felt to be uncomfortable in her own skin. And she knew how long it could take a woman to find herself and blossom into a confident lady who knew who she was and understood what she must do to succeed.

When compared to the rest of the Reeves women, Drucilla Reeves always felt like the person that didn't seem to solidly fit within her family. Alita and Coco were like personality twins: verbally fearless and wild as horses. Burgundy was the thinker, the planner, the one who made sure that everything functioned well and worked properly. When it came to these women, they reminded Dru of *Mystic Pizza* or *Soul Food*. Classic films about sisters who loved hard and had unforgettable personalities.

When she thought about herself and where she fit in, her DNA seemed slightly different. And it made her remember something she once heard: sisters are different flowers from the same garden.

"Elyse dear," Dru said. "I am here to support you and love on you as much as I can. But you are grown and will have to make tough decisions for your own life."

"I know. And I love how you give me pointers about men."

"We all have to learn. You'll figure it out."

Elyse held her phone in her hand and decided to make what she hoped would be a good move.

She tapped on 'missed call' feature on her phone and waited for Gamba to pick up.

"Hi baby," he immediately answered.

"Gamba, I am so sorry."

"Don't be sorry. I acted like an ass," he replied. "I should know that you would never intentionally do anything to hurt me."

"You got that right. I'm not that type of woman. I'm nothing like Coco."

"Good," he laughed. Needing to laugh as well, Elyse chuckled. Her whole insides turned over until she began to feel much better.

Elyse had a sudden yearning to see her man. She stood to her feet. "Gamba, we will put this behind us, okay?"

"Sounds like a plan."

Dru's doorbell rang. Elyse remained on the couch talking to Gamba. Dru quietly walked to the door and soon let him inside.

Elyse's back was turned. She continued speaking to him and hadn't realized he had approached her from behind.

"I've been wondering what're we going to do on our next date night," she told him. Dru gestured at Elyse to stand up.

She did. "I really want to check out a good movie, or we can go to TopGolf."

Gamba hung up on her.

"Hello?" she said.

Elyse felt a tap on her shoulder. Furious, she swung around ready to berate Dru for her awful piece of advice that obviously did not work. Her man had never hung up on her before and he was starting to piss her off again.

But as she turned around her eyes met Gamba's, which were lit up with joy.

"Gamba?"

He picked her up by the waist, gave her rapid kisses on her cheek. He swung Elyse around so many times that she began to feel dizzy, the room wildly spinning like a carnival ride. She felt wobbly yet happy. Calmer and more confident. And more than ever, Elyse felt poised to develop into a strong woman who knew what she wanted in life and wasn't afraid to get it.

That weekend Alita rounded up all the sisters. They gathered in her tiny apartment, all gladly squeezed into her home to do their thing.

"I know it's not an official Sister Day meeting," Alita told them. "But I just felt like we should spend some quality time together."

Coco wanted to read between the lines. She had told Alita her fears about potentially getting questioned by the police and maybe her sister was as scared as her about Coco's fate. "Look, I resent that you're treating this thing like the Last Supper," she said to Alita. The spread of food was impressive. Burgundy had gotten one of her caterer friends to cook and deliver stuffed mushrooms, crab cakes, shrimp cocktail, and chicken tenders.

Coco complained, but steadily filled her plate with food. "Going out your way to get us to meet up and forcing me eat all this food. You know I'm on a diet."

"Coco, you ain't on a diet. Don't even try it." Alita laughed at her own joke.

"But we never eat this good at our meetings. I feel like it's like a bon voyage party for me."

"Stop being spooked, Coco. This isn't about you. It's about the Reeves sisters," Alita explained. "Tomorrow isn't promised to any of us."

"She's right," Burgundy said. "We must love on each other as much as we can. Plus this can be our own version of *Red Table Talk*. We can learn to deal with each other through raw conversations just like Jada Pinkett Smith and her family."

"I happen to love that show," Coco said finally realizing that what they were suggesting was actually sensible and potentially helpful.

"Is there anything y'all want to discuss," Burgundy asked to no one in particular. But Coco almost lost her breath. "No, not me. I'm so hungry I could pass out. And once I finish eating, I'm sure y'all can think of something juicy to talk about. As long as it's not about me."

"Ain't nobody thinking about you, Coco." That was Alita.

"Good," Coco said knowing that her sister was lying through her teeth.

All the women helped themselves to some grub and beverages and took their seats in the living room.

In no time at all the women got caught up doing what they loved the most.

"My first question is to the one who paid for all of these delicious snacks. How you holding up, Sis?" Alita already knew that Burgundy had been spending time with Edmund and had been introduced to him recently when they were at Morning Glory. "I'm sure you must be lonely at times."

"Yes, I try to stay busy, but late at night when the house gets really quiet, it kind of hits me. I am single," she said and stared at Alita. "I am widowed, but I am single too, you know what I mean?"

"Yeah, I know exactly what you mean. And there comes a time when a lot of women have to jump back into the dating game. I had to do it after me and Leonard broke up. And Coco is trying to do it too, God bless her little heart."

"I just want to know what to look out for," Burgundy said.

"Oh, Sis, I can help you with that," Alita replied. "Stay away from tall, black, and broke."

"Or short, rich, and white, but can never do right." That was Dru.

"Tall, cute, and brown, but a total clown." Coco had to throw in her two cents.

"Tall, fat, and yellow, with a stomach that moves like Jell-O." Alita was on a roll. "How about this 'tall, dark, and handsome and perfect,' as in 'perfectly married'? Don't you hate when a married man tries to holler at you? Don't get me started. He trying to text me when his wife is right next to him in bed. What's he trying to do? Set up a threesome? I don't think so!"

All the women fell back in their chairs, talking loud,

playfully teasing each other, and eager to get into some juicy conversation.

"Let's talk about sex," Alita said. "Which reminds me of this guy I used to mess around with named Alphonso. Having sex with him reminded me of a streaming service. Picture this: It's a Friday night. You're sitting in front of the TV, enjoying your show. Things are going well; you're really into it. But suddenly, the streaming service stops working. The show gets interrupted; it starts buffering. You wait around and after a while you get pissed. You're sick of waiting for things to crank back up again. That's the type of lover Alphonso was . . . totally undependable. I call him my Netflix lover."

"Aw Sis," Coco said in sympathy. "I feel you. But I can do you one better than that. Have you ever had a drone lover?"

"No, what's that?"

"A drone lover is when that man pops over out of nowhere. But you're glad to see him so you let him in. He races straight to your bedroom and you let him tap that ass. He's doing a good job too, but before you know it, he's up and running out the door and flying away towards some other woman's house."

"Hmm, that's cold-blooded," Alita said with a chuckle. "I think I can put up with a Netflix lover more than a drone lover."

"Y'all are officially nuts," Dru said with a loud chuckle. "I'm glad I don't have to deal with all of that. Tyrique and I are solid."

"Are you sure?" Alita bluntly asked.

"I am."

"But are you solid enough to finally let that man marry you? You know you've turned him down more times than we can count."

"I know that. But if I'm not ready to marry him, why mess things up over a piece of paper?"

"You on that again?" Coco said. Talk about marriage always hurt her since her own dreams fell apart when Calhoun unceremoniously dumped her and then married Samira. "If I would have kept my big mouth shut and just been content to have Calhoun in my life without the ring, and without the ceremony, I'm positive we'd still be together. We could have grown old together. We could have ended up raising our kids and being with each other till the very end."

"But Coco," Dru said, "This is where you and I don't see eye-to-eye. To me happiness isn't just finding some man that you want to spend the rest of your life with. Of course, there are many happily married people out here. But on the flip side, there are couples who've been together thirty or forty years and they aren't necessarily fulfilled. They feel stuck. They're more like roommates who share bills because the romance is long gone. And they feel too old to start over again. To me, as long as you're happy, whether you're single or married, that's what life is about. Be happy with what you have. Of course, that's easier said than done." She winced as she continued. "Because I am happy with my life yet there is still something missing. If I could have a baby, that would make things so much sweeter."

"Why don't you adopt?" Coco asked. "Hell, you can adopt one of my ragamuffins."

"Stop being silly. I am okay with being an aunt, but it kills me that I'll never know how it feels to be a mother."

"Life is strange like that," Alita said. "We always want what we don't have."

"Let me interject," Burgundy said. "I agree with all of you, which is really an unusual phenomenon." They all laughed. "Because I don't care what anyone says, we always take each other for granted. We treat each other like old shoes that you throw in the back of the closet and forget all about. But we treat the new shoes with much more respect."

"That sounds like the song that says you don't know what you got till it's gone," Coco said. "And if that ain't the truth I don't know what is."

"Exactly." Burgundy's eyes gleamed as she reminisced. "Mama used to tell me 'Enjoy what you have right now, Daughter. Enjoy the life that you've been given because there are no guarantees.' She told me that when I was in my early twenties. Back then I was way too young to understand what she meant. I was new in my marriage and I wanted to have babies, and Mama would just laugh at me. I can see her even now. Her skinny shoulders would shake so hard when she laughed that she had to stop talking. She would finally pat me on my back and tell me to take my time and to live each day just as it came. Mama practically begged me to not try and rush through anything because in this life, nothing is guaranteed. Then years later when she got sick, you know what she said? 'Told ya.' That's it. Like she was proving her prophesy. Like she had to show us girls just what she was talking about. And life was almost over for her so the rest of the things she told me grew more desperate."

"I feel sad. Don't talk about it anymore," Coco said. "I miss my mama."

"We all do," Alita said, "But B needs to finish telling us her story. Go ahead, B."

"Long before Mama died and when I had youth and beauty and brains and all kinds of energy and hope, I would tell her all the Big Dreams that Nate and I had. We wanted to become business owners. I'd tell her all the plans we had of opening up our own restaurant and how excited we were. And Mama would listen. She would always be good at listening to whatever I told her. And she'd smile at me and she would say, "'Dream on my daughter, dream big.' And she told me that out of all the daughters that she had, I probably was the one to actually see my dreams come true. Because she saw that I was focused and goal-oriented and I knew how to get things done with no excuses."

"You are blessed when it comes to that," Dru told her. "I think that is probably one thing we have in common. Focus and determination." The two sisters beamed at each other. The love was getting stirred around in large doses and it all felt so good for this unofficial Sister Day.

But leave it up to Coco and Alita to throw some drama into the mix. The ladies took a short break to enjoy some more snacks that Burgundy had picked up from the store just in case they ran out of food: pizza crackers, cheese balls, and fresh fruit.

"What is this shit," Coco asked. "Where're the hot wings, the blue cheese dip?"

"I thought you were on a diet."

"I am, Lita, shut up."

"That's why you look the way you look right now," Alita said as she stuffed her mouth with the crackers. "It won't hurt you to eat some low cal food every once in a while."

Coco bristled. "Are you calling me fat? Are you calling me fat?"

"No, she's not," Dru told her.

"Call her fat and just get it over with." Burgundy couldn't help but cackle.

"My weight is fine," Coco snapped back. "And someone real special loves the way I look."

"Who?" Alita asked. "You don't have a man."

"You don't know what I have."

"You two, please." That was Dru. "Can we have one meeting without your getting into an argument?"

"No, we can't," Alita said with a laugh. "We've been acting like this since we were kids. Remember, Coco?"

"No. I don't."

"Yeah, you do."

The ladies quieted down so they could continue enjoying the food.

"I think I've come up with a juicy topic," Alita spoke up. "B, you're the only one who can answer this."

"Go ahead."

"How much you getting from those insurance policies?"

"Oh, wow, she really went there," Dru said to no one in particular.

"Um, the attorneys are still ironing out those details," Burgundy answered. "That's about all I can tell you for now, Alita."

"I guess we'll know what's up once we see you renovate the house or if you get a brand new whip or some new diamonds that sparkle on your wrist or your finger."

"Don't hold your breath, Alita. I have a lot of plans, a few good ones at that, as to how I will spend the money. It's mostly going toward the girls' care and livelihood, and their college tuition, of course."

"How much care and livelihood are we talking?" Coco asked. She'd been very quiet when it came to discussions about Nate's will and his finances. "Will the girls be like, millionaires?" she continued.

"Why you asking?" Alita asked.

"I was just wondering," Coco told her.

"I'll bet you were."

"Ladies, please," Dru said.

All Coco could think about was Chance, and how he'd

been cheated out of life so far. He never knew that Nate was his biological father.

"Coco," Alita asked. "Is there a reason why you want to know if Sidnee and Natalia are going to be millionaires?"

"Alita," Dru said, "Don't start."

"Why are you sisters talking in riddles?" Burgundy eyed the ladies one after the other. The topic of conversation was starting to make her uncomfortable. She already knew which sister would have her hand stuck out and expect to be financially assisted from the insurance payouts. But still she wished they'd have a little bit of class and self-control and not be so predictable.

Yet everybody knows how their family is. You think in advance *she's like this so I can't do that. And if I do this then she'll do that. And if I don't want THAT to happen then I gotta avoid this.* And you have to strategize and damn near keep a flowchart just to remember everybody's quirks and personalities.

And some family can get on your nerves so bad that they'll make you change your mind. And if that happens you are screwed, like the lid from a jar of peanut butter.

"B, I think Coco is trying to say once you get that insurance money don't forget about us little people." Alita eyed her sister as though she was challenging her.

"Lita, when have I ever forgotten about you? Sometimes I've had to turn my phone off at night so your desperate pleas for payday loans can't be heard."

"And that's why that brilliant engineer, Matti Makkonen, invented texting," Alita said with a laugh.

"And how would you know *that*?" Burgundy asked.

"Sis, trust me. I know a lot of things that folk would be surprised I know."

"And we don't care to hear about any of it right now," Coco told her.

"No, but seriously B, we know you already know that you're about to be rolling in even more dough. And I told y'all how I just got a second job a couple of days ago. It'll help out but still I think that a little bit of a payday loan for your big sister won't hurt you."

Burgundy decided to play with Alita. "But you're older than I am. You are the true big sister. You need to be helping me out sometimes."

"I do."

"No, you don't, Lita. You have never given me ten dollars."

"I, um, hmm. If I had it I would."

Burgundy laughed and decided to end the conversation. She started nibbling on snacks again.

But Alita wasn't done. "This is ridiculous. The lady is loaded. She acted like losing four thousand dollars in a burglary was pocket change. Must be nice to be so rich."

"Alita, what are you talking about now?" Burgundy asked.

"Can you pull yourself away from yourself? For once? Please?"

"What are you trying to say, Lita?"

"I'm not trying to say, I'm telling you, B, is that you are too stuck on you. That God made a lot of other people besides you."

"I know that."

"Do you?"

Burgundy hesitated. "Is this about you seriously wanting a payday loan?"

"Christmas will be here before you know it. Five hundred will be nice. Two grand would be nicer."

"Sorry. I'm not doing that." Burgundy's voice was firm.

"You're not going help me?" Alita asked.

"No!"

"You are so selfish. The big people always forget about the little people when they make it big."

"Seriously, Lita? How could you even begin to try and throw me, *me*, under a bus? After all I've already done for you? It's like when people ask for your help and you bend over backwards to do it, they tell you you're the greatest ever, but the first time you establish boundaries and you put your foot down, especially when they're family, they get a case of amnesia and claim you've never done a single thing for them. And it's total bullshit. Because if you gave me back all the money I've ever given to you, Lita, you'd have to file for bankruptcy."

"Ha, that's not a bad idea."

"Girl stop. You've got two jobs now. Manage your money. Do something good with it besides spending every penny."

"Okay, alright, sheesh."

Dru sat back and quietly observed the family dynamics. There'd always be people in the family that didn't see eye to eye. They were combative and arguing didn't faze them. But then there were the ones who avoided conflict. That was Elyse and Dru to a certain extent. Dru didn't like all the fussing and wanted to redirect their gathering to make sure it ended on a positive note.

"Burgundy, thanks again for all you do for all of us. We are loving the food and beverages. You really don't get enough credit."

"I agree. Thank you, sis," Coco said.

"You've been more than good to us," Elyse chimed in. Even Alita couldn't help but nod. What else could she do?

Dru said, "You seem to be doing okay, Burgundy, but how are you adjusting to Nate being gone?"

"It's a day to day type of thing to be honest."

Dru asked, "What do you miss most about him?"

"His voice."

"Really? Why is that?"

"Because it's kind of like when there is someone always in your ear. Always saying this and that to you, and at the time just want them to hush up so you can have some peace and quiet." Burgundy grinned at Alita and tried hard not to burst out laughing.

She came and twisted Burgundy's arm behind her back till she felt a bone pop.

"Would you please stop, Lita?"

"Who you gone tell huh? You don't have a husband anymore."

"Oh, Lita, now even I can't believe you'd say that to a widow."

"I-I didn't mean it like that."

"Alita, you meant it how you said it," Burgundy told her in an angry voice. "You know just what to do to push my buttons."

"What?"

"Alita, ever since we were young, you push and push like you want to fight. You want to hurt. We're not kids anymore and you've got to grow up one day. Everything isn't worth an argument. Pick your fights."

Alita could only nod her head very slowly, hopefully in a thoughtful way. Burgundy and everyone else knew that Alita was good at changing and altering the energy of any room that she entered. It was like an invisible force, a type of magnetic power that she held. Did she even know she was doing it? Was she aware that she had that type of power?

Burgundy shuddered and felt somewhat afraid. But then she struggled to push down the fear, push it out until it left her. She did not want to be a prisoner of fear. *No! No running.*

"Look Alita, I love you to pieces, God knows I do, but the next time Dru asks me a question can you please be quiet and let me respond? Can you do me that favor? Please?"

Alita pretended like her mouth was a long zipper and ran her hand across it . . . Her unusual way of promising Burgundy that she'd be quiet.

"Like I was saying, I miss my husband's voice because now that it's clear he has been silenced, because he is no longer with us, the only thing I have are the memories of what his voice used to sound like." She laughed. "And that is why to this day I still can't erase a few of the voice mail messages he left on my cell phone."

Alita nodded but held her tongue.

"And his voice is the one that you hear when you call the house and the old answering machine picks up."

"I noticed that," Dru said.

"And so, yeah, that about sums it up. That, plus a few more minor little things that can catch me unexpectedly. His scent. I still have a few unopened bottles of his favorite colognes. Givenchy. Tom Ford. Sean John."

"Okay, that's fine and dandy," Alita spoke up looking like she was about to explode for having to be quiet for two full minutes. "But we know Edmund Murray is your lover and I know for a fact no man wants to smell another man's cologne. So how exactly do you handle that?"

"None. Of. Your. Business. That's how."

Dru burst out laughing. Alita gave her a frustrated look. And Dru rose to her feet quickly, with her arms outstretched and a big smile on her face. But before she could reach Alita, Dru stopped in her tracks. She swayed back and forth, then massaged her temples.

"Are you alright, Sis?" Alita asked.

"I don't know. I felt weird all of a sudden. I need to take it easy." Alita came over and escorted Dru back to her seat.

"Describe how you feel," Burgundy said and sat next to her.

"It's like how I feel sometimes when I need to put eye drops in my eyes." Dru got rid of the eyeglasses that she wore occasionally and had switched to contact lenses.

"When I first wake up in the morning, my eyes feel bone dry. Like the lenses are stuck to my eyeballs. And I'll go get the drops. I tilt my head back and that's when it hits me sometimes. I felt very dizzy very quickly."

"You're too young to be feeling like a damned senior citizen," Alita said in a cautious tone. "Go and get that checked out, Sis."

"I've been so busy. Studying. Working. And let me admit something. Ever since Nate died, I feel a little bit clingy about my own relationship."

"What?" Burgundy asked.

"Yeah. When we're in bed, I reach over to make sure Tyrique is still lying next to me. And I hate to say it, but when I call him and he doesn't hit me back within fifteen minutes, my mind starts torturing me—"

"Oh, wow. I had no idea, Dru."

Then Dru twisted up her face as if she'd been sucking on lemons. She coughed, then completely vomited all the Sister Day snacks she just ate on Alita's floor.

"Damn," Alita said. "Just damn. You need to go get yourself checked out and hire yourself a maid while you're at it, because I love you to death but I ain't about to clean up after you. Ain't that much love in the world."

And at that she grumbled and went to find a large, clean dishrag. Alita turned on the hot water, squirted some soap on it, and got on her knees to clean up the entire mess. Once she was done and got back on her feet, Burgundy couldn't help herself.

"You do love Dru, huh, Alita?"

"I love all of my knucklehead sisters. It's why I act the

way I do. You see it as crazy, but I see it as . . ." Alita couldn't speak.

Burgundy grabbed her in her arms. They tightly clung to each other. They wept and didn't care who saw. The sisters mourned the tragedies and difficulties of life that had made their existence seem so challenging, so bitter and sad.

Within seconds, the other sisters joined them. The women held hands and prayed. They asked for total healing and recovery from any wounds they had suffered and any wounds they had caused. The road might be difficult but the sisters were determined to make it.

Many things were changing but some things remained the same.

For the first time in a long time, it felt like Sister Day and it also felt like the start of a brand new, different type of day.

Chapter 7

Planting Seeds

Burgundy awoke feeling antsy one late October morning.

She rose out of bed at four-thirty. As soon as the girls got up, she told them to take their baths and get dressed. They ate a fine breakfast of toast, fresh fruit, sausage, and their favorite cereal.

Right after the sun rose, she and the girls gathered outside the house. The expansive backyard was marked by mature live oaks, white oaks, sycamore trees, and landscaping that had been planted long ago according to Burgundy's specifications.

She placed a tiny shovel in Sid's hand. The little girl laughed with delight as she took the shovel and waved it around like a sword.

But Natalia simply eyed the shovel, then gawked at her mother.

"Mama, what are we doing?" That was Sid.

"We're about to plant a garden."

Sid joyfully leaped up and down. The girl was so spirited, in Burgundy's eyes it looked as if Sidnee had run a marathon and had just crossed a finish line.

She remembered how Sid too had been found unresponsive from the gas leak last fall. But she miraculously survived the coma and was now doing well.

These days anything that her baby girl did made her very happy.

But Natalia's curious stare drilled holes into Burgundy's back as she turned away from her.

"Come on. Get in the golf cart."

The girls climbed in the back of their four-seater Club Cart and Burgundy secured their seat belts. Burgundy sat in front and inserted the key into the ignition.

They rode along for a few minutes until they reached the rear area of their yard and got out.

"Here," Burgundy said and pointed. "Before he left us, I asked Marty to dig up some dirt so we can make a garden. I'm just now getting around to doing it. And I have some seeds that we can plant: asparagus, garlic, winter lettuce, and lily."

Burgundy dug inside an oversized tote bag that was filled with packets of seeds, fertilizer, garden gloves, and cute little water buckets with the tiny spout.

She handed Sid her gloves which she gladly took. When she tried to give Natalia a pair, the girl wrinkled her nose and took two steps back.

"I don't like dirt," she proclaimed.

Shocked, Burgundy told her, "That's no concern of mine."

Burgundy ignored Natalia. She and Sid started digging into a patch of dirt with their shovels. The ground was cold, hard, and Burgundy's knees hurt so bad from bending that she was tempted to quit. But she hung in there.

"Why are we doing this?"

"We want to plant seeds, Sidnee, all kinds of beautiful flowers and we want to water them, take care of them and see how they'll end up."

"That's dumb," Natalia said. "We can get Marty to do this."

"Marty isn't our landscaper anymore, remember? We'll be doing what he used to do."

"But he's better at it."

"I know that and guess what, we're still going to try. Now get moving."

Natalia continued as if she just came up with a brilliant idea. "Mommy, you know we don't have to do this. You have enough money to go to a florist and just buy all the flowers you want."

"You have no idea how much money I have, and you definitely can't tell me how to spend it. Do you understand me, little girl?"

Natalia locked eyes with her mom.

"I'm talking to you, Natalia Taylor."

"Yes ma'am."

"What did you say? I can't hear you."

"Yes ma'am."

"Yes ma'am what?"

"Yes, ma'am I won't tell you how to spend your money even though Daddy left us that money."

Burgundy sighed heavily. "You don't know what daddy did. I think you've been snooping again at grown folks' conversations. Have you?"

"Yes."

"That's unacceptable, Natalia. I've told you over and again not to do that. Just for that you are on a punishment. One week. No television, no video games, no tablet, no dance classes or acting classes."

"No *dance* classes? Why not?"

"You heard me and I mean it, Natalia."

Burgundy watched Natalia swing her little metal shovel around. Widely waving it back and forth with her slender fingers.

"Give that to me," Burgundy commanded.

Natalia hesitated.

After waiting a few seconds, Burgundy grabbed the shovel and firmly yanked it from Natalia.

"I want my daddy. I want my daddy." Natalia's screeches were loud and seemed to echo across the massive backyard.

Right then Edmund could be seen rapidly walking towards them. He was out of breath.

"Burgundy, your backyard gate was unlocked."

"Was it?" she asked, feeling distracted. "I need to do a better job. God, I have so many things to remember."

"I was trying to call you first before I stopped by, but the phone kept ringing."

Burgundy patted her jacket pocket. "Right. Sorry. Must have left the phone in the house. On the bathroom counter. Or it is in the kitchen? Hell, I don't know, Elm."

"Why do you call him Elm?" Natalia asked.

"Um, it's a nickname, Natalia. Just like we call you Nat."

"I prefer Natalia. Only my daddy can call me Nat." She spit out the words. She stared at her mother then grabbed the shovel from her hands. Natalia began to punch at the dirt with the tip of her shovel. She twisted the shovel around, placed her small sneaker on top of it, and tried to dig deeper in the dirt. But the tool was a bit heavy and she was having difficulty.

Edmund quietly approached her. "Hey, if you don't mind, I can help you out with that."

"I don't need your help."

"Edmund, I am sorry," Burgundy told him. "Sometimes she sees things through a child's eyes and doesn't realize her limitations."

"I don't *have* limitations, Mommy."

"Oh God," Burgundy muttered, feeling somewhat embarrassed. "My daughter can be stubborn. She's very independent and likes to try things on her own, until she realizes that she's unable to do certain things by herself."

"Mommy, I *can* do this alone. I can swing by myself. I can do a lot of things by myself."

Her declaration broke Burgundy's heart, but Natalia wasn't aware. She ignored her mother and tried even harder to dig into the soil, to drop the seeds into the little holes she made and to create a flower bed, based on her own hard work and determination. In fact, she ended up managing to do the job so well that she left her mother speechless.

"Just for trying to help out instead of quitting before you start, I am modifying your punishment. No TV, tablet, or video games for a week, but you may still go to dance and acting classes."

"I can? Oh, thank you, Mommy," she said with pure delight. Natalia finally smiled and Burgundy felt glad to see her daughter cheer up.

"Why are we doing this in the fall?" Natalia asked. "I thought you're supposed to plant seeds in the spring."

"Because there is such a thing as fall gardens, sweetie, that's why," Burgundy told her. "And we're doing this so you girls can see the hard work that goes into making things grow and come alive. Then God helps us out with the things that we can't do on our own."

"Like make it rain?"

"Exactly sweetheart." Burgundy beamed at Edmund who had jumped alongside her to help her dig in the dirt and prepare the soil.

"The earth opens its mouth every time the rain falls from the sky," Burgundy continued. "And it drinks the water and feeds the earth so that it gets renewed, refreshed, nourished, and fed. And we, all of us that eat, benefit from that renewal."

"Huh?" Natalia said.

"We must do our part, sweetie, and get out of the way so that the good Lord may do his."

"Oh, okay," Natalia said. She continued helping out with the garden without another single comment. And for that precious moment of progress, Burgundy was very grateful.

By mid-day on the following Monday, Burgundy had been at Morning Glory performing her usual duties. She happened to be near the hostess station when she heard a little bit of a commotion. She and Elyse looked up at the same time.

A thin, barefoot woman ran inside the restaurant. It was packed as usual. The young lady looked to be in her late twenties, but her appearance seemed so haggard it was difficult to guess her true age. Noticing the panicky look on her face, Burgundy took the woman by the hand and quickly escorted her to the business office. She placed a call to Jordan Andrews who was elsewhere in the store. Elyse came into the office, locked the door firmly behind her, and took a seat.

The young lady's shoulders trembled as she gasped for breath.

"Need anything?" Burgundy asked. "Do you want some water?"

The woman nodded. But when Elyse moved to unlock the door, the woman nearly screamed. It was a quiet yelp.

"No. Please ma'am. If you don't already have water in this office, I don't want any. Please don't open that door."

"Is someone following you?"

"Yes, ma'am."

"Who is it?"

She stared at the floor and held herself by the arms.

"Tell you what. I will call the store manager and ask him to bring you some water. Are you hungry?"

The woman's cheeks reddened. It was then that Burgundy

noticed a long trail of purple and blue wounds on her arm. It was chilly outside. The woman wore no jacket.

"Elyse, she looks like she's your size. Can you go and get a uniform shirt? Size small or medium. But we can wait till Jordan arrives before you go and find some uniforms."

"Okay."

"Have a seat, sweetie. We're here to help. Do you need us to call the police?"

"I don't know what to do. I just don't know."

"Did someone beat you up?"

The girl shook her head no.

"Where do you live?"

"A few miles from here. I-I was on the bus. And my boyfriend got mad at me because this guy . . . a guy I don't even know . . . he was staring at me and smiling when we were on the bus. I wasn't doing anything. But my boyfriend thought I knew him . . . thought I was cheating. But I don't know him . . . I tried to tell him. But he didn't believe me. And he pinched me hard. It hurt so bad. Then he punched me."

"On the bus?" Burgundy asked.

"Yes."

Burgundy looked distressed.

"I tried to stand up and leave . . . and he grabbed my arm. Pulled at me. Twisted my arm till the bone almost popped. He wouldn't let me go. We got into it. M-my shoes fell off when I tried to run. He snatched my phone and broke it . . . He took my purse. Some people saw what was happening. They held him back and the driver let me off. And I looked back and saw him break down that bus door. So I ran as fast as I could. I heard him screaming behind me. I was scared he was going to kill me." Her voice had fallen to a whisper. She placed her hands in her face and wept.

Elyse went and rubbed her shoulder. By then, Jordan Andrews had opened the door. The woman violently jerked around. Her eyes widened. Jordan held up the glass of ice water and a hot plate of food.

Burgundy offered the meal to the young lady. Then she whispered for a couple of minutes to Jordan. He nodded, closed the door behind him and locked it.

Elyse looked at Burgundy with uncertainty. "Jordan will handle things," Burgundy said with confidence. "We are here to help and serve . . . what's your name?"

"Raven."

"Hi Raven. That's a pretty name. I'm Burgundy Taylor, the owner of Morning Glory. And this is my niece. Her name is Elyse. She's twenty, almost twenty-one. How old are you, Raven?"

"I am. Shit, I can't even remember. I know it sounds crazy, but I hate my birthday. Nothing good ever happens on it so I just kind of forget about my birthday and my age."

"Are you serious?"

"Yeah. I've never had a real birthday party or anything like that."

"My poor child," Burgundy said in a faint whisper.

"It's okay, really. I don't care. My family don't really care about me. I'm used to it."

"No, Raven. You shouldn't get used to being treated poorly. Everyone should know how it feels to be treated special."

"If you say so." Raven tore into her chicken and waffles and kept talking. "If you special you get treated special. But if you ain't," she shrugged, "You get beat up and called names like 'stupid whore' and 'stupid ass bitch' and 'you ain't shit.' That's the type of 'special' I'm used to." She stopped talking but kept eating.

Burgundy couldn't think of anything to say. She watched Raven. Then she looked at Elyse. She knew that Elyse could easily be a statistic. A young woman who got let down by the system, or by her family, or a woman who would continue to come across certain type of man that would use and abuse her. She could easily have run away from home when she was a teenager. She could have run away and then gotten snatched into a world that frightened her, a sex trafficking type of world where she would have no protection, no family, and certainly no good future.

Just watching Raven eat gave Burgundy a powerful sense of gratitude. But she also felt condemned about how she'd treated Elyse when she'd first learned what Nate did to her. She knew she could have been more sympathetic to her when she first discovered her husband's sexual abuse.

She knew that there were other Elyses, and more Ravens out there, in Houston, and other parts of the country.

She sighed and gestured at Elyse. "C'mon over here."

"Why, what's wrong?"

"I just want a hug. That's all."

Elyse waited a few seconds but then fell into Burgundy's arms. Burgundy held her tightly then kissed her braids. "I'm sorry. I-I didn't mean to not believe you last year, to falsely accuse you."

"I'm sure you didn't mean it, but you did hurt me."

"I know. I was wrong. Very wrong. And I wish I could take it all back and make it up to you somehow, someway."

"This hug is a nice start . . . it feels good, B."

They had a couple more minutes of healing and soothing words. More promises of aiming to do better. Then Burgundy pulled herself together after she'd seen that the young woman had devoured her food. Raven was looking better already.

"Raven, I'm sorry about what you're going through, but I'm glad you came into Morning Glory."

"Me too. You have no idea."

"And I don't know what's going to happen to you after you leave here, and even if I don't know you, that actually worries me."

"Don't worry about me ma'am. I'll survive."

"But what does survive mean to you?"

"If I'm lucky, my boyfriend will go to rehab, stop drinking like a fish. If I'm real lucky he'll finally grow up, become a man, and learn to keep his hands to himself."

"But after what you've just been through, do you really want to go back and be around him? I mean, those bruises look pretty bad, and you haven't seen a doctor. What if you get blood clots?"

"I-I dunno."

"Do you have health insurance?"

"Don't need it. I'm my own doctor. I just buy over-the-counter stuff, or get a Band-Aid, wipe away the blood, and hope for the best. It's worked out okay so far."

"Raven, no."

"Ma'am, doctors cost too much. And when I go to places like Ben Taub, you wait twelve hours at least with no promise that you'll be seen. People with cardiac problems are more important than women who got beat up. So, like I said before, I have learned to become my own doctor and my own nurse. I don't need nobody."

"But Raven, being your own doctor and nurse and fearing for your life . . . is that what you call survival?"

The girl just shrugged. A proud look was etched on her tired, wrinkle-lined face. Her cheeks were swollen. Her eyes looked dead and lifeless. She refused to give Burgundy or Elyse any eye contact.

"I want to help you, Raven, but—"

"But what? What can you do? Can you make my man act like he has some sense?"

"Why not get another guy? A different one who will love and respect you? Don't you deserve that?"

"I don't even know what that's like, Ms. Burgundy. I can't even imagine."

Raven accepted the clothes that she'd been handed. She

got dressed in Burgundy's private bathroom that was inside of the office. When she was done, she looked as if she was ready to walk back through the door and return to her uncertain yet violent world.

"Thanks for this food. I haven't had a good meal in two, three days." She looked down at her Morning Glory shirt. The long sleeve polo nicely covered up her arms. She was even wearing a pair of work shoes, a half inch too big but it felt better than having her bare feet scratch against the rough Houston concrete.

"Well, it was sure nice to meet you, Raven. Before you leave, I am going to give you my contact info."

"That's fine."

"And you can have a plate to go if you want."

"Nah, I'm good."

"One more thing. May I have a hug, Raven?"

Raven appeared confused.

"Why would you want to hug me?"

"Because I do." Burgundy walked over to Raven and pulled her into her arms.

Have you ever cried in the arms of a stranger? You don't know that person but they are there at just the right time when you need a firm shoulder to cry on. The two women stood in the business office. At first the young woman felt stiff. But then Raven's initial reserve and pride gave in. She thought about how afraid and ashamed she felt. Soon she placed her swollen face on Burgundy's neck. She wept in the woman's arms. The tears made her neck feel both hot and wet but it didn't matter.

"Everything's going to be alright, Raven. I'm praying for you."

"But you don't know me."

"It doesn't matter. God sees. God knows. God cares." That made Raven cry even harder. She tried to muffle her sobs while Burgundy rubbed her back. She hoped the girl wasn't too embarrassed by Burgundy's display of concern. As the young woman's tears subsided, Burgundy felt an extreme sense of gratitude. It was as if Raven had helped Burgundy as much as she had helped Raven.

What is not firmly planted can easily be uprooted.

Burgundy realized she needed to do more than just talk the talk. It was easy to dream and imagine. But to get the dream to come to pass she'd have to put lots of action behind it. Plant some seeds, water them, nurture the seeds, fertilize the plant, and do whatever she could do to maintain the vision.

The next day, right before dawn, she and Edmund were jogging along a circular path of a park near her subdivision.

They slowed down their pace.

"I am sorry, Edmund. I don't want it to seem like everything is all about me, me, me. How are you doing? Are you good?"

"What are you talking about?"

"Um, I know it's the anniversary of your divorce. I thought you might be in a bad mood."

"You remember the date?" he asked.

"Yeah. October thirtieth."

"I'm impressed."

"Elm. I listen to you and the things you tell me, even when it seems like I'm not listening."

"Babe, you are amazing, because the divorce was the last thing on my mind. Right now I'm good. My catfish businesses are flourishing. I have no complaints."

"I'm glad then. Happy you've adjusted to being single again."

"You can adjust, too. In fact, you are. That's why I'm glad that you are so focused on your daughters, Morning Glory, and this new venture that I know you're seeking."

Burgundy had told him what happened with Raven and how it stirred something big inside of her; she gladly shared with Edmund her desire to help women who'd been through tough times.

"I know there is a need for these kinds of things," he told her. "In one neighborhood where I have a restaurant, I do see a lot of young women, some in their late teens up to forty or so. They seem to have nothing to do. They hang outside a seedy motel. They seem to be either hiding out or searching for something. Your dream can help save someone's life. I'm here for it."

Burgundy nodded, feeling so very happy that as much as she listened to Edmund, she knew that he was an excellent listener for her as well. It wasn't just about the great sexual encounters they'd share every once in a while. Edmund perfectly filled the role of being a gentleman, a lover, a friend, and a take-charge man who could step in when he sensed that she needed him.

"What more do you need to do to get started, Burgundy?"

"I need a facility, number one. A nice, empty space I can lease that's within my price range. Potential donors must be secured too. The best type of money to spend is other people's money. And I need a grant writer or someone to help me develop the mission statement, and a five-year and ten-year master plan for the non-profit."

"I love it. This is good seed."

"Thank you, honey."

"In fact, I know people and I will get in touch with them."

The sparkle in Edmund's eyes matched Burgundy's. They picked up their pace and happily inhaled the fresh morning air. And just like that, from a tiny seed that stirred within her, a dream had been birthed.

Chapter 8

Crime and Punishment

The next day, Coco Reeves's dreaded moment had arrived. She was on her way to give her detailed statement about the last time she saw Nate Taylor. She did not want to face the police, for she didn't trust them, the sheriffs, or their K-9 dogs. Alita volunteered to drive her to the station; it would take almost an hour to get there from Coco's house.

They were now together in the car. Coco sat stiffly in her seat; she clutched her cell phone in one hand. Her gently used, four-inch-wide King James Bible sat firmly on her lap. She cracked open the spine and glanced at its onion skin pages. She thumbed through several psalms, a few proverbs, and feeling distressed, Coco slammed the book shut.

"I don't have a chance in hell," she concluded.

The sisters were headed to Conroe, Texas, a forty-mile distance from downtown Houston. They drove north on I-45 and had just zoomed by the exit to the George Bush Intercontinental Airport.

Coco solemnly peered at the cars heading in the direction of the airport.

"It's too damn quiet in here, Coco. You ain't talking. I

want to hear some hip-hop." Alita turned on the radio. A loud bassline boomed inside the car. The windows vibrated. A group of mumble rappers started spitting out lyrics that Alita couldn't understand, but the beat was hot; she bobbed her head and swayed. It took Coco three seconds to turn off the radio.

"Why'd you do that? I want to hear some music."

"You call that music? It's trash. And I'm not in the mood to be listening to that garbage. It reminds me too much of Calhoun, and I don't want to think about him or any other man right now."

Before long, it grew eerily quiet once again. The only thing that could be heard was Coco's rhythmic tap on that floorboard. She rocked in her seat as if listening to her own soundtrack.

"Coco, please. Will you stop making all that noise? You haven't said much at all since we've been in the car."

"Is that a crime?"

"No, it's not. But I know one thing. I hope your dumb ass did not commit some type of crime that caused Nate to end up dying."

"Why would you say that, Lita? I haven't done a thing to that man."

"Then why're you acting like you've got something to hide?"

Coco ignored Alita and tightly clutched the bible.

"C'mon, Sis. Be straight with me. Did you go over to their house that night and fuck him up because you wanted him to marry you instead of Burgundy?"

"What the hell? Who told you that?"

"Nobody told me anything, Coco. I can tell by your body language and the way you've been acting since the man died that something serious went down between you two. I'm mad as hell that you even slept with Nate and had a baby for him. And now he's dead. And now the police want a second statement from you. And *now*, somehow, you got me involved. You've convinced me to drive you to Conroe, a place I can't stand because of all those racist crackers that live up that way."

"Gee, I'm sorry to put you through this. But you're my fam."

"Coco, I don't give a shit about that. I don't need this. I have my own troubles like trying to get my knucklehead son on the straight and narrow so he can finally grow up and be a man. And I need to give love and guidance to Elyse. And one more thing—"

"Please spare me the details about your life. Shit happens. To you, to me, all of us. Deal with it."

Alita peered at her sister. They locked eyes; eyes that went from hardness to softness.

"Lita, I'm so scared."

"Just go in there and tell the truth, baby girl. The whole truth and nothing but the truth."

"Really? It's not like people haven't told the truth before and it backfired. I think a good ass lie could work out better than admitting the so-called truth."

Truth.

There it was again.

A small yet colossal five-letter word that the Reeves family had been struggling with for the past few years. And Coco wasn't sure if delving even deeper into her ugly truths would cause the messiness of her life to go quietly away.

"I swear to God," Alita was saying, "If you tell me everything that went down, it would make me understand more. I just want to know."

"The only person I may think about telling my business to is God."

They pulled up in the parking lot of the police station. Alita put the car in park.

"You ready to face this, Coco?"

Coco ignored her.

"Alrighty then. I guess this is it." Alita turned off the engine and they sat in silence for a few minutes. Alita popped the locks.

"No matter what has happened, I'll be here when you are done, Sis. Be strong."

Coco opened her side of the car. Before she walked away, she yelled into the car, "Thanks, Lita. I love you. And thank you for loving me too."

Coco shut the door, walked inside and gave the officer her name and her reason for being there. He asked for some identification and typed on a keyboard. He handed back her ID and asked her to wait. A few minutes later a female officer came and got Coco and escorted her to a small office. Two male officers were waiting. So far, everyone she'd seen in the station was Caucasian. Her knees turned to jelly and trembled as she sat at the black tabletop with the black metal chairs.

"Good morning, Ms. Reeves," said one of the cops in a pleasant voice.

"Hi."

"How's your day going so far?" the other guy asked. He gave Coco a half-assed smile.

"Eh, um, it's alright I guess. I just want to answer your questions and be on my way."

"Totally understandable."

The cops were seated on the other table staring at her. They had pads of paper and pens.

"You want a bottle of water?" This cop was very talkative and seemed like he was the one in charge.

"No," she said.

"Let's get started. State your full legal name and spell it for me." He asked for her date of birth, current living address, telephone numbers, employer, and emergency contact person's info.

"I've changed my mind. I want some water. Will this take long?" Coco asked.

"It depends."

"On what?"

"On what you tell us."

"Oh. Well, what else you want to know?"

"As you know we've called you in because we received the autopsy results regarding Nathaniel Taylor. You knew him right?"

That question irritated Coco. "Of course. He was married to my sister for a long time. So of course, I knew him."

"When was the last time you saw Nathaniel? Tell us everything that you remember."

Coco swallowed so damned hard it felt like her tongue disappeared. That other cop brought her a bottle of water; he twisted open the cap and handed it to her.

She tilted her head, took a long swallow. She kept drinking until the bottle was half empty and her stomach had filled up. She felt her eyelashes grow damp and she wanted to wipe her eyes but was too proud.

"Ms. Reeves, are you ready to answer the question?"

"Okay, alright. Um, it was on a Saturday," she answered.

"Be more specific. What date?"

"The last Saturday in August."

The talkative cop pulled out a calendar. "August twenty-fifth. Is that the last time you saw Nathaniel Taylor?"

"Yes. That was the last time I saw that man."

"Do you have anyone who can corroborate with what you're telling me? Any witnesses?"

"Um, sure."

"Who was it? What's the person's name? What happened?"

"Slow your roll, bro," she said in jest but the cop didn't crack a smile.

"Okay, it's like this. Me and my . . . um, Elyse and I had been together that day."

"What all did you do that day when you were with Elyse?"

"She swung by, we chopped it up for a minute, then we drove over to the post office to pick up the mail for my sister and brother-in-law."

"Is picking up the mail something you normally did for the Taylors?"

"Yeah, I work for them."

"And what's the address of this post office?"

She paused, wanting to run out of the room.

"Ma'am, can you answer the question? Is there an address you want to share with us about the post office location?"

Coco nodded.

"Give us your answers out loud, ma'am. A tape recorder can't record your body language."

"Okay. Um, I feel embarrassed because I don't know the exact address. I just know what streets to take to get there."

"Tell us the zip code. Or the street name and cross streets and the landmarks. We'll make sure to find out exactly where it is."

"But why?" she asked as she felt her chest tightening.

"Why not?"

Coco did as she was asked and took another sip of water for her throat was starting to feel extremely dry.

"Okay, you go to the post office and what happened after that? Did you stop anywhere after that?"

She described how she waited for Elyse to get her things from her bedroom.

"And where exactly were you during this time?"

"Downstairs. I went in the kitchen. I think I got something to drink." She nervously laughed and held up her now empty bottle of water.

"Want more?" Feisty Cop asked her.

"Um, yeah, but the more I drink the more I'm going to have to use the ladies' room. I have a weak bladder."

"Just a few more questions, then you can be excused. Ms. Reeves, you were in the kitchen but we know that at one point you saw Mr. Taylor. Did he come downstairs or did you go find him?"

"No, I-I went upstairs."

This time the quieter officer confronted Coco. "And what happened that led to your blood being discovered at the crime scene?"

Coco's face grew darker.

"Crime scene? Why would you say that?"

The feisty cop was no nonsense. "We collected forensic evidence, Ms. Reeves. Several deep scratches were noted on the deceased's body. Drops of blood was found as well. And DNA results show that you and he had a physical encounter. Is that correct?"

"Look, how would you even know all that? I was just there to help out my niece."

"Regardless of your intentions, something happened between you and Mr. Taylor. If you don't want to be considered a suspect and want to clear your name, you are going to have to tell us everything, Ms. Reeves."

"I-I don't want to remember all that, sir. Please. It was a silly, stupid thing. It's embarrassing."

He sat back and crossed his legs, his eyes alight with excitement. "Even so, tell us everything that happened. I don't want you to relive that experience if it's something that bothers you, but we understand that people fight." He shrugged. "I have it out with my brother-in-law all the time. It happens. You're not alone, Ms. Reeves."

Coco's eyes teared up even more. This time she wiped her eyes on her sleeve. Her breathing intensified. Just being that close to officers with loaded guns made her feel trapped.

The pleasant officer looked at her with sympathy but Coco wasn't buying it.

He's trying to act like he can relate to me and as if I can relate to him. But I can't. He's a cop. A white one at that. He has a thick policy book that was written to benefit him. He has an entire city behind him. Plus the State of Texas.

The feisty officer said, "Did you and Mr. Taylor have it out? A lover's quarrel maybe?"

"No," she said. "Why would you say that?"

"Unless you tell me your story, I'm pretty much going to make up whatever I think happened. Now tell me!"

"Oh God." They waited for her to continue. Coco was starting to feel like a hundred pair of eyes were staring at her; as if every inch of her body was exposed.

As she thought of many headlines, viral videos, and faces of angry protestors filled every place in Coco's head, she remembered people who'd died while in custody. A lifeless body slumped up against a steel bar, with a stool sitting underneath them, two legs dangling back and forth from a rope or a sheet tied to a ceiling.

"Ms. Reeves," she heard the cop saying. She had zoned out really bad. And in spite of her nervousness, she decided to take her chances regardless of their discovery of forensic evidence.

"Okay, sir. See, it's like this. Long story short, me and him had it out because he was a perv. He'd been sexually assaulting my sister since she was a little bitty thing. Barely one hundred pounds. And on that night, Nate tried to get Elyse to have sex with him. He was married and messing around on my sister Burgundy."

"Why would you care about who he sleeps with?"

"Huh?"

"That's your sister's husband. Am I correct?"

"Yeah, but—"

"But if he isn't *your* husband, why would you care?"

"Um, well damn. She's my sister. If it hurts my sister it hurts me."

"But did your *married* sister know what he'd been doing with the other sister?"

"I don't see what that has to do with anything."

"Um, let's get back to the relevant testimony." That was the calmer, seemingly gentler cop trying to restore order.

"Go on Ms. Reeves," he said. "What happened after you saw him attempt to have sex with Elyse?"

"I-I felt angry at his trash behavior. And so, I asked him about it. He didn't like me questioning him. And he got mad and sarcastic and . . ." She cast her eyes downward. She was getting to the hard part.

"Go on."

"He seemed to be getting more aggressive. I-I feared for our safety. And I ran downstairs and I came back up holding a gun."

"Whose gun was it?"

"My-my sister's."

"As in Burgundy?"

"Yes."

"And where is it now?"

That was a great question. After the entire incident that went down with Nate, Coco had tried to get rid of the gun. And now she really didn't know where it was.

"I don't know." She paused. "Anyway, basically, that's how he got scratches on his chin. 'Cause we fought over the gun. We traded a couple hits. And that was that. He never pulled the gun on me. But he snatched it out my hands and I got it back from him. And so, after that, Elyse was like 'Coco, he ain't worth it, let's go.' And we left."

"You left?"

"Yeah. We got the hell out."

"What time was that?"

"Honestly, I don't remember. Why would I be looking at my watch at a time like that?"

"Clearly understandable. But would Elyse remember?"

"I dunno. You'll have to ask her." They jotted down more notes and took a long time doing so.

Coco was sick of all the non-stop questions. She stood up and headed for the door.

"Where do you think you're going?"

"We're done, right?"

"No ma'am. We need to ask you a few more questions. It shouldn't take that long. Sit down."

She returned to her chair and slumped in her seat. Thirty minutes later Coco was still in that same room answering the same questions and trying to stay awake. Her bladder was good and full. And an hour after that Coco despised the taste of water; so, she switched it up to some Seven-Up. Then she asked for a Coke.

"Ms. Reeves, what were you wearing that night?"

"Excuse me?"

"Can you recall what you were wearing that night?"

"No. That's crazy. Why would I remember that?"

Right then the feisty cop retrieved what appeared to be a blank CDR. She watched him slide the disc inside of a DVD player.

"Are you sure you don't remember what you had on? Just take a wild guess. What clothes? What shoes?"

Coco began to sweat under the arms. Her mind started racing.

"I don't know. I don't remember the shoes I wore."

The two men lowered their voices as they spoke amongst themselves.

"Ms. Reeves, we need you to log into all of your social media accounts right now. Facebook, Twitter, Instagram."

The two officers stood over her waiting for her to log in.

She accessed her Facebook account and felt mostly safe and that none of her current posts would incriminate her.

"Let's find the posts that were right around the time Nathaniel Taylor died."

The officers looked but couldn't find much of anything. Coco happily logged out and stared at them. But one of the officers turned on a projector; he pulled up a jpeg of a color graphic. It showed her wearing a taupe colored blouse, taupe slacks, and a new pair of flip flops. It was a picture from inside the lobby of the post office.

This was the exact outfit she wore the last time she saw Nate.

"We asked you about the shoes you had on? Weren't you wearing these flip flops, Coco? Do you remember now?"

"No."

"Okay, how about this one?" They pulled up another photo, one more recognizable.

"Where'd you get this photo?"

"From your real Facebook. Not the one that you just showed to us."

"But how? I-I didn't post that. Someone must have hacked my account."

"Nice try, Coco. You did post it. You posted it on August twenty-fifth, at 6:32 p.m."

Coco said nothing.

"And you wore these flip flops. They were brand new."

"How you know that?"

"Because when our officers first went to investigate at the house in The Woodlands, they found a Ross store sales sticker on the kitchen floor, next to the stove. Isn't that where you bought those shoes, Coco?"

"What? That means nothing. So what you found a sticker. Doesn't mean it's mine."

"But isn't Ross where you purchased those shoes?"

"What?"

"Answer the question, Coco."

"Don't yell at me, you—"

The feisty cop jumped in her face with a quickness. "Excuse me. Were you about to say something?"

She shook her head, angry and too afraid to say anything more.

"All I need to know is if those were the shoes you wore that day. Answer the fucking question and I won't have to yell."

"Yes, I bought them at Ross. But that proves nothing. They're just shoes."

"Ms. Reeves, you posted that photo the day you went to Nate's house, right? And after he was found dead, you deleted the photos. Lots of photos."

"But how would you know that?"

"We know this because we know if anyone posts anything on social media. A photo, a tweet. Even if you shut down your account or delete everything, we still can get a hold of your social media footprint. Bottom line is you took a selfie that day. Standing in the mirror. Was it before you killed your brother-in-law, or are you the type to kill someone, go out to eat, and then take selfies afterward?"

"What? Are you accusing me of killing him?"

"You turned on that stove, didn't you? Turned on that oven with all that gas and hoped he'd fall asleep."

"No," she cried. "It's not true."

"Ms. Reeves, if that's what you did, and we plan to prove that you did it, you are a coldblooded murderer, and you're going to pay for your crime."

"Sir, I did not kill that man."

"Alright, I'll give you a chance to prove that you're innocent. Do you have your cell phone on you?"

"Yeah. Why?"

"I need you to pull it out so we can take a look at emails, texts, and photos. Right now."

"Really?" she asked in disbelief.

"Really!"

"But I-I don't want to do that."

"Well, you have no choice, Ms. Reeves. If you cooperate, then it shouldn't be a problem. If you don't, you're going to run into all kinds of problems, young lady."

Her heart beat wildly inside of her chest.

"If you didn't kill him you have nothing to be scared of. Now hand over your phone."

The penetrating looks that they gave Coco made her feel like she'd forced Nate to stick his head inside a gas-lit oven.

"Look, I wish I had an attorney with me."

"Because?"

"Because these days . . . when you are black and living in America and you have to deal with the police, some things are going to automatically cross your mind."

"Such as?"

"You wonder if you reach for your phone, are you going to get shot. If you make any sudden moves, no matter how innocent it is, it could cause you to get killed." She glanced at the exit door. "And I don't feel safe here. It seems like you're forcing me into a confession. Because that's what y'all do sometimes to people who look like me."

They said nothing even though they wanted to interrupt her.

"And the fact that these things have happened from north to south to east to west, to the best of black people and the worst of black people, I can't help but feel scared as hell." She wanted to feel brave. To fight for her rights. But their blank, unemotional looks made her words seem meaningless. The strength of who she believed herself to be began to leave her very lungs.

Feisty Cop finally spoke up. "You people make things harder for yourselves. You make all these excuses, blame the government for this and good white folks for that. You're always screaming like you're a victim."

She wanted to scream.

"We tell you to put your hands up, but you reach in your pocket."

She wanted to reach across the table and slap him.

"You make things harder for yourself because you don't know how to listen and how to respect the law."

She wanted to kill him.

"And if you'd just do as we instruct you, there wouldn't be these problems. You'd then save your own lives."

She couldn't take it anymore.

"Comply, you say? Is that what you mean? Comply?"

"Exactly." The feisty cop sneered. "You do know what that word means, don't you?"

"Sorry to burst your bubble but compliance, which means to conform, to be agreeable, to do as you're told, none of that means shit to my people." Coco wanted to cry but she was too enraged. Her blood felt as hot as chicken grease and so did her skin.

"We don't give a fuck," she continued "And not because we don't know what the damned word means. We know. We do know."

"If you really knew it, then you'd just do it. Like Nike." He sneered again.

Coco sneered back. She couldn't help herself. She didn't know how she could be scared to death yet have the guts to speak her mind. Saying how she felt could cause her to get busted across the lip, her head slammed against the floor, or worse. But at least these men could hear where she was coming from. And if they beat her or killed her, at least things she strongly believed in had been said.

"We don't care that your people don't care. That's a stupid way to look at things because we're the law, don't you agree."

"I-I don't know. I'm confused."

"Then let me explain. If your people would learn how to shut the fuck up and simply respect law and order, hey, wait a second. Why are we even having this conversation? We are the law, dammit. There is no discussion." Now the officer sounded wounded, like he'd been picked on, like he was the victim.

"I'm not done yet, sir."

"Excuse me?"

"No. I need to say one more thing." She took a deep breath. "If complying makes things better, then what about the ones like Philando Castile? He did as he was told, he was in his car, tried to get his ID, his wallet . . . The cop still shot the man . . . in front of his kid . . . his woman. And Philando died. Over a simple traffic stop? He was only thirty-two. He complied. Yet he died. Why did he get shot? Can you answer me that?"

Feisty cop was speechless for once. "Uh, no. I can't answer that."

"How was he protected? How was he served?"

"Again, I can't tell you."

"This shit was so wrong. It's government approved genocide. It's . . ." Coco couldn't speak any longer.

The tougher policeman's entire face went from pale pink to dark red. He started desperately coughing like something big got wedged in his throat.

The gentler cop told her, "I'm sorry for what happened in those other cases, but all I know is that is all cops ain't the same."

"I should hope not."

"Ms. Reeves, what I'm trying to say is MCSO is different. We really are here to protect and serve."

Coco had heard it all before. "Officer, I'm not trying to be a pain in the ass, but this whole thing freaks me out. You're going to protect me, you say?"

The officer eyes softened. "Put it like this, Ms. Reeves. Let's pretend like we weren't even here. If we were somewhere like a protest, and I could see that the crowd was getting unruly. People start pushing, shoving, throwing bottles and rocks, and it's getting loud. Folks are getting threatened and everyone is closing in on you to the point you can't even breathe. And if you slipped and fell to the ground and were about to get crushed to death, it would be my duty to protect you."

"Nice story. But I don't believe it though."

"Ms. Reeves, let's try that again. If you were at home and your boyfriend was beating you in the head with a hammer and threatening to kill you, who would you call?"

"911—"

"You'd call 911. You'd have us come out to your home, you'd put our lives in danger to save yours. We'd rescue you from a perilous situation, arrest your boyfriend, testify on your behalf in court. If that happened you wouldn't hate us. Suddenly we'd be your best friend."

His partner chuckled like he couldn't believe they were still talking about the same old crap. He slammed his big white fist on the black table.

"Now, if you two can stop chatting it up like you're best buddies, maybe she can hand over her damned cell phone so we may proceed with this investigation. This is serious. It's not a game. A man is dead. We need to find out what happened."

"Oh okay, sir. I'm sorry. Woo, I just can't believe any of this," Coco told him. The Asshole smiled, but she didn't.

She felt like she couldn't smile. She was alone in a tiny, shrinking, windowless, camera-monitored room with two unsympathetic strangers.

"With all due respect sir, tell your protect and serve speech to those dead motherfuckers who got killed by a cop's gun. If you want my phone you're going to have to go in my purse and get it yourselves. I don't trust you guys. I'm sorry, but that's just how it is."

"Ms. Reeves, may I ask you something?" This was the less aggressive officer. She saw sincerity in his eyes so she mumbled, "Go ahead, Officer."

"Do you believe in God?"

"Hell yeah."

"I do too. I am a Christian, I believe in the Bible and I believe that police officers have a special assignment, a special duty."

"Oh, is that what they call it these days?"

He ignored her. "And if you believe in God then you have to believe that your higher power won't let anything happen to you if it wasn't in his will."

"Huh? You're saying that God wants me to be here in this stinking police station?"

"I'm saying even when you believe in Him, it won't always prevent bad things from happening. Remember the story of when Jesus was arrested? And he wasn't a criminal."

"Look, man. I appreciate you're trying to comfort me, or whatever it is you're doing, but I seriously doubt that God wants me here in this place. I'm nothing like Jesus. I ain't white. So please, Officer, let me go. I've told you everything."

Aggravated cop said, "We'll let you go but we need to see that phone of yours."

"The only way you'll see my phone is if God himself comes and takes it from me."

He frowned at Coco and got up to remove her purse from her lap.

"Hi," he said with a smirk. "I guess my new name is God." He shuffled around through her big, bulky handbag. He handled it with the utmost delicacy even though she'd already passed through a metal detector when she first arrived.

They got her cell phone and asked for her password and she gave it to them. She watched while they filtered through all of her texts, emails, and photo gallery. She squirmed when they looked at the topless selfies that she'd sent to Calhoun but never deleted.

"Did you find anything interesting yet?" she asked. Her voice sounded scratchy and exhausted.

"We're taking your phone and will be back shortly." Before she knew it, they'd left her alone in the room. They locked the door behind them so she couldn't even use the restroom.

Coco's hands were free, but she still felt trapped, like her freedom as she'd known it only one day earlier had vanished before her eyes.

Within twenty minutes, they returned; the Smirking cop asked her to stand up.

"Coco Chanel Reeves, you are under arrest for the murder of Nathaniel Taylor."

"What? Are you serious?"

"You have the right to remain silent."

They read Coco her rights.

"Thanks you guys. I really appreciate this. Can you pick me up some Burger King before you cuff me?" They ignored her sarcasm and soon the metal handcuffs were tightly clamped around her wrists.

She stood on her wobbly legs. The nicer cop could barely look her in the eye. "What's your name again?" she asked.

"Sergeant Cohen."

"I appreciate the stuff you told me, Officer Cohen. The things you said about it being God's will when bad things happen to people. And I will try to remember it the next time I get in trouble."

"Sorry ma'am, but we're just doing our job."

"You doing your job is making me suffer for something I didn't do. I didn't kill that man."

"The evidence suggests otherwise."

"Look Sergeant Cohen. Everyone has a point of view depending on what side of the street they're standing on. You're standing on your side of the street and that's why you see things your way. But you're going to have to stand on my side of the street to understand where I'm coming from. You feel me?"

"I don't get it."

Coco was so exhausted all she could do was laugh. "No problem Sergeant Cohen. It's all good. But you know what? If you were married to a woman who looks like me, I wouldn't be going through this."

"What's that supposed to mean?"

"If I was born looking like you, the outcome would be much different, much better. Don't you agree?"

Sergeant Cohen looked like he finally understood.

"Hey, that's not fair."

"It sure isn't," she said, and felt the handcuffs cut into her skin as she held her hands behind her back.

Cohen had no words; his partner whisked Coco away.

She got processed, fingerprinted, and was assigned a number. She was forced to turn in her street clothes for the standard Montgomery County prison garb, a pink and white striped uniform with a plain white T-shirt underneath.

She winced when a guard thrust three fingers deep into her anus to search for contraband.

"Really?" Coco said. "I just got here, I haven't had time to sneak shit in this place."

"We still have to check; now shut up before I really shove something hard up your ass."

Coco felt like she'd been socked in the jaw. She fought back hot tears, anger, and a hundred regrets.

All she could think about was how she got here, and what it would take to get out.

Chapter 9

So Emotional

The news spread quickly.

Alita called Burgundy and told her that she needed to round up the Reeves sisters.

"I'm on my way to your crib."

"Lita, are you serious? It's almost eleven at night."

"Coco's been arrested."

"What?"

"They think she murdered your husband and now she's cuffed and uniformed in Montgomery County Jail."

By the time Alita had arrived at Burgundy's house, she was waiting in the family room along with Dru and Elyse.

Alita strolled through the house. "They got her. My baby sister is locked up."

"I feel so bad for Coco," Dru said. "What's the plan?"

"I think she'll be arraigned sometime in the next day or so," Alita said. "This is some bullshit. They have no solid evidence that she did anything. It's all circumstantial."

"How's she doing, Lita?" That was Elyse. "I feel it's my fault."

"What? Why?" Alita asked. "You shouldn't feel bad at all since Nate started all this mess."

Burgundy finally spoke up. "Leave him out of it. He's not here to defend himself."

"Ha! And I guess you think it's your job to do it, B?"

"None of you will fight for his legacy. So leave him out of this. Stay focused."

"Ain't no way we can leave his ass out of it. If he had kept his hands to himself, we wouldn't be going through this. All I can think about is Coco. She's probably in there pulling her hair out, fighting with folks, cussing out the guards. You know how she gets when she feels cornered."

"Again, what's the plan?" Dru asked.

The doorbell rang and Dru went to open the door.

There was Calhoun and all of Coco's kids: Cadee, Chloe, and even Cypress who was asleep in a baby carrier. The kids looked so confused and out of place. Just seeing how exhausted they looked caused Alita to burst into tears. She went to comfort the children with hugs and kisses.

"Why are you crying, Aunt Lita?" Cadee asked. "You look sad."

"Oh. I-I'm just happy to see y'all. That's all. I love my nieces."

Alita had already given Calhoun a heads up about Coco. Thankfully, the kids were already with their dad when Coco had been questioned by the police.

"Where's Chance?" Elyse asked.

Alita spoke up. "Um, he's fine. Don't even worry about him."

Calhoun spoke up. "Is he with that bonehead nigga, Q?"

"Um, aren't you married now?" Alita asked. "How would your new wife feel if she knew you were still salty about your ex?"

"Alita, that ain't none of ya business. I ain't salty either."

"Sure as hell looks like you are to me."

"I was just wondering," Calhoun said. "Wondering where little Chance is."

"Why do you care?" Alita asked. "You dropped out the boy's life and you can't get an attitude because some other man has stepped up to the plate to do the job even if he is your former best friend."

"Former is right. I got nothing good to say about that dude. Or about Coco."

Alita stepped up to Calhoun. "You know what? I can't believe my sister used to be sprung over your ass. If you would have done what you vowed to do, maybe none of this shit wouldn't have happened. If you had been a real man from jump street and not fucked over a woman who loved you with all of her heart, my sister wouldn't be in jail."

Calhoun was stunned at Alita's outburst. So was everyone else.

"Lita, I'm glad that you're sticking up for Coco," Dru said with pride in her voice. "And you all can argue back and forth about this, but you'd be wasting your time. This is not about Calhoun or Q. We've got to think about Coco's kids and what's going to happen to them. Trust me, they're all she cares about right now, not about a man. Any man."

"What are you talking about?" Cadee asked. "Where's my Mommy?"

Calhoun crouched next to his daughter. He hugged her then whispered a few words in her ear. She yawned, nodded, and looked like she was about to fall asleep.

Burgundy had enough. "Look at you all. I love you to pieces but this whole thing is crazy."

"What do you mean?" Elyse asked.

"Lita, why'd you ask Calhoun to come out here with the kids? We know they're in a good, stable environment with their dad."

"They are," Calhoun said. "I take damned good care of my kids."

"And I think you should drive them home, Calhoun, let them go to sleep so they can be ready for school tomorrow," Burgundy said to him. "And one more thing, keep doing everything you've been doing. Coco will be alright. She's a grownup. A hell of a survivor. She'll be okay."

Everyone stared at Burgundy in shock. But she didn't care at that point. This was one family crisis that she wasn't equipped to handle in that moment. She said a prayer for her sister and asked everyone to excuse her.

She needed to think, think real hard, and being alone in the immediate aftermath of everything that had gone down was the best solution she could come up with.

The flurry of excitement about Coco's arrest settled within a few days. And on Friday, Dru had a rare day off from her occupational therapist job. A doctor's appointment had been scheduled in the afternoon. But that morning she took time to pick up Elyse and drive her to Morning Glory.

"Thanks Dru, for everything you do for me."

"You don't have to thank me. I'm happy to help out."

"Helping me out takes a lot of time."

"What are you talking about?"

"You like to coach me and teach me things about being a woman, balancing my checkbook, and investing money. I'm learning a lot. But sometimes I feel guilty. I feel like I take you away from your man. And I would never want anyone else to do that to me."

They were in Dru's car, having a grownup conversation. Elyse had come a long way but still hadn't progressed into the woman that Dru felt Elyse could one day become.

"I don't mind doing whatever I can because I know it's working, Elyse." Dru laughed. "You make me so proud that the sacrifices don't bother me a bit." She shuddered as she thought about the emotionally dark place where Elyse used to dwell.

"Girl, there is no way I'd want to stop your success. But I must admit, although you've come a long way, you do need to handle some more important business."

"Like what?" Elyse asked.

"You need to secure that bag."

"Oh Dru."

"I know you don't like talking about it. But you could be doing so much better and have so much more."

"But I make a little more money now that I'm almost an assistant manager."

"And that's fine, Elyse," Dru gently told her. "But as a strong woman you should never want to grow comfortable with your situation. You always have to set higher goals and stretch yourself."

"I don't know what more I can want than what I've got. It makes me happy."

"And that's great, but there's more. Take me, for example," Dru explained. "I'm about to graduate with honors with a master's degree in occupational therapy."

"I'm so proud of you, Dru. I wish I could go to college."

"That's just it, baby girl. You can go to college. You can do whatever you set your mind to do. I can see it, Elyse. You can do way more."

The excitement that Elyse heard in Dru's voice began to make her insides tingle. What did Dru see in Elyse that the girl could not see in herself?

"Tell me more."

"Not only should you take advantage of the trust fund that in my opinion Burgundy owes to you, but it's time that you get your own car. You should not be content with accepting rides from me, Lita, Coco, and Gamba. And Uber is fine when you're in a pinch, but it's nothing like having your own. I can envision you in a brand new SUV."

"Dru, are you serious?"

"Elyse, I am very serious. You must believe good things, speak them out loud until you believe that they can be yours. You should never agree to a negative life that someone else thinks you should live. Take our dear sister, Coco, for example. She's been labeled everything but a child of God. Once the news got out that she was arrested, it's been pure hell. The press has called her a thug, and they know nothing about her. She's never been in trouble with the law before. That's why we must prove people wrong."

"Why they do that to Coco?"

"Because they don't know her. They know what they've heard about her. Or maybe some are stuck in a systematic way of reporting the news when it comes to certain issues. When was the last time you saw *USA Today*, CNN, or Fox go out of their way to highlight the wonderful, outstanding contributions that are made daily by people of color? Ph.D. candidates, people graduating *summa cum laude* from Ivy League schools, inventors, all kinds of magnificent things, but as usual the only media that will broadcast our positive stories are the smaller, black media outlets."

"That's true now that you mention it. But what can we do about it? We're not the media."

"We're not the media but we can be the opposite of the images they like to post about us." Dru paused. "We have to be better than what they think. Like, for myself, I have something to prove too."

"Like what?"

"I plan to walk across that stage and hold my head up high when I am handed my graduate degree from TWU, and I'm also looking into opening up my own OT clinic."

"You are?"

"I can count on one hand how many black-owned OT clinics exist in the Houston area. And part of my thesis was on the feasibility of the operation of a privately-owned clinic that catered to school children up to college age. And I learned for myself that it's doable. That and much more."

When Dru pulled in the parking lot of Morning Glory she decided at the last minute to walk inside with Elyse. This wasn't going to be the usual drop off and 'see you later' type of situation. Bigger matters were at stake. And critical conversations needed to be held.

Dru entered the front lobby and waved at the other workers while Elyse dashed away to the ladies' room so she could spruce up her makeup and comb her hair. She'd been taught by Dru that appearance was important. She wanted to look the part of an assistant manager and she was willing to do whatever it took to succeed. Feeling newly inspired, Elyse attended to her hair and face then went to put on her work jacket.

Meanwhile, Dru decided to take a few moments to order a coffee and one slice of French toast.

She took a seat at a booth and when she saw Burgundy walk past, she waved at her.

They engaged in perfectly decent small talk for several minutes. Then Dru gazed at her sister and asked her to sit down.

"Burgundy, I know this is probably something that you aren't necessarily thinking about these days, but do any of your businesses have a formal sexual harassment policy?"

"Um, not really."

"You might want to think about having one."

"Why should I?"

"Burgundy, I'm serious about this. Your company should implement it like ASAP."

"Thanks, Dru, for your very unsolicited advice—"

"I'm only trying to make a suggestion that may protect your interests."

"I doubt that you're concerned about my interests, Dru."

Her underlying meaning did not go unnoticed. Dru could understand why Burgundy was so touchy these days, considering what she'd been through. But Dru was inclined to believe that had Burgundy instituted a strict sexual harassment policy at her place of business, maybe none of what happened with Nate would still be dogging her. And maybe Coco would never have gotten arrested.

"In case you forgot, our sister is locked up," Dru said in a rare heated tone.

"I know Coco is in jail," Burgundy told Dru. "Is that my fault too?"

"In my opinion, if you would have been more aware of what was going on with him and Elyse, or with him *period*, maybe none of these tragedies would have happened. From what I understand, Coco just wanted to protect Elyse on the night that she came to help the girl move out. She called him out on his shit and Nate didn't like it. They got into it. And when he died the next day, of course, it made Coco look like the culprit."

"Is that right, Dru?"

"Yes, it is."

"I'm glad you've become such an expert . . . on so many things . . . such as criminal evidence, marital relationships, and more."

"I'm not an expert but I do believe that if you'd had courage enough to confront your husband about the accusations made to you by Elyse, accusations you didn't take seriously, Coco wouldn't be locked up. Part of this is your fault. You should have stayed more on top of your man's whereabouts . . . not because he was a man, but because he was a risky type of man . . . one that needed to be watched and checked on."

"My my my. Amazing how people's truths just suddenly come tumbling out of their mouths. I didn't know you had it in you, Dru."

"It's been on my mind, in addition to some other things that I've kept inside."

"I see." Burgundy gazed at Dru. "Do you know exactly where Tyrique is right now?"

"Yes, I do."

"You only think you know where your man is. You can only assume what he's doing." Burgundy felt insulted. She would not allow herself to take the full blame for Nate's choices. "Hell, do I look like I have the power of God with eyes that are in every place all at the same time?"

"Of course not, B—"

"Then stop placing the *blame* for what happened to *Coco* and *Elyse* on me. God knows I am sorry for everything, but it's not the type of sorry in which I feel completely responsible for their downfall. That's bullshit!"

"Now wait a minute—"

"No, Dru, you wait a minute. The only thing I did, the only thing I can always do, is be the best that I can be under the circumstances. And whether you believe it or not, I had no idea what Nate was doing to Elyse. Is there a penalty against wives or family members who trust what they've been told? Because if there are then you're guilty too. If we didn't trust our partners, we wouldn't be with them. And if we find out that they've lied, betrayed us, and made us look like fools because we honestly took them at their word, guess what? It's devastating. It hurts. I was and I still am hurt."

"From what I've been told you're not hurting too bad at all. You've bounced back and have a new lover to help you get through the sad, lonely nights. You refuse to bail out Coco, and to me that's a damned shame."

"If you care so much, you do it."

"If I was in the position to do it, I would. I would. But I'm not."

"And I am?"

"Of course, you are. Are you kidding? That man left you loads of money."

"And how would you know that?"

"Everyone knows. Stop coming at me sideways and keep it real with me. And if you think I sound like Coco, then you're right. I'm siding with Coco."

Dru's words dug deep. Burgundy wanted to release a piercing scream. But she held it together. For God's sake, she was at Morning Glory. The restaurant was one thing that she owned that she never wanted to let her down. Working made her feel stable, secure, and in control. And she would be damned if she let anything or anybody, or a damning media story, destroy what she had built up.

"You know what your problem is, Dru?"

"I wasn't aware that I had a problem."

"You do. You're smug and judgmental. You can dole out advice to Elyse because she's young and hasn't been through a lot."

"Wait a minute, she's been through a whole lot."

"But she's never been a wife," Burgundy argued. "Never been a mother. And neither have you."

"How dare you say such ugly things to me, Burgundy Taylor."

"Words hurt, don't they? And so does the truth."

Tears slipped from Dru's eyes. Embarrassed, she swiped a napkin from the napkin holder and tried to pat her eyes dry. She thought of her inability to maintain a pregnancy. And as she blinked her eyes, the stream of tears increased, flowing across her cheeks and resting underneath her chin.

Elyse happened to be walking past their booth. She locked eyes with Dru, whose distressed face shook Elyse to her core.

"What's going on here?" she demanded as she stood next to their table. "Is everything okay?"

"It's fine, Elyse. Get back to work," Burgundy said with a forced smile.

"I'm not going anywhere. I know Dru and she's crying. What's wrong?"

Dru picked up a fresh napkin and patted her eyes. "It's nothing, Elyse. My contacts are bothering me."

"It doesn't look like that to me. I heard y'all fussing over here a minute ago. But I didn't say anything. I was always told to stay out of grown folks business," Elyse calmly responded. "But I love you all too much to watch you hurt each other with stupid words. We are family. We stick together. You understand that? Do you?"

Her small face looked both angry and crushed.

"Elyse," Dru finally spoke up. "You're right. B and I spoke out of turn. We said some not so nice things to one another. I have no excuse. I started it and I was wrong. Burgundy, please forgive me."

Burgundy said nothing. She stared straight ahead. She drowned out Dru's additional pleas for mercy.

"I was out of line, B. If I hadn't said what I said, you never would have lashed out at me. I know this. Am I right?"

Burgundy remained quiet; she was pondering words, the power of all kinds of words. The words of Dru, the words of Elyse, the words of Coco and Calhoun, and how she was going to deal with the ones that were now orbiting inside her head.

Burgundy was home when her doorbell rang later that evening. She'd fixed her girls a pasta and salad dinner, played games with them, and was trying to relax with a glass of Moscato. She held the glass in her hand as Natalia rushed ahead of her and opened the door.

"Excuse me young lady. Did you at least look through the peep hole first to see who it was?"

"No. I was hoping it was the Fed Ex guy."

"What?"

Natalia laughed and then stopped once she saw that their visitor wasn't delivering a package. Edmund slid past her disappointed face and waved hello.

"Hey, Burgundy. Is this a bad time?" he asked.

"Yes," Natalia said.

"Hold on, Nat. We're not going through this again. I asked my special company to come over so we can discuss some things. Mommy needs some adult time."

Natalia turned around and sprinted into the kitchen where she had been enjoying a cup of rainbow sherbet.

"I'm sorry, Edmund," Burgundy apologized. "I don't know where she gets that from. She's been that way ever since she was two. I think the first words she learned were 'why' 'No' and 'Dada.'" Burgundy couldn't help but laugh out loud.

"Let's go to the family room," she told him. They went and got comfortable on the sofa. He immediately sat close to her and placed his arm around her shoulders.

"You have no idea how glad I am that you came over."

"I've been missing you, Burgundy, and I know you've been through a lot. I could hear it in your voice when you called."

"Yeah," she said as she held her glass of wine. "One way to get through the troubles of the day is to sip on this," she said. Burgundy took a long swallow and drained her glass. "And then to kiss on this." She leaned over and gave Edmund a hot, juicy kiss on his lips.

When they let up for air, Burgundy stood to her feet and shook her hair loose. She was already barefoot and was wearing a Texans T-shirt and leggings. The entire day had been draining so far. With the argument with Dru, and

Coco's complicated predicament still plaguing the family, she needed to relax. And she started to feel much better now that Edmund was there with her.

"Did you have quality time with the girls?" Edmund asked.

"Yep. Work was pure hell after that misunderstanding with Dru. And I left early today. Picked up the kids from school and we hung out and had a good time, that is, until Natalia begged me to go to the store and buy her a couple more gallons of ice cream."

Edmund smiled. "Let me guess how that turned out."

"I told her 'no.' And it hurt to tell her that but we already have loads of sweets in the freezer."

"How'd she take it?"

"She pouted, acted like she was about to die, threatened to call CPS, all kinds of nonsense." Burgundy laughed. "But I had to teach Natalia that sometimes a mother has to say no. Sometimes a sister has to say no. It's hard to do it but it had to be done."

"Just because you say no to Natalia doesn't mean you're a bad parent."

She paused. "I hope not. And now, after the stress of arguing again with my child and feeling like somehow, I lost that fight, I am so ready to fucking chill and relieve some stress. Today really was the day from hell."

Burgundy sighed, and stretched, and began to sing the lyrics to "I Wanna Dance with Somebody (Who Loves Me)".

"I love me some Whitney Houston," she continued. "My mama and daddy would play Nippy's music ever since I was young. I loved her music and her movies. I cried like crazy when she died. But right now, I'm about to party like she's still alive and standing right here in my living room."

"You're in a mood," Edmund told her in an amused tone.

"You bet I am. I have to make myself have fun or else I'll go crazy." Burgundy raced over to the stereo. It was an old fashioned record player that she'd bought from Sam's Club. She had a vinyl copy of the *Whitney* album.

"Let me do the honors," Edmund said. Soon Whitney's sweet vocals bounced off the walls. Burgundy and Edmund moved around to the music, and it felt really good to let her hair down.

Burgundy gyrated back and forth. And she went into complete orbit when the song ended and she skipped over a few to hear her favorite off the album: "So Emotional."

I get so emotional baby, every time I think of you.

She couldn't think of a better way to spend her evening. The man she adored was there by her side. She sang her heart out and stared deep into Edmund's eyes as they moved in sync.

The fact was, Burgundy's entire family loved to get down on the dance floor. It was in their DNA. Dancing felt like freedom and power, like releasing every care from their souls until a joyful exuberance took over. Many African tribes, such as the Kenga people, held a ritual of dancing after a loved one died. It was called a death dance: a way of celebrating life and not just mourning a death. Other times the ritual meant passing down family traditions. Burgundy was more than ready to be freed from all the worries that held her down.

"C'mon baby," she said. "You better move a lot faster than that if you wanna keep up with me and Nippy."

"Oh yeah?" Edmund asked.

"Damn skippy. I'm Whitney." She pointed at his chest. "You're Bobby. Now get to dancing." They laughed and fell cozily into each other's arms. Edmund enjoyed shuffling his feet to music as much as Burgundy. He wasn't very good at it and definitely didn't know any of the latest moves but it didn't matter. He loved to have fun.

Burgundy turned around and backed herself against his chest. She twisted her ass against his package. It felt naughty, erotic, and liberating.

She and Edmund made such a ruckus that Natalia entered the room. Sidnee followed right behind her. Sidnee hadn't seen her mom act this wild and loose in quite some time. She clapped her hands, cheering her mother on.

Edmund saw Sidnee and jiggled right up to her; then got down on his knees so he that he could be eye level. He grabbed her little hands and made her dance with him. Sidnee laughed and played along. But Natalia stood watching the two of them with her arms folded tight across her chest.

When Edmund noticed how intently Natalia was staring at them, he asked his dance partner to excuse him.

"Hello there, Natalia."

She simply stared at him.

"Would you like to dance?" he asked.

"Don't talk to me."

"Natalia, I won't have you disrespecting Edmund," Burgundy told her.

"You love him more than you love daddy. You never danced with my daddy."

"W-what? How would you know that Natalia?"

"Because I do."

"You know nothing. You are assuming or you're repeating what you've heard someone else say."

"No, I'm not."

"Oh God. Why am I even arguing with a little girl about my relationships? This is insane. Natalia, we aren't doing anything wrong. And if you can't chill out and join in on the fun, you may as well go upstairs to your room."

"Mommy, I can dance with Mr. Murray. I was having fun," Sidnee told her.

"I know, sweetie. And that's all I want us to do," Burgundy said, her voice cracking. "I-I just wanted us to have some fun."

"Why do you want to have fun?" Natalia asked.

Even though the music was going strong, Burgundy felt ridiculous all of a sudden.

"What the hell? The man is gone, Natalia. I can't bring his ass back. I don't even know if I'd want him back."

Edmund cleared his throat. Burgundy left the room. Edmund followed behind her. Natalia finally left. But Sidnee continued dancing alone.

It was mid-November. The days were getting shorter. And so was Burgundy's patience. Some days she'd be on top of her game, other days were a struggle. She had a lot on her mind, and when that happened the way she got centered was to stay busy or do something that challenged her.

One morning, she went to work but left mid-day. She drove and ended up at a women's center. It's one that she'd heard about and supported by writing out big checks every year but she had never stopped to actually visit it. Until then.

Burgundy met with the director of the center. Alice Keith was her name.

"It's nice to finally put a face to a name," they both uttered the same sentence at the same time and laughed.

"It's an honor to meet one of our dedicated benefactors," Alice said.

"No, the honor is actually mine," Burgundy replied. They walked down the long hallway that extended from one building to another.

"I see it's well-lit in here," Burgundy mumbled.

"It has to be. That is for the safety of the patrons and the workers. Come this way."

Very shortly they walked into a room that was filled with women. Tables, chairs, cubbies, and shelves filled just about every corner of the rectangular shaped room. It reminded Burgundy of an art and crafts class that she took when she was in middle school.

"What's this?" Burgundy asked.

"This is where the women are encouraged to express themselves artistically and creatively through making whatever they want to make. We fill the shelves with paint brushes, fabrics, scissors, clay—"

"You said scissors?" Burgundy eyed some of the women with caution. They glanced at her for several seconds then resumed doing their projects.

"Oh, you don't have to worry," Alice remarked with a slight smile. "Only the best-behaved women get to attend this class. We don't want anyone to get any ideas, especially being around the scissors. And the glue. And the other bottles filled with what I called artistic poisons."

"I see." Burgundy stood still and glanced over the shoulder of one short-haired woman who looked to be in her sixties.

"That's Miriam. She was the victim of a husband who'd frequently showed up at her job unannounced. He would yell, scream, hit and punch her in front of her boss and coworkers. They fired her. Miriam couldn't find another job. So she came here. She's a good woman who just found herself in a bad situation with a man twenty-five years younger than her."

"Are you serious?"

"Yes. When a woman is desperate for love she'll do just about anything, put up with all kinds of dangerous living situations, just to say she has a man." Alice frowned. "Luckily, Miriam woke up before it was too late. We send her off on job interviews and tried to teach her other skills to keep up her self-esteem which, by the way, took a huge blow when she got out of her marriage."

"But how do you know that her violent husband—"

"Ex-husband."

"What if he comes by here?" Burgundy cautiously eyed the doorway of the classroom. She held in her breath unable to imagine the type of fear that probably existed in such a place as this women's center.

"We have security guards, and we aren't even publicly listed in a directory. If you noticed, when you came in you had to give your name, hand over your ID and be approved to even gain entrance into the living center of this facility. We are serious about security."

"Then how do people find out. I mean, I see you listed in the list of charitable organizations directory but now that I think of it, I had to call and go through a battery of questions to get this address."

"They know you because you are a donor," Alice told her. "You were already checked out, and pre-checked out, before you even set foot on our property."

She gave Burgundy numerous facts and figures. Alice invited her to meet some of the women who had their own survival stories.

By the time their visit was over, Burgundy was brimming with hope.

Burgundy recently learned that when Nate died, his insurance policy was enough to keep her and the girls comfortable for the rest of their lives. The checks had been cashed and their financial future was stable. And now that she felt secure that her immediate family would be alright, she started thinking about other women too.

Burgundy drove back home, settled down and called Dru.

"Hey there," she told her. "I have an idea, and I think you're just the person who can help."

"What is it?"

Burgundy started to describe her plans.

"I've been toying with an idea that sounds crazy, but it keeps nagging at me. I want to create a rape crisis center for whoever would need it. Hispanic. White. Black. Everyone."

"What brought this on, B?"

Burgundy glanced around her house. The house with five bedrooms, tons of quality furniture, and rooms with spacious closets that were filled with clothes, shoes, purses, and more.

"I'm stressed but I'm also blessed, Dru. That's what brought it on."

"Oh, I see. And what made you realize that? Because for a minute there you sounded like one of those people I hate running into when I'm at the mall, the grocery store, the bank."

"People like who?"

"Ingrates. People who complain about everything when they already have everything. When nothing they have is ever enough."

Dru suddenly gasped, as if she was in deep pain. Burgundy's eyebrows flew up. "Sis, is everything okay?"

Dru didn't respond, but Burgundy could hear her sniffling.

"Hey, if you need me, I can be there in thirty minutes depending on traffic."

"Really?" Dru said in surprise.

"Are you serious? How dare you assume that I don't care about you? That no one in the family will toss aside anything we're dealing with to help you out."

"I just didn't want to intrude. I think about you and what you're going through, and how nasty I've been treating you lately."

"Dru, dear, all is forgiven."

"Really?"

"Really. Fundamentally, as a family, we have to work on our issues and forgive each other. Nothing else matters."

"I'm glad you feel that way, but, whoa. Compared to what you've dealt with lately, my issues simply can't compare."

"Why compare problems, Sis? This is about you."

Dru began to stammer. "No. I'm good. It's fine. It'll be alright."

"Now, don't you lie to me, Dru. If you need help, if you need a listening ear you'll have to speak up. If we try to help you and you refuse us, it's like you're acting too self-reliant."

"Self-reliant?"

"Or maybe you're more like me than I ever realized." Burgundy recognized the signs of someone who pretended as though everything was fine but the exact opposite was true. Burgundy knew hurting people when she saw or heard them. Right then she quietly gathered her purse and a tote bag. She set the security alarm on "Away."

When Burgundy went out to the garage and was ready to start the car engine, she placed the call on mute to drown out the sound of the car starting up.

Burgundy backed out of the garage and was soon on her way. And she hoped to hell that Dru wouldn't ask her if she was driving when she heard the sounds of tires on the road and her turn signals.

They continued chatting on the phone.

"B, I need to ask you something."

"What is it, Dru?"

"Don't you feel a bit weird to try and open a rape crisis center?"

"No, I don't. It's a good thing. It's called making lemons out of lemonade."

"And do you feel odd helping out other women, virtual

strangers, when your own sister is still in jail and you've refused to accept her collect calls?"

Burgundy was momentarily silent. Sure, she knew that her other sisters had given her the side-eye when she told them point blank that she could not bail out Coco.

"Even though I have the money to help her, I think that Coco has to learn from whatever she did to put herself in that situation." That was Burgundy's cryptic response.

"Okay, but doesn't she still have the right to be out and try to pull herself together for her case?"

"If you care that much you can bond her out, Dru."

"Like I said before I'm not in the position to help. I don't know why the judge imposed such a high amount anyway. It's not like she's a flight risk."

"Well, murder is a serious thing."

"You really think Coco murdered Nate?"

"I don't know, Dru. And that's an honest truth. But let's change the subject."

Soon Burgundy was standing in front of Dru's front door.

Tyrique answered her knock. Burgundy placed a finger against her lips. He nodded conspiratorially. Pointed to the kitchen. She removed both of her pumps and tiptoed into the kitchen. Dru's back was turned as she cradled the phone between her chin and her ear while looking inside the refrigerator.

Burgundy suppressed a giggle then walked up to Dru. She placed her hands over her sister's eyes.

"Guess who?" Burgundy asked in a gruff voice.

"B?" she asked and swung around.

Burgundy burst out laughing. "How'd you know it was me?"

"Your expensive, divine perfume always gives you away." They stood there stupidly grinning at each other. That's when Burgundy knew exactly what love felt like.

Love went above and beyond. Love didn't hold grudges. Love could be fun, surprising, and deliciously spontaneous.

Burgundy held her baby sister in her arms. But the baby was growing up. Dru looked healthier and had filled out.

"I'm here for you," Burgundy told her, and it felt good to say something positive, words that she meant with every ounce of her heart.

Dru said nothing. She simply nodded with her nose pressed against Burgundy's bosom.

And in an odd way, Burgundy felt like she was holding in her arms all the women she desperately wanted to help.

Dru let go and asked Burgundy to have a seat at the breakfast bar. She fed her some leftover homemade Asian soup and a cup of tea.

"So anyway," Burgundy continued to say. "Like I was telling you earlier, I have this idea. Let me know if I sound nuts or not. It won't hurt my feelings. I have a bit of money and I think I know exactly how to use it. Every week we read or hear about people in crisis. I even see men on the streets walking around with a dazed look in their eyes, like they have nowhere to go and no one to turn to."

"Like the mentally ill?"

"Good answer, but no. My mission isn't to help the mentally ill, although I do sympathize. No, this is more like a safe house for women who are trying to get out of bad relationships. A wife that needs to leave a husband but has no family, no money, no resources. What is she supposed to do, stay there and take it?"

"What if she still wants to work it out?"

"That's fine but I want to help those that are fed up. I'd hire a few professionals to keep the center safe, the women—"

"Or men—"

"Right. To keep everybody safe as possible. We'd provide counseling, job opportunities, career assistance, help these people get back on their feet." With every sentence that Burgundy heard spring from her mouth, she felt her mental juices stirring. That's what hope does.

At that point in her life Burgundy needed something that clearly let her know that pain wasn't for nothing.

"I like your idea," Dru said. "You need to get a proposal together. Maybe apply for a grant."

"I don't want nobody's grant money. That comes with all kinds of stipulations. I want to do it my way. No interference."

"That's understandable. But at the same time, it's always better to spend someone else's money instead of your own. Why not apply for a grant anyway? And then, if approved, you can supplement it with your own money as well, and ask for donations from your wealthy colleagues."

"Yes, accepting money from donors is also what I plan on doing. No matter where we get the money, I'm going to make this happen. It's a dream that I will not give up on."

Dru nodded. "Although I'm still pissed at you for how you've handled this Coco situation, I'm excited about your proposal."

"The Coco thing will work out. I'm sure of it. Meanwhile, I think this is something I can do to get my mind off me. Off Nate. And so on."

Dru agreed. "Look back, reach back, and give back."

"Yes. That's what I want to try and do."

"Do you have a name for this center?"

"The Sidnee Taylor Safe House."

"Really?"

"Yes."

"Why that name?"

"Last fall, when it wasn't looking good, when Sidnee was in that coma, I nearly lost it. So much death seemed to be hovering around me. But we prayed, we believed, me and the entire church. When she recovered a few days later, and her life was restored, I knew I had to give back. I had to do something that honored what I felt was God's way of restoring her little life. And that's why the center will be named after her."

At hearing Burgundy's determination, Dru agreed to help. She promised to notify her contacts and then they'd prepare to ask for grant money.

The more Burgundy thought about it, the more encouraged she felt. And having something positive to focus on rejuvenated her spirit.

Burgundy was feeling great and wanted to take a few risks. She invited Edmund to come spend the night. He agreed. It was that Sunday evening and he wasn't doing anything that he couldn't set aside in order to please her.

"I will need you to be very quiet. Little Miss Nosey goes to bed around eight. You can show up by eight-thirty."

"Sounds like a plan."

Burgundy had gotten used to it but sometimes she was tired of sleeping alone. She went to her dresser drawer and found some adult underwear and a sexy nightgown that she would wear.

She made sure to play with her kids till they were happily exhausted. It was actually wonderful to see Natalia and Sidnee laugh. She had a good time with the girls.

But when playtime was over, Burgundy tucked them in bed and waited until they were fast asleep. She closed their bedroom door and went downstairs.

A little after eight-thirty, Edmund showed up. She took him by the hand and led him into her bedroom. She shut and locked the door and proceeded to turn up the volume of her television, which was airing Sunday night football.

"Perfect," he told her.

"Oh, but you aren't over here to watch the game," she laughed and reminded him.

"I know that."

"I only turned that on real loud to drown out the noises I know we'll be making."

"Damn, baby, you're making me so hot," he told her.

They kissed then retreated to her exquisite master bedroom.

"God, I have missed you," Edmund said as he kissed the top of her messy looking hair.

"Me too. I hate that we have to schedule these kinds of things, but I just want to get it in whenever I can. Family first. But you definitely must fit into my equation."

"Is this your equation?" he asked and reached inside her underwear and patted her on the vagina.

"Oh, Edmund. Let's get this party started, since I see that you cannot control yourself."

Burgundy beamed from ear to ear. It felt so good to feel wanted, to be with someone who made her feel beautiful and desired.

Burgundy and Edmund decided to take a bubble bath together. For obvious reasons, he had never been in her bedroom. Tonight was the first time.

He looked around.

"Nice room," he said.

"Yeah."

She had taken care to remove most of Nate's remaining belongings and hidden them out of sight.

"I'm still debating about redecorating the whole house, or maybe I should scale down and move. The house is so big. But it's the one that the girls have known most of their lives."

"They need that stability."

"True, but there are a few ghosts here."

"I get it. I had the same dilemma when I got divorced. I

was able to keep the house. Kyra moved out. And I had to get rid of all those things that she left behind. Tons of stuff. It kind of made me feel bad. I asked if I was that bad of a person that she didn't even want to take the time to pack up all of her things."

Edmund's voice sounded hurt, which was a rarity. Burgundy walked over to him and gave him a hug and a kiss on the lips.

"And so, after the divorce was final, it felt a little weird to invite women to my house. In fact, I rarely did it."

"Oh yeah," Burgundy said with a teasing sound in her voice. "I'm sure you were fighting off all the single women once they knew you were on the market again."

"It wasn't the single ones. It was the married ones that came after me."

"Really?" Burgundy asked.

"Yep." He shook his head in amazement. "There are some married women who can't stand their husbands. They are living with men who make them miserable and they are on the hunt for a replacement. They see me as a good man. My ex-wife, she just wasn't happy, even though I did everything possible to make her happy." His eyes looked distant and sad.

"Even with you, Burgundy, God knows I've come to like you a whole lot, and I can say I am crazy about you, but I still—"

"You still what?" Her heart wildly pounded inside of her.

"Don't look so scared. You are a great woman. But I don't want to complicate your life. I don't want to become an extra burden."

"Oh Elm. You are one of the few people I know who lightens my burdens. I don't know what I'd do without you, babe."

She wanted to cry, because sometimes people honestly did not realize how much they meant to others. People assumed all kinds of things. Sometimes they felt invisible, like they don't mean much to others, and that if anything happened to them, if they disappeared for any reason, that they would not be missed. But it wasn't true. It wasn't!

She took Edmund by the hand. They sat together on a love seat in her bedroom.

"Look at me," she demanded. "I may be going through some challenges, but make no mistake, Edmund Langston Murray. You are a very important part of my life." She gasped and let one tear fall from her eye.

"Don't cry. I didn't mean to make you cry or make you sad."

"I'm not sad," she answered. "I'm mad."

"I'm sorry."

"No, I'm mad at myself. I didn't always appreciate Mr. Taylor. And I am not trying to compare you two because you're definitely individual men. But I want to say this . . ." she paused and made sure she felt it in her heart before she said it. "Maybe it sounds premature and if it is, I will deal with that, but as of right now, you are one of the first things I think of when I wake up in the morning. Edmund, I long to hear your voice every single day. I've given you your space but I know I wouldn't like it if we went two or three days without hearing from one another." She squeezed his hand. Following the love that was in her heart felt scary at times. Could true love really show up for her that quickly?

"I love you to pieces, Edmund. I-I know it sounds silly or it doesn't make a whole lot of sense and I would never want you to think you are a rebound man because I became a sudden widow. God knows," she gasped and closed her eyes. "If I am doing that then you deserve to not be around me. You'd deserve something better."

He nodded slowly. He understood what she was saying. Here they were, two individuals whose marriages ended in the ways they never imagined. It felt so embarrassing for him to tell his family that his wife did not want him anymore. It made him feel like a loser, as if he were tainted goods, and for a while Edmund did not want to date any woman. They were far too emotional and very difficult to understand at times.

"I'm glad I know where you stand, Burgundy. Truth is important. At our age, bullshit is not where it's at." He paused, then smiled. "It's been a long time since a woman has said she loves me and meant it."

She smiled. "I feel it and I wanted to tell you how I feel. Love is odd, it's strange and inexplicable at times."

"I agree," he said. "Now let's get to that bubble bath."

"Sure," she said. "But first allow me to fix us some nice hot tea. Tea relaxes me. I'll be right back." She hurried to the kitchen feeling peaceful and delighted about how the evening was going. And nothing could make it even better than her favorite hot beverage.

Good tasting tea is like good sex. It makes you moan, your eyes roll to the back of your head, and you want more. And when you make good love and have more fun than you have ever had in your life, you just want to enjoy the moment and stop caring what people think.

And that night, Burgundy and Edmund had lots of good sex and lots of good tea.

Chapter 10

Love and Happiness

Alita was at her stock clerk job. She was busy placing bottles of shampoo and conditioner on the shelves. She was working hard to make her shelf look nice and presentable when she felt a presence behind her back. Alita slowly looked up. At first, she couldn't recognize the elderly man who was leering at her. But she could never forget a face covered with moles. It was the ugly, wrinkled face of the man who raped her when she was a teenager.

"Hey there," he said.

"Jack Dawson! W-what you doing here?"

"I'm out now. Did my time."

"Oh." she told him. "That's nice." Alita wondered why the prison system didn't warn her about his release. And how the hell did Jack know where she worked?

She got her answer soon enough. Jerrod Dawson walked up to his daddy and cheerfully patted him on the back.

"Hey, what's up, Alita. It's good to see you're busy working at your job."

She felt as if Jerrod had taken a finger nail file and jabbed it into her neck. She tightly clutched a tall heavy bottle of deep conditioner.

"You know how big this store is? How'd you end up

here in my aisle during my shift? What do you want?" She stared at the two men and slowly rose to her feet with the bottle held close to her side.

"We were in the area, Alita."

"I don't believe that, Jerrod. I've blocked you from calling me so now you think you can walk up on my job and start more shit. But I already told you last time we talked . . . I have nothing for you. Elyse knows everything. And so does Leno."

"Elyse knows what? What is she talking about, son?"

Jerrod failed to answer his dad. It seemed that the words that Alita spoke took the wind out of his sails. He looked flustered. He coughed. Then said nothing.

"If you don't mind, I have a job to do. I don't want you here, and I will call security if I have to."

"Are you threatening us?" Jerrod asked.

"I'm asking you nicely to leave. I don't feel comfortable seeing you here, Jerrod. You or your daddy."

"But Jack is your baby daddy."

"He raped me. It's not the same." Alita was angry. "He hasn't been around all of her life so what difference does it make now?"

"He wasn't around because you had him locked up for those false charges." She and Jerrod went at it for another minute. Jack stood in the background looking aggravated.

"Look, Jerrod. I said what I said and now you need to go. You don't live around here and I know you're still trying to shake me down. But it won't work this time." Alita still regretted the many times in the past that she gave in to Jerrod and forked over hundreds of dollars to him because he threatened to expose her.

"Alita, because of you, my dad is a felon. Nobody will hire him."

"That ain't my problem! I've told you that a thousand times."

"What is Jack supposed to do about money?"

"You work. Your sisters work."

"My sisters work part-time."

"What about Roro?" Roro had been Alita's best friend when they were in high school. The two teens were thick as thieves until Jack impregnated Alita, was found guilty of sexual assault, and sent to prison. She hadn't talked to Roro since then.

"Speaking of the devil," Jack finally said. Jerrod's two sisters entered the aisle. They were helping to steer a wheelchair, one of the older models, operable by hand. And in the chair was a woman who appeared to be in her late thirties.

"There's your answer," Jerrod said in a bitter tone.

Alita gasped. "Roro?"

"Yep, it's me. How you doing, Alita? You seem to be doing great. Much better than me."

Alita felt a painful tug in her heart. She couldn't believe that this was the young spirited girl that she used to run the streets with. They'd hang out at the mall, go swimming, play softball. But now, her childhood friend was slumped in a wheelchair.

"Aren't you going to ask what happened?" Jerrod's smirk made Alita feel closed in, outnumbered.

"You know what, I don't like this at all." Alita's tone was heated. She shook the bottle of deep conditioner at Jerrod as she fled past him. "You all have to leave. This is harassment. I don't want to hear it, none of it."

She briskly walked away. She felt Roro's sad eyes on her, but she didn't care. She could hear Jerrod's voice taunting her. "We still know where you live. You can run but you can't hide, Alita. You owe me and my family."

Alita hated hearing his shrill voice, a voice that continued to haunt her, a voice that made her feel afraid and insecure.

She went to store management and explained what

happened. It made her very nervous to do it because this job was her only means of financial support. She thought about her kids, and her man. Shade Wilkins had been so patient with her, in spite of all of her family troubles. She did not want anything to happen to cause him to see her in a different, more negative light.

That night, Shade Wilkins popped by Alita's spot unexpectedly. He only gave her a ten-minute notice before he showed up at her front door.

Opening the door, she placed one hand on her hip.

He grinned then and softly crushed her inside his big strong arms.

"Don't even try it," she told him.

"Aren't you glad to see me?" he asked.

"No."

"No?" He released his grip then turned around and looked behind him. Feeling nosy, Alita looked too. She noticed five oversized bags sitting on the sidewalk like sacks of groceries.

"What's in those bags, Shade?"

"Don't matter now. You're not even glad to see me."

"Oh, c'mon, baby, don't be like that."

"Oh okay. I'm 'baby' now?"

"You're always my baby."

He shrugged and started walking away.

"Where you going?" Alita hurriedly followed him.

Shade lifted two bags in one hand, three in the other. Alita read the names etched on the sides: Dillard's, Coach. Nordstrom. Saks Fifth Avenue. And MAC.

He walked toward his car and popped open the locks.

"Hey, what are you doing? Where you going, Shade?"

He said nothing.

She froze. Her eyes teared up. She kicked off her flip flops and ran to him, her bare feet stomping upon the pavement.

"Baby, I'm sorry. You can come over anytime you want. You don't need to call first. You know that already."

As she thought about how important Shade was to her, she wanted to cry. She'd been through far too much to simply let this good man walk out of her life.

This was no time to play games. Love was at stake. Happiness was trying to get away.

"Baby, did you hear me? Please, Shade."

Shade turned and faced her. "I don't know what to make of you sometimes."

"But why not? What did I do?"

"It's just . . . everything . . . sometimes. Then it's nothing . . . the rest of the time."

"Speak in plain English."

"How do you feel about me, Alita?"

"You already know that. You know I care about you."

"Alita, I know what you tell me. And sometimes you give me mixed signals. And sometimes? I just get tired of it."

"Baby, calm down. We can get through this. I know that I've been acting a little crazy lately."

"Lately?" He eyed her warily. "You've been acting like this since day one. At first it was cute, intriguing, and slightly amusing. But lately, I've been thinking."

"Shade, don't do that. Don't think!"

Alita wished he would laugh like he normally did. But he didn't crack a smile.

Her mind flashed backward in time. When she first hooked up with her ex, she and Leonard were in love, true partners. But after a few years, things grew distant, then ugly, then tense. Love turned to confusion. And before she knew it, her marriage was over.

And it seemed like the hurt from that breakup never left. She wanted to do better. She knew that holding onto the past made her look bitter and powerless.

"Shade, baby," her voice trembled. "You are the best

damned thing that ever happened to me. And that's the truth."

"You sure don't act like it. Sometimes you act like you don't want the best, like you don't want me."

"Oh, c'mon, Shade. Are you serious?" Feeling afraid, she hugged him around his waist. She tried to make him kiss her. He pushed her away and increased the distance between them.

"Why are you acting like this, Shade? This isn't like you at all." She stared at the shopping bags, beautiful, enticing-looking bags that seemed like they were filled with treasures that weren't meant to be hers. Love and happiness. That's all Alita wanted. But what would it take for her to have it?

"Shade, how can you buy me stuff and not give it to me?"

"Is that all you care about? Stuff?"

"You know that ain't true."

"Then what do you care about?"

"Are you serious? You. Us. Our happiness."

He shook his head as if he did not believe a single word she told him. "I think I'd better bounce," he said.

"Bounce?"

"Yeah," he confirmed. The look on his face exhibited confusion, something she wasn't accustomed to seeing from him. Shade Wilkins was the first man in a long time that Alita believed could handle everything that she was.

"Don't leave. Why can't you just come in the house, have a seat, and calmly explain yourself so I can know where you are coming from. I-I thought we were tight and that you were secure in how I feel about you."

"You give me mixed signals. And at times, I feel like you're hiding something from me." He stared at her and she felt as if she was being scrutinized in a way that suggested he did not totally trust her.

"I ain't hiding nothing," she claimed in a forceful way. "What you see is what you get."

"That's what I thought when we first met. Because you were blunt. Defensive. But I knew a decent, passionate woman was hiding behind all that loud talking you'd be doing."

"And underneath the loud talk," she replied in a humble quiet voice, "is the real me, babe. I thought you saw that and knew it too. But now it feels like you changing your mind. Like you're the one with something to hide and not just me."

Her blunt reply made his eyebrows lift with a swiftness.

"I'm not hiding anything."

She felt hope stir inside of her. Hope felt better than fear. She let go of him and forced him to drop the shopping bags.

"I want us to talk some more," she told him. "I-I feel we can get things straight and get back on the same page."

When Shade remained silent, Alita kissed his lips and pressed her torso against his body. She grinded against him, using her feminine wiles to stir things up below his belt.

She moaned when she felt Shade hardening right against her.

It felt good yet she felt guilty. Like she was sexually manipulating a man to get what she wanted from him. She didn't want to act that way with him. She knew she needed to do better.

"Alita, I want you to tell me how you feel about me."

"Why do you keep asking me this?"

"You can be confusing and defensive. And it makes me wonder . . . sometimes."

"I know I can act hard. Yes, I do, Shade. But you can't tell me that I don't love you with all of my heart. I think I always have. I was just scared to admit it. I love how it feels to love you and I never, ever want to lose that feeling. Maybe that explains everything you need to know. I don't want to lose your love." Her loud voice fell to an anguished whisper. "I completely love you, Shade Wilkins." Her voice became hoarse. "And if you can't see it or believe it, and if you think I'm lying or saying something just to be saying it, then that's on you." Alita had no more strength. All she had was her truth and the only way that she knew how to express it. Shade silently watched her. She didn't know if she should stay or walk away.

Finally, a tiny smile spread across Shade's lips. He pressed his warm chest against Alita's bosom. Her nipples responded. She felt them grow harder. Human contact never felt so good. She closed her eyes and enjoyed the tenderness he offered.

Love. Happiness. She needed it. And she hated how it felt like she could easily lose it.

"I love you too, Alita."

"I know you do, babe. Thank you for loving me. I mean that." She felt incredibly grateful for that simple moment and never wanted to take love for granted. Love was like money. You can have it one day and lose it all the next. But true love had to be different.

Finally, when it felt safe to release him, she looked down at those bags.

"Looks like somebody's been shopping," she said in a teasing voice.

"Sure have."

"Galleria Mall?"

"Yep."

"Is-is that for me? I mean, you know, I don't want to assume it's for me so I need to ask."

He paused and looked up at the sky. "Um, I dunno," Shade said in a sing-song voice.

Alita playfully punched him in his arm.

He laughed.

"I was in the Galleria area yesterday. And at the spur of

the moment I decided to go in there to the Apple store just to browse. But I wound up going from one store to another. And I saw a couple things that I thought you'd like and . . ."

Alita began to smile as any happy woman could.

Shade kept talking. And Alita kissed him while he was jabbering away.

"Mmm mmm mmm, you're the best."

He could only laugh and let Alita have her way. She gave him lustful kisses right there on the sidewalk. When she came up for air, he grabbed two bags and placed them in her hand.

"We can go back inside and you can see what you got."

"Humph. I don't think so," she told him. She defiantly opened the Coach bag first. And when she saw what he got her, she nearly screamed her head off.

"Man, you something else." She retrieved a pair of brown cat eye sunglasses and quickly slid them on. She tilted her head back and forth pulled out her cell phone and took a few selfies.

"How I look?"

"Like a million bucks. But keep looking. There's something else in that bag."

Alita gasped and dug inside and felt something small, slender and lightweight.

"A watch?"

"You know what time it is," he said with a laugh.

Shade grabbed the beautiful piece of jewelry and buckled the strap so that it fit snugly on her thin wrist. With its black face, cherry colored leather strap and yellow stitching, this piece was the most glamorous watch she'd ever owned. Her eyes settled on it in admiration.

"Whoa! I needed a watch. And it's perfect. You did great, babe. But I'm shocked you didn't buy me a purse like I assumed you did when I first saw the bag. You're full of surprises. I love that about you."

"I'm glad you like it," he said, with a warm twinkle in his gorgeous eyes.

She felt dizzy with happiness then grew serious. "You know me, Shade. I don't worship material things. And I know it's the thought that counts." Looking at all those shopping bags that were different colors and sizes, she felt inadequate all of a sudden. "Shade, I appreciate what you've done, but look. I-I can't match what you've bought me, though. I don't make your type of bread. I barely make enough to pay the rent and buy food."

"I did not get this for you so you could pay me back. In my mind, that's not how it works."

She knew he felt insulted. He had a kind, genuine heart, a male type that she wasn't used to, but the kind that she wanted to get used to. "I know you got good intentions, Shade, but I can't help but remember . . . and I don't mean to bring up the past. But—"

"Then why do it?"

"Because it helps me to appreciate what I have now, that's why."

"The past has no place in your present or your future."

"I know it doesn't, but please don't get mad, Shade. Let me finish."

"Go on."

"I remember I dated this one guy a little while ago. And we'd kick it every other day. Go out to eat, go to the movies, go to the rodeo and the carnival. And he'd stop by my place after work and bring me things now and then. But it always seemed to be something that someone else was getting rid of. Something that another person gave him. And he'd accept the stuff they were going to throw away and somehow he'd think of me."

She winced at the way the past could still unearth a painful memory. Even after all this time she knew that old memories could still impact her. But oh how she wished they wouldn't.

"Oh babe, I'm so sorry that happened to you."

"Don't be. It's not your fault. But I tried not to be too hard on old boy at first. Like one time he gave me a T-shirt that his job was giving away. Or he brought by a few house plants that a store was offering to customers for free. They were beautiful and blooming. And I'd take them, of course, hell, it was all free. But after a while those gifts seemed like that's how he felt about me. I didn't understand why he couldn't come out of his pockets to buy some flowers or a box of candy or even a decent bracelet. Yet he always told me 'Lita, you know how much I'm feeling you. Lita, you my gal, and I'm feeling you big time.' He was feeling me alright. And when I felt some type of way over his gifts and stopped giving up the ass, he and all his hand-me-down gifts scattered like a bunch of pigeons."

"No woman deserves that type of treatment, Alita. Sounds like he was a little on the cheap side or he didn't know how to show you how he felt in a way that was meaningful to you."

"Like I said before, I'm no material girl, yet, Shade, I feel bad accepting your very nice gifts." Alita sadly glanced at her new watch. "I can't do what you do or buy what you buy."

"And I'm not asking you to. I don't judge you for where you are right now. Your struggles are just temporary."

"Are they? How do you know?"

"Everything is temporary, Alita. Nothing lasts forever."

"I don't like how that sounds."

"I don't mean for it to sound negative. But tough times don't last."

"Prove it."

"You're not with El Cheapo anymore are you?"

She had to laugh out loud. Then she smiled. He could always say just the right thing.

"Go on, my dear. Relax, accept the gifts, and enjoy them."

"Okay. I will."

"Plus it makes me happy to see you happy."

"But." She wanted to reach out and let the happiness take over her entire being. And right now was all she had even with the bad memories that still tried to linger. Right now was her new reality.

"Shade, baby, I appreciate all you're doing and telling me, but isn't it true that old boy was trying to make me happy too?"

"I can't speak for him, Alita. Maybe he was clueless about what you would like and appreciate."

"You know what, Shade, I remember another time when I told that guy that I love strawberry-scented shampoo and shower gel, but he kept bringing me some pumpkin smelling stuff that I hated. I kept telling him, 'Strawberries, strawberries.' And he kept bringing me the pumpkins."

"If you don't stop talking about your exes . . ."

Alita laughed again. "I'm done. Done with staying stuck in the past."

"Thank you."

She gleamed with happiness. A happiness that she prayed to have and then when she got it, it seemed like a dream. But as she stared at Shade and felt his love and tenderness, it felt good to know that her new man was the real deal.

"Shade, baby, I don't know what I'd do if you weren't in my life."

"I feel the same way, Alita."

They kissed again. Alita felt so lucky. She felt like the Lord was finally noticing her and maybe answering one or two of her prayers.

Suddenly, out of nowhere, the sky crackled with a bolt of lightning.

"Grab my shit," she yelled. "Oh, and you be safe too."

They laughed and yelled then made a mad dash inside the house before the first bucket of rain could pour down on them.

Shade let her open up the rest of her gifts. Two lipsticks from MAC. A beautiful striped maxi dress plus sandals from Dillard's. A crystal choker from Saks.

She wasted no time trying on everything and everything looked good on Alita.

But two bags remained. One smaller one stuffed inside a larger one.

"I'll do the honors," Shade remarked and dramatically pulled up one bag and held it up high.

He made her wait to open one of the bags that he'd saved for last.

She looked inside and jumped up and down and yelped. Shade bought her a genuine leather and snakeskin shoulder bag.

A *Coach* bag.

From Nordstrom.

That's love.

Chapter 11

Old Wounds

Dru and Jerrod Dawson stood face to face. It had been years since she'd seen her high school sweetheart in person. Once Jerrod broke up with her, they had no further contact. Dru gave him his space and then attempted to get in touch with him, but he rejected her. She felt hurt and confused, as if she'd been ghosted after being what she thought was a good girlfriend. Dru moved on with her life and that's when she enrolled in undergraduate school and ended up meeting Tyrique. Their bond was immediate and filled with warmth, mutual support, and loads of common courtesy toward one another. Dru finally felt like she could forget about her ex and enjoy a new and better relationship with a man like Tyrique.

Jerrod had friended her on social media months ago, but other than that, they'd had no true connection. And now, standing only six inches away from the man, Jerrod managed to drum up feelings she hadn't experienced in years.

"Drucilla Reeves, how's it going?"

"It's fine. Thanks for meeting with me. I think we have a lot to discuss, Jerrod. Have a seat." They were in the food court of Memorial Mall. It was a busy Saturday and the presence of lots of others, although strangers, offered Dru some comfort.

"I don't want to beat around the bush, Jerrod. Bottom line is that I've heard a lot of things about you. Most of it is very disturbing. I just wanted to hear your side of the story."

"About my dad? My half-sister, Elyse? Is that what you mean?"

"That's just for starters." Dru thought about the threats he'd used against Alita and she wanted to reach across the table and slap his face.

"What can I say? It's true. I have nothing to do with it though. If you want to get mad at someone, you may want to start with that whack ass sister of yours."

"One thing you're not going to do is disrespect my sister. Not my niece, nobody in my family, you understand?"

"Whoa, why you copping an attitude?"

"Because I have a right. I-I must admit, Jerrod, the things I've been told about you trying to get money from my sister and the terrible threats you've made to her if she didn't do what you asked, they hurt me. It didn't sound like you'd do anything like that."

"Baby girl, listen up."

"I'm not your baby."

She stared at Jerrod but in her peripheral view she knew that Tyrique was a few feet away, carefully observing.

"Jerrod, I don't know what's going on or why you would do the things you've been accused of, but if you don't want to end up like Jack, you need to lay off threatening my family."

His eyes darkened then lit back up. Tyrique walked over. "Is everything alright?"

"Yeah, baby. We are just talking. This won't take long."

When Tyrique walked away, Jerrod grabbed Dru's hands. "Look, don't be like this. It's a misunderstanding."

She tried to snatch back her hands but he held on. "Stop tripping. I'm not going to hurt you. I won't hurt you, Dru. I loved you."

"Love doesn't act like you do, Jerrod. If you hurt my family then you're hurting me. Those two things don't mix." She wondered what she ever saw in him in the first place. Their love had started so early that it all seemed silly and juvenile. He would shoplift her favorite snacks from the neighborhood store and present them to her as gifts. Back then it was cute. But his recent extortion attempts made her see something different in him.

"Jerrod, look. We can have a grown-up conversation right now, but you are going to have to release my hands."

"It's only because of how I feel. I love you."

She said nothing.

"Don't you miss what we had, Dru?"

"No, I don't. 'Cause you're nothing like you used to be. And you need to get over it and accept that we're not together anymore!"

"But—"

"There is no 'but'." She tried to look over her shoulder but couldn't. "My man is the one you just saw."

"But—"

"And don't forget, you broke up with me when we were in twelfth grade. You never gave me closure. Why should I give you any? Why should I treat you any better than you treated me?"

He angrily let go of her hands. She could see the frustration on his face. Right then he appeared to her as a complete stranger.

"I messed up, Dru. Because of what went on with my father, I didn't know how to handle it. I think that's why I acted how I did. Your family took my father away from me."

"Jerrod, it sounds like some misplaced anger. Because

my family did nothing. Your daddy forced himself on Alita. Place the responsibility on the adult who should have known better, and stop messing over my sister. Alita was the victim. Your dad was the predator."

She watched as his face crumbled with each damning word she spoke.

"I feel bad about your daddy being taken away like that. I wouldn't wish that on anyone, but right is right and wrong is wrong." She paused. "Have you ever talked to your father about what happened?"

He stared into space for so long that Dru was tempted to walk away from him. But she waited.

"No," he finally replied. "If I ever did try to ask him, he'd play like he didn't hear me. He didn't want to talk about it. He told me it was none of my business. He blamed Alita. He said he was being railroaded. He told me all kinds of shit and I guess none of it was true. Daddy was my hero back then. He taught me how to play baseball, football, how to build a rocket, how to do everything." His voice was filled with emotion. "See, Dru, when your father is your hero, he can do no wrong. I couldn't see his faults. I didn't want to see them. He was my *hero*; you understand that?"

"I understand looking up to people and making them your hero even if they don't deserve it. But your dad, he's no hero. He's hurt people."

Jerrod's eyes welled with tears. It seemed as though he was finally understanding the impact of his dad's choices. And Dru felt very bad for both men in that moment.

"Dru, I'm sorry about everything that happened. And I don't know how to make things right. I just don't—"

"Jerrod, I know the old you. You had dreams. Now look at you. You've aged twenty years, and for what?"

"Dru, please."

"If you're serious about making things right, don't follow in your dad's footsteps." Dru felt angry and upset that people didn't seem to think about their choices and how important it was to make good ones.

"You're still young and it's not too late for you to start all over again." She looked over at Tyrique. "When you broke up with me, I wanted to hurt you because you refused to give me closure. I wanted to hunt you down and find you and make you pay for all the heartache you put me through. Jerrod, I loved you like crazy back then."

"But now?" He lifted her chin. He moved his mouth closer to hers, but before their lips could touch, she smacked him across his face and made his cheek sting with pain. She stood up.

"Jerrod, you deserved much worse than what I just gave you. And if you keep fucking with my family, and you end up in prison for all your dirty deeds, you'll be just like your hero. It's over. Go on with your life. Please."

"You mean that, don't you?"

She nodded and told him goodbye. She could see that he was having a moment. And she wanted to give him space to reconcile all those confusing, awful feelings that he must have been dealing with.

She quietly walked over to Tyrique who accepted her into his waiting arms. They kissed and began to rapidly walk away.

"Whoa," she said. "That was one of the hardest conversations I've ever had with anybody."

"Why is that?"

"Because I found out I had some feelings that I didn't know I had. I had to speak them. Jerrod needed to hear them. I'm glad we talked. And I'm glad about something else." She had a devious smile on her face as she watched Tyrique. Her man was so good, patient, sensible, and so *there*.

"It took my talking to my high school sweetheart to realize that I dodged a bullet." She laughed incredulously. "Yeah, that's just what happened. If he hadn't dumped me, I wouldn't have you, Tyrique. And I can't imagine life without you."

His face brightened. "Thanks for saying that. It feels good to hear where you're coming from."

"Tyrique, I hope that you weren't worried."

"No, I wasn't."

"I think you were. I think if we are human, we always feel we are competing with the ex. My ex-boyfriend, your ex-girlfriend. Especially in this new age of social media and people getting reconnected with people they used to know. Hey, maybe some people are into that. Finding their old loves via Facebook. That's not me. I'm not looking for anybody, past or future, to take your place."

Tyrique picked Dru up and swirled her around until she got nice and dizzy.

"Put me down, Tyrique. Or else I may throw up on your shirt. And your Jordans."

He immediately sat her on her feet and chuckled good-naturedly. "I deserved that. But you just made me the happiest man on earth."

"I don't quite believe that."

"Why not, Dru."

"I know you want more from me. I know it."

"Look, about that getting married thing."

"I know you want me to be Mrs. Tyrique Evans. And damn it, I ask myself all the time, why mess up a good thing? I mean, we have no issues, Tyrique. We work well together, you're supportive of my studies and my career, my ambitions, and I feel the same for you. I-I feel like there's not much else we can do to improve this."

"I think there is. We should add to our family."

"I know you want a child. But tell that to my body. Tell

that to my dead uterus." She went from feeling very complete and satisfied to feeling inadequate.

"If I could have a baby tomorrow, I would. But that's not in my power."

"Tell me something. If you could never have a child, and I already know adoption is out of the question, what about getting a surrogate?"

"No, Tyrique. It's fine. I'm happy with you right now the way things are. If I could freeze this moment in time, I would be content."

"Seriously?"

"Yes."

"I don't believe you."

She laughed. "You know me well. Because if I had the ability to give myself everything that we lack, and it isn't much, I'd be the happiest woman on earth. But at the same time, I am still the happiest woman on earth as long as I have you, Tyrique Evans. And that's the truth."

Chapter 12

Sleeping with the One I Love

It was all Gamba's idea. He had received his orders to report to the base for the weekend. And he booked a flight for Elyse to join him once his three-day assignment ended. He rented a car and drove up to the base which was located near San Antonio. When his military duties were complete, he went to the airport to pick up Elyse and drive her around to see the city.

"We'll try and check out the Alamo and the Riverwalk if we have time."

"What do you mean, if we have time?" she asked. She sat beside him in their rental car. This was her first time going out of town with a man and she felt excited yet nervous.

"There's so much to do here. Like, I know you've never been to Six Flags or Sea World. But we can't do both so you'll have to pick one."

Elyse laughed. "Both sound good, Gamba. I want to do it all. I've never flown by myself before." She paused. "I actually hated it."

"We'll be flying together back to Houston. Don't even sweat it. You're here with me now and I got you."

"Then I don't care what we do," she happily exclaimed. "But I do want to see the animals, so let's do Sea World."

"It's a plan."

They headed to the water park where they spent hours riding roller coasters and swimming with sea lions. Later, after they left the park, Elyse was exhausted yet content. They checked into their hotel which was located near the airport.

They got situated and made a quick run for a seafood dinner and brought the raw oysters back to their room. By the time they enjoyed a late supper and took a shower, it was almost midnight. Elyse couldn't wait to find out what happened next. She had never spent the night with a man in a hotel.

"This is kind of like an early birthday present," Gamba told her as they settled in the king size bed. He kissed her and held her in his arms. She enjoyed snuggling against Gamba, feeling the heat of his skin and his tender touch.

"You're so good to me, Gamba. It seems like all you want to do is protect me and make sure I'm happy."

His voice sounded husky. "I want to do that, Elyse, plus a whole lot more."

Elyse took one look at Gamba and knew it was time. She sat up and removed the more conservative pajamas that she'd first dressed in after they showered. Then she got up, totally naked and walked to her suitcase. She removed a sheer babydoll nightie and slid it on her body. Her breasts stood at attention. The entire atmosphere made her feel grown and ready. She sat on the foot of the bed and looked at Gamba who was waiting on her. She crawled across the bed and stopped at his knees.

"You look so beautiful." The first time a man sees a woman in her nakedness is like observing a painting for the very first time. He takes it all in and examines every lovely square inch. The tone, the shape, the color, the texture, and he enjoys the way he feels as he gazes at its beauty.

Elyse simply smiled and laid her face on his thighs. Elyse expelled a deep breath and grabbed his penis. She kissed it several times in quick succession.

"Damn, that feels good," Gamba said through clenched teeth. She nodded then took him into her mouth. She felt his hands caress her back and shoulders as she continued to do everything she could to please him.

"I've wanted you for so long, Elyse." He gasped as she sucked on him and made him groan with pleasure. "I've never waited this long before."

She looked up. "I hope it's worth it."

"It is," he told her, then let her continue loving his body with her delicate fingers and wet tongue. She told him to turn over and she proceeded to kiss the side of his neck, shoulders, upper and lower back, and his ass. He squirmed and cursed as she stroked the sensitive parts of his body.

"You sure this is your first time?"

"Mmm hmm," she coyly told him. "I've masturbated a lot so I know what feels good to my body. And I'm guessing what feels good to yours."

She got him totally worked up and then lay on her back so he could return the favor. He positioned himself on his side and looked adoringly at her. They kissed each other for what seemed like hours but it couldn't have been more than twenty minutes.

He lay between her legs and hungrily sucked on her mound, licking and teasing it with his tongue until she cried out. Her entire body tingled and she couldn't believe how good he was making her feel.

"I can't believe how much I've been missing out," she gasped. "C'mon. Give it to me. Now!" He rolled on a condom and then immediately started shoving his hips and punching against her vagina until their bodies became unified. She felt his thickness fill her up completely, and it felt so unusual she almost lost her mind.

"Ouch, it hurts," she said.

"It's supposed to, but try to take it. I'm not going to hurt you."

"But you already are."

"Do you want me to stop?"

"No, keep going."

He moved his hips slowly and steadily and was pleased when Elyse began to move with him. She spread her legs wider so he could reach the deepest parts of her. After a while she didn't notice any pain, just tons of sweet pleasure. When her orgasm swirled through her body, she felt like a real woman for the first time in her life. This felt way better than when Nate used to violate her. She loved Gamba and Gamba loved her.

As she lay there experiencing what felt like pure joy, Elyse cried, and it felt natural when Gamba cried with her.

Her cheeks were wet with her tears and his too. She laughed and gasped and scratched his back with her long nails.

"I-I did it. I finally made love the way it was meant to be done."

"What did you think?"

"It was good, baby. Let's do it again."

He laughed and scooped Elyse in his arms, sticking his tongue deeper in her mouth so they could seal their love with amorous kisses.

They continued to talk as they lay there exhausted. Then Gamba had an idea. "Let's put on our swimsuits again and go up on the roof. They have an outdoor pool."

"Okay."

Elyse and Gamba changed outfits and headed to the top floor. The stars were twinkling in the black sky. They found some lounge chairs and pushed them together. Sitting side by side, they held hands and gazed up. Occasionally, an airplane would fly over the hotel. They watched and entertained quiet thoughts, happy to be there together.

And when Elyse climbed on top of him so that the lounge chair held both of them, he let her. He pulled her hair through his hands and stroked it. They kissed with such passion that Elyse knew that she had found the greatest happiness she had ever known.

"Why does good love feel so good?" she finally asked him.

"Because it's right and it's the best thing that two people can share."

"I'm glad about that. Because I do love you, Gamba. I do."

"I love you back, Elyse."

They were the only ones there on the roof. Even though there were security cameras stationed in the pool area, the two lovers did not care. Gamba covered their bodies with a large beach towel and he made love to her under the stars.

Gamba told her to get on birth control and she agreed that was the best thing to do. Life had transitioned from what felt like hopeless darkness to a marvelous light. Hatred gave birth to love and it was starting to bloom.

For Elyse Reeves, it was a happy birthday indeed.

Elyse's birthday wishes seemed to come true even more just two days later. When she arrived at work, courtesy of Alita's curbside service, Burgundy met them in the parking lot. It was eight o'clock.

"Guess I ought to let you two know something," Burgundy told them. "We have a meeting with Judge Mallow about some legal matters that have to do with Nate. Alita, I already mentioned that to you the other day."

"Yeah, I forgot. But actually it works out because it's my day off."

"Fine. We'll all drive down after we eat a little breakfast. I-I hope you'll be happy with the outcome." She gave Elyse a pensive look then walked back into Morning Glory.

An hour and a half later, the three women were seated in the judge's office.

"Finally. We're all together in one room instead of having all these separate little meetings," Judge Mallow said with a smile.

"I'm glad we're finally getting to do this," Burgundy replied.

"I am so very sorry again for your loss, Mrs. Taylor. But the good thing is that your husband really knew how to manage his affairs. We already had the reading of the will but that's not why we're here. Before he even died, we discussed a settlement of sorts that will benefit this young lady, Elyse Reeves."

"It's about time," Alita said.

"Sis, please hush."

"Bottom line is Elyse is entitled to compensation for her pain and suffering."

The judge went on to explain how the attorneys came to an agreement as well as the insurance company, however most of the funds would be allocated over a period of time.

"It's like you're getting paid by the estate in certain increments over a twenty-year period."

"How much we talking?" Alita asked.

"Since Elyse turned twenty-one a couple of days ago, she is now considered an adult and unfortunately, we do not have to disclose these amounts to you."

"Then why the hell am I here?" Alita wanted to know.

"Out of courtesy. And because your sister, this lady right here, asked you to be present. I guess she wanted you to hear it from the horse's mouth, so to speak."

Alita sat there bristling. The judge went on to talk a lot of lawyer gibberish. And when they got out of the meeting, Burgundy held up her hand in front of Alita's open mouth. "I really don't want to hear it right now, Lita. Just follow me, okay? Can you just do that?"

Alita nodded. She got in her car and they followed behind Burgundy. She rode up to the Nissan dealership where her ex-husband Leonard Washington worked.

Her son Leno was there and he greeted them with a bright smile. He led the group to a golf cart then drove them to a rear new car lot. They hopped off the cart and Leno pointed at a black SUV.

"These are hot off the line. That's why they're back here. And no other customer has even touched this one, looked inside, or taken it for a test drive." Leno smiled at his mother and sister.

"Go ahead." He handed them the keys. "Get in."

When Elyse and Alita saw a brand new Nissan Murano, they both began to shout.

"Noo, is this for me?" Elyse asked Burgundy.

"Yes, my dear. This beautiful new SUV is for you. Happy birthday, fam."

"*Whatttt?*" Alita's shriek was loud. She couldn't help herself. This was more than she could have imagined.

"But I thought the money was tied up," she said to Burgundy.

"It is. But there are still ways to get things done when you really need them to happen. She deserves it. She's earned it, God knows she has. And I'm happy to do this for her."

"Does it have insurance?" Alita asked.

"Fully covered, Mom," Leno told her. "And I want to

drive her around." He was good natured about it all even though his mother wasn't able to buy him his own car when he was seventeen. But this was different. Elyse got enriched from a lawsuit and he couldn't be upset with her.

After Elyse stopped laughing enough to calm herself down, she took a brief test drive around the parking lot. She got out of the car. Burgundy had another announcement.

"One more thing," she said. "I need you two to follow me again, and after that you're all on your own. Leno, you can come too if your dad doesn't mind."

Instead of arguing and questioning Burgundy, the two women eagerly followed her again, this time Elyse driving her own car. They ended up at a fairly new apartment complex in a suburb of Houston.

They parked in front of the building. Both Alita and Elyse shrugged at one another but waited while Burgundy spoke with a leasing agent. And after a while, they took an elevator up three flights and followed the woman inside an apartment.

"Lita," Burgundy said with a grin she could barely contain, "Welcome to your new spot."

"Wait, what?"

"This is your new home, Lita."

"You serious?"

"Yep."

"Stop lying? Don't play, B." Alita looked around and fought the idea that she was being tricked. But Burgundy seemed serious. Alita looked at the leasing agent. She stared at the granite counters, the Oriental rug that sat in front of the black leather couch, love seat, and recliner. There were even a few nice paintings on the wall.

"Well, I must say that this is a shocker. A nice surprise."

"I had a hell of a time planning this whole surprise," Burgundy said. "And it's all yours."

"You serious? You paying? I don't have to pay a dime? Are you pulling my leg?"

Burgundy hesitated, prayed she wasn't making the biggest mistake of her life, then handed her sister the keys.

"How's this for pulling your leg? This key is for you, and this one is yours, Elyse."

"B, this place is so fucking amazing." She glided her fingers across the black leather sofa and drank in the fragrance of brand new furnishings.

"Damn, I feel like I'm at my ex-husband's place . . ."

"You're not at Leonard's spot. It's your spot. Well, technically, it's rented, so it's not like you may live here forever, but for now, enjoy it, Sis."

"But what about my current little dump?"

"Pack up. And move here. I'll pay out the rest of your current lease so none of that is an issue."

Alita took a brief tour so her bedazzled eyes could take it all in. She returned to the living room and sprawled out on the couch. She kicked off her shoes and lay back on the pillows that were neatly arranged. When it finally sunk in that she had a decent, luxurious apartment home that was big enough to store all of her belongings and then some, she had to bite her own hand to keep from yelling.

"Leno, I see there are three bedrooms. That means there's an extra room for you to come chill out in when you want to hang out with me and your sister." Alita was pleased and kept fighting the strong urge to laugh with joy. She looked so silly trying to contain her joy that they all ended up giggling.

"You have to forgive my big sister," Burgundy explained to the leasing agent. "She is very emotional and could have been the next Angela Bassett or Loretta Devine."

"Are you calling me a drama queen?"

"That's exactly what I'm calling you, Lita."

Everyone smiled and continued the tour of Alita and Elyse's new home.

And when Alita grew humbly quiet and started another tour, this time taking her time as she walked about from room to room, Burgundy understood completely. She loved the feeling of giving and going above and beyond when it was least expected. And she loved to see the look of sheer delight on her family's faces. God knows they'd been through a lot.

But letting go of past hurts and focusing on others felt too damned good.

Elyse had telephoned Dru and given her the new address of her and Alita's condo. Dru came over right away. Elyse met her at the front entrance and led her inside to give her a brief tour of the kitchen. But then Elyse's fingers started tingling. It felt like her entire body was sizzling.

"Dru?" she said in a whisper

"What?"

"Can you keep a secret?"

"Sure. You know you can trust me, Sis. What's up?"

Elyse looked both ways. Alita and Burgundy were cackling at some joke. This was Elyse's moment to steal away her favorite sister and tell her what was in her heart before she exploded.

They retreated into Elyse's bedroom. She crawled into the bed and watched Dru sit on a nearby chair.

"Girl, you have an odd look in your eyes. Is everything all right?"

"Everything is perfect. We finally did it."

"Did what?"

"We made love." Her cheeks spread into a wide smile. Dru jumped up off of the chair and leaped into the bed next to Elyse. She yelped then quickly quieted down.

"No wonder you're glowing. You got some loving. I'm so happy for you. It's about time, Elyse."

She shared with Dru what happened when she met Gamba in San Antonio. "He is my man, but not because we made love. I can feel our connection in my soul. And that's why, when we finally did it, it felt right. It felt real good."

"I can tell. The changes in you are so inspirational. You haven't let your past hold you down."

"No. I haven't. I won't. And I have Gamba, and you, Dru. Both of you have really helped me out. Plus Alita, and now look what B has done for me. I never thought she would be so kind to me." Her smile turned sober. "I'm happy that I survived to see this. Because at one time, I really wanted to just die. Just shove a whole bottle of aspirin down my throat. Lie down and never wake up again."

"Oh my sweet baby, I am so glad you didn't go through with that, Elyse."

"Me too." Elyse took the time to hop up and grab a few sheets of tissue from a box sitting on the dresser drawer.

"Get me a couple too while you're at it, alright?"

Elyse obliged, crawled back beside her, and handed Dru a tissue so she could dab at her moistened eyes.

Elyse laughed. "I don't know why I got up because I'm not even crying, but in case I do, they are going to be happy tears."

Elyse smiled at the memories of her first time. "Gamba taught me how to please him and then he pleased me too."

"From now on, girl, I will be able to tell every time you two do it. Ha!"

"I hope it's a lot." Elyse suddenly dashed out of bed and ran to the dresser drawer. "Oh, I forgot to tell you. I threw out all my old panties and got a whole bunch of new ones. See!" Elyse proceeded to show Dru all the silky, satiny, sexy underwear and negligees that she'd bought with the money she'd gotten.

"The sales clerks in Victoria's Secret know me by my face," she laughed.

"What are your plans now, Elyse? I mean, I know you probably want to tear that man up every time you see him, but love and relationships require more than just a good sexual chemistry. Um, I don't know if I should be even asking you this, but can you cook mac and cheese?"

Elyse burst out laughing.

"No," she said. "And no, I don't want you trying to teach me either. I'll get Coco or Lita to do that."

"Okay, Sis. That's fair." Dru happily sighed. It was about time that good news came in waves for the Reeves family.

"I can tell you are hopeful about your future, but have a plan, Elyse."

"What do you mean?"

"What type of vision do you have for your life? Where do you want to end up in five years, ten years?"

"God, I don't know. I just want to be around Gamba. Me and him. Together."

"That's nice. But there's more to life than being around your man."

"Okay, then. What do you want, Dru? What are you doing, other than getting a fancy degree?" Elyse sounded somewhat insecure and as if she were attacking Dru.

But Dru understood. She knew how it felt to be so young that you rarely thought beyond the next few days, let alone the next few years.

"Oh, trust and believe, there are many things, good things, precious things that I want. I don't want to just go through the motions of life, to act like the status quo, and look like I'm normal only on paper."

"Huh?"

Dru laughed. "In other words, I have dreams beyond just kicking it with Tyrique."

"Why hasn't he married you? You're a good woman. You're pretty, smart, kind, generous, thoughtful. Any other man would be happy to make you his wife."

"I don't measure my worth and value on those sorts of things. And as much as you love your man, you shouldn't do that either. You have so much going for you and I love the new changes in you."

"I get what you're saying, Dru." Her eyes brightened and her voice exuded excitement and determination. "I want to move up in the world and do well in my career, love my man, and spend time with my family. And to answer your question, in five years, I want to be somebody."

"You already are somebody, Elyse."

Chapter 13

Red Table Talk

After a terrible Friday night in which Coco had cried herself to sleep, she pulled herself together to go through her daily routine. By mid-afternoon, the prison guard informed her that someone was there to see her. Six weeks had passed since she'd been locked up. It was almost Christmas and knowing she had a visitor instantly lifted her mood.

Coco rested her swollen eyes on Alita's pretty face as soon as she entered the designated area. Coco inched her way toward the thick plate of glass that separated her and Alita. She sat down on the stiff, black stool and sighed when she felt her entire butt spread over the sides of the chair until it seemed to disappear.

"What's up with you, girl?" Alita finally spoke up after noticing the dazed, angry look on her sister's face. "I've been worried sick about you since the last time I checked on you. How you holding up?"

"I'll let you decide."

"Okay. How they treating you in here?"

"How you think?"

"They treating you any better than I treat you?"

"Not a chance."

"Uh oh, you in big trouble then, Sis." Alita heartily

laughed, thinking that a joke would lighten the mood. Then she abruptly stopped.

"Seriously, what's going on, Sis?"

"All I can tell you is that the prosecutor wants this case to move forward, Lita. Like real fast. Like why the hell is he in that big a hurry?"

"Mmm, I wouldn't know."

"But then again, where the hell am I going anyway? Not like I can go see Beyoncé and Jay-Z anytime soon."

It pained Alita to see Coco, her fun-loving, life-of-the-party sister, not cackling like she used to whenever they'd kick it.

"What you doing with your time in here?"

"Same thing as always. Sleeping, playing spades, going to the law library, or staying bored out of my mind. Every other day my attorney comes in. He tries to keep my spirits up and talks to me about a bunch of shit I halfway understand. Then the rest of the time I think about how I got here. And how mad I am—"

"He ain't worth it—"

"Not mad at Nate. I get mad at me. The choices I've made."

"He made some fucked up choices too."

"But who's in jail, though, Lita?"

"And who's dead, Coco? And which is worse?"

Alita let her sister vent.

"I'm just saying. I should have stopped loving men that don't deserve my love. I should have focused more on loving me and doing what's best for me and my babies."

"You loved Nate?"

"No chance in hell. But I'm thinking about my other lovers: Calhoun, Q, Ricky, and so on. The way my life has been going, I need an upgrade on everything."

Coco felt that as much as the truth hurt it was the only way that she could begin to make wiser choices.

Alita observed her surroundings. She openly gaped at the fellow visitors: old men crouched over from osteoporosis. Women hobbling on crutches. Young men wearing doo-rags and sagging pants, and young chicks carrying knee-high kids on their hip.

"Look at this shit. I'm shocked that a lot of 'em are white. And I'll bet most of these people they're coming to see were locked up for stupid shit. Public intoxication or selling weed."

"Save it, Lita. Your going on and on won't change anything. It never helped me." Coco laughed as she remembered her pointless rants at Sergeant Cohen and his partner. "It seems like we're powerless sometimes. Like we can't stop bad things from happening. We just got to roll with the punches."

"No, Coco. Don't think like that. There's a silver lining to every cloud. You might not see it, but believe me, it's there."

"I hope so. Do me a favor. Put money on my books and try to cast a vote in all the next primaries. That's something I failed to do because I didn't think it was important. But now that I'm here, and I could end up with a crooked judge . . ."

"I hear you, Coco. I don't think you'll be here that long, but if you are, I promise to do what you've asked and more."

"We need to stop tweeting, bitching, and complaining; we got to show up at those polls."

"You're right again. Sitting around whining about injustice never changes injustice."

Coco gave her sister a nervous look.

"Girl, if I'm found guilty, I will be classified as a felon. Then I can't vote until I have served my entire sentence."

"That's not going to happen, Coco. You had poor judgment but you are not a criminal. The jury will realize that.

You'll be out soon and then you can get back to your babies."

"How are my kids by the way?"

"Doing as good as can be expected." Alita hesitated and stared at her hands.

"What Lita, what?"

"You know Calhoun has the kids."

"What? You mean, like permanently?"

"Yes. At least for now he does. I mean, those're his kids."

"I know but, shit." Coco's eyes quickly filled with water. She used the sleeve of her pink and white shirt to pat her tears dry.

"I miss my babies. Cypress is so young. She's probably walking by now. Saying a few words too. I hate I'm missing out."

"I know. But you have no worries. They're doing a great job raising her."

"They?"

"Calhoun . . . and his wife."

"Samira's stuck up ass is taking care of my baby?"

"You ought to be glad. At least the state didn't come take Cypress. They tried to take her, believe me. But Calhoun stepped up to the plate, Sis. He had his act totally together and made sure to prove that he's her father. And now they're like one big happy family."

Alita went on and on as she got Coco caught up.

"From what I understand, on Friday nights, Calhoun has this 'family night' event for all the kids. Y'all's four, plus Natalia and Sid. I'm shocked that B even lets her girls hang out over there but she does. And I've seen B drop the kids off and a few times she's even hung around. I've been there too. Me and Dru. Elyse and Gamba."

At that point Coco didn't want to imagine her family able to exist without her.

"And the family nights are based on themes. It was all Samira's idea. She got on Calhoun to get more involved. And they came up with a Slime Night. And so," Alita said with a hearty chuckle. "The kids got together in Calhoun's dining room. Natalia and Sidnee ran into the room juggling cans of shaving cream. Cadee was carrying a tub of Tide, glue, and some green food coloring. It was a big fat mess but so much fun. And after that, Natalia turned up the Bluetooth stereo and tried to get me to do the floss dance and the orange justice challenge. I was shocked Natalia got so involved, dancing and playing around with all her cousins."

"And are you saying that y'all had the nerve to have a good old time, while I was rotting away in this fucking jail?"

"Oh shit. I'm sorry, Sis. I-I shouldn't have told you."

"No. I'm glad you did. I like to know everything that's going on behind my back. I mean, my former man is now married and moved on, but you would think he'd try to get me out of here."

"Coco, you seem to be forgetting you aren't exactly Calhoun's priority these days. But give him credit for taking care of his responsibilities as a father."

"But Samira?"

"Samira is an excellent bonus mother. You ought to be glad. I didn't know old girl had it in her, being that she's all elegant and graceful and sophisticated."

Coco couldn't stand to hear anymore. The words of truth were like daggers in her already fragile heart. Yet hearing what was going on in the outside world gave her something different to focus on.

"Did my kids like playing in the slime?"

"They loved it. They threw most of it on Calhoun."

"On Samira, too?"

"Yes, Coco. Damn!"

"Good. That's all I wanted to know."

"Coco, you ought to be ashamed of yourself. The village has shown up in full force to keep the family together during a helluva crisis. That's what a real family does. And Coco, believe it or not, you have a real family."

"And I miss my family. Especially Cypress. Will a baby that young still remember her mama?"

"Don't even worry about that. When we were over there, Calhoun let me and Dru show Cypress all kinds of videos that we filmed before you got locked up. We show her the silly faces you were making when you were holding Cypress in your arms on the Fourth of July, when you dressed her up in an American flag outfit. Remember that?"

"Yeah, I remember. I was tired as hell that day. 'Cause I did all that cooking. And y'all dragged me outside to see those fireworks. And I complained but ended up having the time of my life. Boy, I miss little things like that."

"And that's why we put these videos in front of the baby. We tell Cypress all the time 'That's Coco, that's your mama.'"

"I sure wish I could see her face when she sees that video."

"I'll tell you what she does. Her little face lights up. She laughs and points. She gets real turned up anytime she sees your videos and photos. In fact, we're trying to get her to talk and say all kinds of cute little words. Stuff that you would say."

"You do?" Coco asked, feeling impressed.

"Yes, ma'am."

"Oh, shit don't do that."

"Too late. Cypress has a potty mouth."

They both cracked up and Coco knew Alita was just teasing her.

Coco allowed herself to relax. She felt happy and confident that her kids were in a stable environment. Yet the question of 'what if' kept her frozen with fear.

"I appreciate the things you're doing for me, Lita, but I still feel scared."

"It's easy for me to tell you not to worry 'cause I'm not in your shoes. But you gotta know that we have your back, Coco."

"When y'all going to bring the kids here to see me?"

"Uh, I dunno about that. Chance, Cadee and Chloe, they don't need to see you like this."

"Oh Lita. You're right. I don't want them to see me in here."

Alita pressed her palm against the glass. Coco reached over and did the same. It looked as though they were touching one another.

"I love you girl," Alita told her.

"Love you back."

"This too shall pass," Alita assured her. "So, Coco. Tell your big sister what really happened that day. Because I know your lawyers are coaching you about what you can and can't say when you go to trial. We won't get the full story in that courtroom. But you can tell me what went down. Go ahead."

"Are you serious?"

Alita sat back and waited like she was a Catholic priest.

"Damn, Lita. I only have so much time—"

"Then stop wasting it and get to talking."

Coco took a deep breath and soon began to tell her what had been inside of her for a long time.

"I drove Elyse to Nate and Burgundy's to get her stuff. I waited downstairs. But it was taking her a long time so I went up to her room. Long story short, I heard some stuff going down behind that locked door. You know how Nate liked to lock Elyse's door. And it pissed me off. I managed to break the lock and I saw them. And Lita, he had big beads of sweat sitting on his forehead. And I'd been through so much hell up to that point that all my frustrations came pouring out. We argued. Nate denied being the father of our baby. That made me want to whip his ass. I know it sounds stupid after the fact but that's how I felt back then."

Coco looked up at Alita to see if she believed what she was telling her.

"Damn, sis." Alita could only shake her head. "Are you sure there isn't more to the story?"

"Yeah. I told him something like how I wanted to just splatter his brains on the walls for everything he'd done, but how he wasn't worth it."

"How did Nate react to that?"

"Lita, he told me he felt like a piece of shit for what he'd done."

"He did?"

"Yeah, he startled babbling and talking about how when he was a teenager his brother touched his dick. And how he hated it. And how he couldn't stand to be around his brother after that. And how he wasn't even sorry when his brother unexpectedly died. And how he thought that once his brother couldn't molest him anymore, then he'd be free. But he told me how messed up it felt when he ended up doing the same type of shit that was done to him."

"Coco, did Elyse hear him make this confession? This is like key info."

"No, by then Elyse had gone downstairs to wait for me in the car. She and Natalia had left. It was just me and Nate all alone in that big old house."

"What else? Go on."

Coco hesitated. "He made me promise not to tell anyone."

"So fucking what? Why would you be loyal to a rapist and a dead one at that? This is important."

"I know it but I swore to him not to say a word."

"Sis, your life is on the line and you care more about him than yourself?"

"But—"

"But nothing, Coco. You're really sounding stupid right now."

"Lita, I'd never seen Nate look so desperate. He looked weak and that was something I never saw in him before. And I felt sorry for him yet hated him at the same time."

"You sound crazy. A man like that doesn't deserve sympathy. And people like you make it worse for real victims."

"I am a real victim."

"Then stop protecting him by keeping his secrets. Don't you know how stupid you sound?"

"I know. I know. Oh God, I hate that this shit ever happened. It's messed up all of us, Lita. You just don't understand."

Coco sounded so confused, Alita decided not to judge. "Oh well. It is what it is. If you get a murder rap for his ass I hope it's all worth it."

Coco said nothing.

"Well, finish your story. Then what happened?"

"And then, he told me that a lot of times he felt like he had no control of himself and his impulses, and he struggled with so many things in his head."

"So he was crazy, crazy?" Alita asked.

"I guess. I asked him why he never got any help. And he told me he had his reputation to think about. People looked up to him and he felt like a shithead for making the family look bad."

"Sounds like in the end, our brother-in-law was in a bad space. We already knew that. And it's kind of a shame. If he could've gotten the help he needed who knows what would have happened?"

"His confessions blew me away, Lita. I just stared at

that man like I never knew him. And guess what? I was glad that he wasn't claiming Chance as his son. I didn't want my child to have his DNA. I didn't want any part of Nate. At that point, I felt like he was a bum ass bitch. Because instead of getting the help he deserved, he kept it all inside. And he told me he was glad that Elyse was moving out. Because maybe with her not being near him, he could get her out of his mind. And he told me that he planned on assigning her to work at a different Morning Glory so that he wouldn't have to see her at their main restaurant. But you know, before any of that could happen, he died."

"Nate had a chance to do the right thing long before then, but it sounds like God took him out of here before he could do any more damage."

"I guess." She paused. "So, now you know."

"Thanks for telling me, sis. I know it was hard for you to tell me these things."

"It was." Coco had a distant look in her eyes. "I swear to God I never wanted to think about it or talk about it to anybody. Ever. I wanted to take all these secrets to my grave."

"One more question."

"What, Lita, what?"

"Did you have anything to do with him dying?"

"What? Hell no."

"Hell no, as in 'not really'?"

Coco looked at Alita. "Nate died because he wanted to die. That's the only way I can put it."

"But how do you know this for sure?"

"I just do. He started talking about Natalia and Sidnee. And that's why I feel so bad. I know he loved them and he would do anything for them, but he felt like his behavior had left a black mark on their lives. He felt like if he got arrested he would mess up their happy, innocent lives. He worried about what would happen to them."

"Why wouldn't you just give up this info from the jump, Coco? If you did you might not even be here. I don't know why you didn't tell me this before now."

Coco's eyes dropped. She had no answer. She could only wrestle with the tormenting thoughts that continued to plague her mind.

Is it possible for someone to be guilty yet not guilty at the same time? When you have information that you should tell, but if nobody knows that you know, are you still liable? Coco found herself in that state of awkwardness, a purgatory type of situation, where she was damned if she did and damned if she didn't.

"Am I supposed to honor someone even though they had some evil and messed up ways hidden in their personality?" Coco knew Alita didn't have the answers but she still wanted to ask.

"Girl, the evilest person in the world can be called an angel after he's taken his last breath."

"Ain't that the truth. Because we feel sorry they died. We forget the evil they did. And we try to focus on the good."

"We want to pay our respects and it's too fucking rude to stand up at someone's funeral and expose their wicked side." Alita paused. "And I hope when I die y'all say a lot of good stuff about me."

"Really?" Coco smiled. "Good like what? Help a sister out."

"Coco, you know you're wrong for that." Alita had to release a chuckle. "I guess I come across as tough and no nonsense, but you know there is a lot of love behind my words and actions."

"It's all good, Sis. Because if I needed someone on my

team, guess who I'd pick? It wouldn't be Dru even though she's an angel. And of course, Burgundy wouldn't want to be on my team."

"So that leaves me?"

"I'd purposely pick you, Alita Reeves Washington. Because people know where they stand with you. You're blunt as hell, but where's the lies?"

"Oh, from where I'm sitting, Coco, I think you have all of them."

They both burst into laughter. Being around Alita, her spirit animal, ignited Coco's soul. She knew that there'd be words of caution, but also words of comfort. And in this perilous time of her life, that's exactly what she needed.

Once the New Year began, Coco's case grew in publicity. Every local newspaper carried the story about the man who may have been intentionally poisoned by gas by his sister-in-law. The section below the news story was filled with all sorts of random comments about the case from readers who had much to say:

DirtyBastard: Too bad she didn't inhale that gas and die a slow death right along with him. Poor man.

Trump2020: What else do you expect from these ppl? Thugs. The whole lot of 'em.

The action outside the jail where Coco was housed wasn't much different. Little old women wearing flowered hats and men wearing Western shirts and cowboy boots assembled out front. People held up hastily constructed posters scribbled with words "Murderess," "Convict Her," "Death Row for Coco."

The protestors started as soon as the sun rose, and

wouldn't leave until the evening news caught them on camera.

Montgomery County police were aware.

"These people are causing a ruckus on purpose. They're trying to incite a riot. The blacks are gathering to defend Coco because they see too many white faces that want her to be found guilty."

One afternoon in mid-January, a security guard went to tell Coco what was happening since she purposely avoided all live news shows.

"You've become quite the celebrity."

"I don't know why," Coco said. "They act like I'm Lizzie Borden."

"You may as well be," he told her.

"This is nuts. But what's going on?"

"Coco, the blacks are gathering around outside the police station and—"

"Excuse me, sir, but I'm not a 'black' and they are not 'the blacks.' I'm a black *person*. Not a color; I'm a human being."

"No harm intended ma'am. I just wanted you to be aware of what was happening. Maybe it is scaring you to know that what you allegedly did has people all riled up."

"Right. You'd have thought I killed someone with value."

"Is that a confession?"

"No, siree, Bob. No confession here."

Coco just continued her daily routine and dreamed of better days.

The next time Alita came to see her, Coco wondered why the other sisters didn't visit her as often as Alita.

"Dru has been sick off and on. And you know Elyse has come see you a few times. And B, well, that's a whole other story."

Coco nodded.

"But would you even want B to come see you?" Alita asked.

"I just want her to bond me out. She doesn't have to come see me."

"You're wrong for that, Coco."

And before she ended their visit, Alita told Coco that she needed to face all the things that she'd been avoiding. "There comes a time when every woman has to 'man up' and face her demons."

Coco agreed. They said their goodbyes.

A couple days later, Alita invited Burgundy over to her new spot. She had bought some additional items to make the place reflect her decorating tastes. She told Burgundy that she wanted her to check out how well her apartment was coming along.

"Sweetie," Alita told her while they were on the phone. "I just want you to stop over for a minute. I won't take up a lot of your time. Come through."

Burgundy felt delighted at getting a personal invite. She arrived shortly thereafter. She walked through the entire apartment, all twenty-five hundred square feet of it. She saw Elyse's bedroom and was impressed at the extra items both she and Alita added to make their place feel like a home. Throw rugs, decorative wall art, and accent pillows with matching fabric storage bins courtesy of Wayfair, which had become their favorite online store.

When Burgundy ventured into Alita's bedroom, she came to an abrupt stop.

"Alita," she said as she walked around closely observing her surroundings.

"Look, B. I know we need to talk about this."

"I thought that you and Shade were going to have your own separate places. But I see his shoes, some of his clothes, his weights are stored in the closet. I even smell his scent. Are y'all shacking? Did I pay for your man to live here?"

"B, that's the thing. You set this up for me and Elyse, but you already knew I had a man and she does too. But it's not like you're paying to take care of Shade."

"But I paid the rent on this place for a whole year."

"And I never asked you to do that either."

"Well, if that isn't the most ungrateful—"

"See, that's what I'm talking about. You are very generous but there are always strings attached. It's like you want to give us money and gifts but we are restricted. Like you're the government or the welfare lady coming over to see if we have extra TVs and toasters and boyfriends that we're hiding. I don't want to hide my life. I don't roll like that."

"I don't like spending money on a man that's not mine. Don't get me wrong. Shade is cool. He's my good friend, but I feel like you two went behind my back and did this anyway." Burgundy stormed across the room, made an exit, and ventured into Elyse's.

"Are you hiding Gamba's shit somewhere in here too?" She pulled opened drawers and slammed them when she couldn't find anything that seemed to belong to Gamba.

"I know you think I'm nuts, but I hate feeling used."

Alita joined her. "B, no one is trying to use you. You need to get real."

"Why should I, and what about, Lita?"

"Hello? Me and Shade are lovers. We love each other. We're together, B. And we want to be around each other every chance we get. Just like you want to be around your boy, Edmund. You definitely haven't apologized about having that man in your life. And if you have needs why can't you see that I have them too."

"Shade should pay for your needs on his dime, not mine."

"Okay, B. How about this? Do you want Shade to cut you a check for half the rent that was paid upfront? Would that make you feel better?"

"What would make me feel better is to be around a family that isn't so shady. To be forthright with me instead of throwing heavy shit on me at the last minute. You all do that way too often. With Sister Day we always talk about speaking our truth, but your truth always comes a day late and a dollar short. Over and over again, I'm the fucking last to know."

"Because you can't handle the truth."

"I can handle it if only you'd give it to me straight, no chaser, much sooner than you do. The longer you hold out on the truth, the worse things get. And the harder it will be to really get me to fully trust anything that comes out of y'all mouths."

"Okay, hold that thought." Alita glanced at her watch. She counted to one hundred. Just like she wanted, her phone rang. She whispered a few words into the receiver. Then she placed the caller on speaker.

"Coco," Alita told her. "B is here with me right now. At my spot. We're talking about getting stuff out in the open and not holding things in anymore. This is your final chance to let her know what happened between you and Nate. You understand me? This is your *chance,* Coco."

"Lita," Coco's shrill voice rang out over the speaker phone. It sounded peculiar. "I don't know about this. I'm starting to have second thoughts."

"I know you're scared but it needs to be done. Tell B everything. No holding back."

Burgundy's eyes were filled with panic. Getting blindsided always felt like a set-up.

"B, this is the hardest thing I've ever had to say to you." Coco closed her eyes and imagined the expression on Burgundy's face. "It's time that I tell you about some real stupid shit that happened back in the day. I've been scared to tell you, but um. Me and Nate," she paused. "Yes, we made a big mistake. We hooked up and made love." Burgundy groaned.

"But one time only, B. I swear to God."

"Famous last words."

"It's true though, B, you gotta believe me," Coco pleaded.

"Whether it was one time or twenty times, it doesn't really matter does it, Coco?"

"You're right. Once was enough to make it feel wrong. But I was young, out of control; I wasn't thinking, and I regret everything."

"Am I supposed to believe that my husband was fucking around with two of my family members?" Burgundy's voice sounded cold. "That two family members were messing around with my man?"

"Wait, B," Alita said. "What happened to Elyse was different, and you know it. You'd better not blame her anymore. You promised you wouldn't."

Burgundy thought about it. She conceded. "You're right, Lita. I can't blame Elyse for what happened. She didn't want him. But it sounds like he wanted her, and you too, Coco. How could you? Even though you were young, how?"

"I dunno. It just happened. I wasn't thinking. And if I could take it all back I would."

Burgundy wanted to forgive Coco. But she couldn't forget her husband's share of the blame. The many ways he'd disappointed her, how he had misled her. And she didn't want to mourn him. She felt angry. And she realized how certain secrets might always be exposed when people died.

"Where did this happen?" she asked Coco.

"In your house."

"What? My house? In my bed?"

"B, I'm sorry."

"You don't have the decency enough to go to a hotel? At least that's a little more respectful. You stupid ass bitch. You deserve to be locked up. And worse."

"Calm down, B," Alita told her. "She has a lot more to tell you."

"I've heard more than enough. I don't need to hear any more secrets."

"Trust me, you need to hear it."

Burgundy quieted down. All she could do was listen.

Coco continued. "Burgundy, like I said before, my mind wasn't right that day. And . . . we did it without protection."

"Are you saying you—"

"I got pregnant."

Burgundy covered her ears. Alita forcibly removed the woman's hands. And she made her listen.

Burgundy sighed with resignation. "And now you want to tell me that Chance is Nate's son. That he hid another secret from me. And you did too. Same old story. Same old shit."

"Huh?" Coco said.

"I already knew, Coco. Calhoun had the decency to tell me this little horrible secret because he felt as used, dumb, and as stupid as I did. He actually told me the whole story at one of his slime parties."

"Oh wow," Coco said.

"So you already knew?" Alita asked.

"Of course, I did. I wish I didn't, but I knew."

"And is that why—" Alita started to say. "You never came to see her in Montgomery County Jail."

"Exactly. I just couldn't. I felt frozen with anger. Frozen with indecision. Back then, I was still mourning someone that I didn't understand, a person whose actions made me sick to my stomach. I hated him. Didn't trust him. And that means that I couldn't trust Coco either. Because, unlike Elyse, she was grown when she did it. She already had kids. She had the power to say 'no,' but she didn't. So why would I want to bond out this Benedict Arnold who had the nerve to fuck my husband, suck his dick, bear his child, and hide Chance's paternity from the entire family for years. Years! That's multiple deception. And you sisters are so used to me being stupid, and gullible, and generous . . ." Burgundy looked around at the pricey house that she'd paid for.

"And you expect me to do everything as if I am an emotionless robot that has no feelings whatsoever. You think you can crack a joke and tell me you're sorry a hundred times and then it's supposed to be all kisses and hugs and checks written out to your name only five minutes later."

Burgundy shot to her feet like a dog had bitten her.

"Damn, B. You told not one lie. Not one. Because we do do that."

"And you're one of the main offenders, Lita. You can be very manipulative." Burgundy laughed at the absurdity of it all, dealing with family issues that would have driven any other woman completely out of her mind.

"Again, the generous sister has been made a fool of. Over and over and over again." She looked at Alita. "Is this what family is about?"

"I messed up, B," she heard Coco say over speaker phone. "And the fact that you seemed to rise up and accept the family secrets, like when Lita told you that Elyse is her daughter, well, it made me hope that you could forgive me too. That you could look past all this terrible, awful shit and not hold it against me forever." Coco sniffed and her voice sounded hoarse. "Believe it or not, I love you, Sis. I don't blame you if you hate me, but I hope you don't. I-I don't know how you'll feel about Chance either. But please, even if you hate me forever, please don't blame him or treat him bad. Chance didn't make this mistake. He didn't ask to be born."

"And I didn't ask to be betrayed by my own sister."

Coco gasped. She wanted to weep. And Coco decided that the truth had done what it came to do. It seemed like it was designed to destroy everything that she had ever tried to love.

She'd loved Calhoun and she lost him. She had loved her sister, but would she lose her too?

"Again. I apologize."

"I do not want to ever hear you say those two words, ever again, Coco. Because coming from you, they don't mean a thing, except to make a fool out of me one more time."

Burgundy walked around in a daze, her handbag clutched tightly to her side. She wanted to do something, but couldn't think of a single thing. Sometimes that's what life could do to a person. Leave them as speechless and lifeless as a monument that's eternally stuck in the same position.

"Lita's been begging me to get this out in the open. To have that Red Table Talk that people claim is so important to do."

"Ha!" Alita said. "I doubt that Jada and her family will go through anything as difficult as this situation we got on our hands."

"Jada might not," Burgundy said. "Unless she has a story as devastating as mine. And how I came this close to doing something so out of character that I knew I was on the brink of losing my mind."

"What are you talking about, B?" Alita asked.

"How's this for some red table talk," Burgundy asked.

Coco's stomach did somersaults. "What is this about?"

"When Calhoun pulled me aside to let me know what had happened about Coco and Chance, I was so distraught. I could tell that he regretted telling me. Calhoun didn't know how hurt I'd feel. And he told me he was sorry. He pulled his chest against mine while I cried in his arms. And I swear I was so damned tired that I was on the verge of saying forget it. Forget being a nice, forgiving, honorable woman, who has integrity and is trying to do something powerful with her life. Forget helping other people. What does it get you in the end?"

"B, obviously you changed your mind or else you wouldn't have signed me and Elyse up to get this nice pad."

Burgundy's voice was low and soft. "If I reneged on my promises what would that make me? How would it look? I'd be a vengeful person. I don't want to be that. Not at all."

Hearing her sister's voice made Coco's heart pitter patter. She sounded sincere.

Coco asked, "Does that mean you forgive me?"

There was a brief silence. "It means that I must think long and hard about some things. Because that night that Calhoun told me some things, he also told me that . . ." She stared at the phone and laughed. "He told me that I was the one that he'd wanted to be with."

"B, don't do this," Alita warned her.

"No, if we want to throw some shit on the table, then let's do it. A while ago, when Nate and I were having trouble, yeah, I almost ended up in Calhoun's bed."

Coco screeched. "Stop lying, B."

"Now hush up, Coco. You had your true confessions moment. Let me have mine."

Alita stared in horror at her sister.

"You and him had gotten back together, Coco. And it was around Christmastime, a couple years ago. And he brought over some gifts for Nat and Sid. He came to our house. Nate wasn't home. He had taken the girls ice skating. I was home alone working. Tired. Lonely. And horny. Horny because back then my husband's dick was too soft and mushy for me to appreciate. He was old. Calhoun was young, virile, and I knew he'd love how I looked in my short little nightgown I was wearing."

"B, you can stop now. I don't think Coco needs to be hearing this."

"Be quiet, Alita. For God's sake, stop interrupting!"

Alita quieted down and snatched a few tissues from a box of Kleenex that was sitting on the table.

"I let Calhoun in the house," Burgundy continued. "He was looking good and smelling even better. Behaving like an active, loving father, and a decent guy. He looked in a way that I'd never noticed before. He smiled in that wonderful way of his. We chilled over a little bit of apple cider and donuts that I had set out for company. And he told me even then, Coco, that he was glad to be back with you but he had mixed feelings. He said he was angry that you got pregnant. And he didn't want to touch you."

"How can he say that? Me being pregnant didn't stop Calhoun from trying to hit it."

"I don't doubt you at all. I could tell that his sex drive was still strong. And Calhoun confided in me, Coco. And I listened. And he told me he liked older women. I laughed. And without saying one word, he reached over and grabbed my hand. He tickled the center of my hand and I knew that it meant he wanted to fuck me."

Alita gasped. "Please, B. Don't do this."

"I'm warning you, I can do a whole lot more confessions that you don't want to hear or believe."

Alita thought of her man Shade and she immediately closed her mouth.

Burgundy recalled more of her memories. "I knew without no doubt that if he thought he could get away with it, Calhoun Humphries would have made love to me, in my house, in my bed, and he would have done a real good job. And I probably would have liked it."

"She said 'would have' Coco. Did you hear that? She didn't fuck your man."

Burgundy said nothing. Her eyes narrowed to tiny slits as she leered at Alita. Burgundy wondered how someone could claim to love her and then torture her with the worst news of her life in the same breath.

"Are you done, B?" Coco asked. She was trembling, and feeling angry and confused. Now she was glad that she hadn't married Calhoun. It would have been a marriage built upon false pretenses.

"I'm done for now," Burgundy said. "Good luck with your case, Coco. Bye-bye."

Alita hung up the phone. "Now what?" she asked. She noticed then that her sister's eyes were red. She handed the tissues to Burgundy and let her quickly dab at her eyes.

"Now we just give it time," she sniffed. "Coco needs time. Lots of time, Lita. And I do too."

"That's fair." Alita felt nervous about the future and how everything would pan out.

Burgundy headed toward the door.

"You leaving now, B?"

"I am."

"That's fair, too." Burgundy placed her hand on the doorknob. "Um, thanks," Alita cried out. "Thanks for everything."

"More redundant words that I've heard a thousand times."

"Oh, B. Don't get mad. I mean it. You're the bomb. You're shocking the hell out of me—"

"That's because you've gotten so familiar with me that you think you know every square inch of me. But you only know what you think you see. How about that?"

"I lie every once in a while, but you ain't never lied, sis."

That comment produced a cheerful laugh out of Burgundy.

"Telling the truth is what we say we want, but it's not always what we expect, is it, Lita?"

"You can say that again. And, um, I sure hope you don't have any truth you're holding onto, that you need to tell me. It can wait, B. Seriously. I'm just saying."

Burgundy's giggles subsided. "That's another conversation for another day." And she waved goodbye, and left.

Chapter 14

Come Monday Morning

The sisters got through their latest crisis and in late March, Coco was informed that her case was about to go before the grand jury. Her public defender, Cedric Lancelot, came to see her.

"Coco, you won't be at the hearing and I won't be either. It's not allowed. But I will let you know the results of the grand jury as soon as it's decided.

"Do you think I have a chance to go free?"

Since they'd been meeting, she'd given him all the info she had forgotten to share with the Montgomery County officers.

"All I can tell you is that these jurors will examine all the evidence and determine if there was probable cause."

"In other words, my fate is left in the hands of a bunch of strangers. God help me."

"Try to stay positive. I believe in you."

"Thank you, sir. You're the one person that I've met in a while who believes in me."

The next day, twelve jurors assembled in a small court room. In addition, there was the bailiff, stenographer, witnesses, and Ethan Ketchum, the prosecutor.

Ketchum began his questioning of the witnesses.

"State your name."

"Latonya Warfield."

"What is your occupation?"

"I am a postal worker for the United States Post office."

"How long have you been employed in that position, Ms. Warfield?"

"My twentieth anniversary is in twenty-one days."

"Congrats."

She was then asked the physical address of her work location.

"What are your duties, Ms. Warfield?"

"I help to sort first class mail and packages. And my job is to place them in the PO boxes."

"And what does that entail?"

"Just making sure every morning to place mail that is addressed to the specific box number by nine forty-five every morning."

"To your knowledge, does every PO box get mail every day?"

"Oh no, sir. Some boxes receive tons of mail and others receive very little or none at all."

"And what happens if an assigned post office box has too much mail? In other words, there's no more room for you to place incoming mail in the intended box?"

"We will either put a yellow card in their box indicating that they have mail that needs to be picked up from the front counter, or we put a little key in their box so they may retrieve it from one of the bigger boxes."

"Very good. Now tell me what happened on the day of Wednesday, August twenty-eighth."

Latonya took a deep breath. "A lot of mail had come in for box number 8285."

"Whose mailbox is that?"

"It's assigned to a Mr. and Mrs. Nathaniel and Burgundy Taylor."

"You're accustomed to getting lots of mail for them, right?"

"Yes, sir. Various letters and packages always get delivered to them."

"And what happened on that day?"

"Since the box was already overflowing, I placed an orange key in their box."

"Are you absolutely positive that you put a key in their box?"

"Yes. I know because we keep record of the notices and keys that we put in applicable mail boxes."

"Now, do you remember what mail was already in the Taylors' PO box?"

"I don't remember one hundred percent, but more likely, if it was a typical day, it would be a lot of first class letters, solicitations, magazines, cardboard boxes, and bubble wrapped packages. Nothing out of the ordinary."

"And did anyone ever come and pick up the mail for that box? The one that had the orange key?"

"No sir."

"Now, for box 8285, how big is it, dimensions-wise?"

"It's definitely one of the biggest boxes when compared to the others."

"Dimensions, please?"

"It's eleven by five point five."

"Inches, right?"

"Yes sir."

"And you eventually noticed that, perhaps, a week later, that some of the mail from box 8285 was being picked up, but one or two in particular were not. Those pieces were left sitting in the box. Am I correct?"

"Yes, sir."

"And you discovered something. Tell us about that."

Latonya sighed again. "There was a big brown padded envelope that was sitting in the box for about eight days. No mailing address on it. No return address. It was just an envelope, there in the box."

"Was the envelope sealed?"

"Yes, it was."

"Then what?"

"I had to ask all my coworkers if they had put that package in the box. They all said they didn't."

"What do you do when you see an unmarked package that finds its way into a postal box?"

"My instincts told me that something was wrong. I considered it a suspicious package."

"I see," Ketchum told her. "Then what happened?"

"I alerted my supervisor. He contacted the Haz Mat people to come out and examine the sealing tape so they could test it for explosives or anthrax. I hate anthrax."

"I don't blame you. Then what happened?"

"Long story short, once the investigators got involved, they set up a robot that discovered a firearm in the envelope."

The jury looked shocked. Everyone was on the edge of their seat.

"Then what?"

"Montgomery County Sheriff's office was brought in."

"Latonya, did you ever unseal the envelope and put your hands on that gun?"

"No sir. I did not."

"And you weren't aware of the contents of the suspicious package until it was later revealed."

"That is correct. I had no idea a gun was in there and I didn't understand why anyone would put in an unmarked envelope."

"Thank you. That will be all."

Their next witness was brought to the stand.

"State your name."

"Michael Morrison."

"And your position?"

"I work for Montgomery County PD."

"And your job?"

"I examine evidence that was confiscated at crime scenes."

"You say you take away evidence from crime scenes?"

"Yes."

"And what evidence did you take from the residence of Nathaniel Taylor last fall?"

"Once the coroner determined there were deep cut flesh wounds on his face, PD decided to obtain a search warrant and return to the house in which Mr. Taylor was found unconscious."

"And what did you take, sir?"

"The gun that was found hidden in the PO Box."

"And why was that gun so important that you confiscated it?"

"It had fingerprints. Those of Mr. Taylor and Ms. Coco Chanel Reeves."

"I see. Anything else?"

"Her DNA was found underneath Mr. Taylor's fingernails. And her blood was discovered on his shirt. It was only two drops, but enough for us to think there was probable cause."

"Anything else?"

"We found lipstick stains on his mouth."

"This was after he had died?"

"Yes, sir."

"And whose lipstick was it?"

"DNA says those stains came from Coco Chanel Reeves."

"Thank you. No further questioning."

Ketchum brought up the next witness.

"State your name please."

"Natalia Anne Taylor."

"Your age?"

"I am eight years old for now."

Everyone laughed.

"You're a smart little girl."

"Thank you."

"We want to ask you some questions."

"I already know," Natalia said.

"What do you mean, you already know?"

"My auntie told me what you'll be asking me about my daddy and the oven."

The jury gasped again.

"Natalia, do you know what lying is?"

"Yeah, everyone does."

"What is it?"

"It's when you don't tell the truth. When you make up something that is false. Like when you wake up in the morning and tell your mother your stomach hurts. But it really doesn't, because you don't feel like going to school that day."

Mr. Ketchum tried not to laugh. "Very good. Now, if I ask you a question, you will tell me the truth, right?"

"Yes, sir. I hope so." Natalia's shoulders began to tremble. She realized that everyone was staring at her. She didn't want to be there anymore.

"Did you turn off the oven on the night of August twenty-fifth before you left the house?"

"I-I think I did." She hesitated.

"Please remember. This is very important."

"Yes, I did turn it off. I remember now."

"What makes you remember?"

"Because it was so hot in the kitchen. I waited a long time for my Aunt Coco to come back downstairs. And I did turn it off. Because I didn't want to be hot anymore."

"Natalia, you are under oath which means you must tell the truth."

"I do remember now. But I was scared to tell. Because I thought that the little bit of gas that was there had killed my daddy. And I never would want to kill him." She burst into tears. "I was scared. I wanted to be sure. I didn't want to go to jail. I plead the Fifth Amendment."

Ketchum told Natalia she was dismissed. A few more witnesses were interviewed such as Liz, the fire fighters who'd arrived on the scene that day, the medical staff at the Woodlands Hospital, the EMS drivers, and a couple more.

Then the prosecutor came back and addressed the grand jury.

"We have presented forensic evidence which concludes that the defendant got into an altercation with the deceased. They fought over a gun. A gun that she tried to hide. Although the gun wasn't fired, she clearly has a motive. Instead of using the gun, she used gas from the man's oven. The State of Texas believe that Coco Chanel Reeves premeditated to murder Nathaniel Taylor. The accident was no accident. Everything that happened was intentional."

The grand jury was allowed to submit questions to the prosecutor. Ketchum read off one of the questions.

"What time did Coco Reeves leave the house that night?"

"We estimate that she left the residence approximately eight forty-five in the evening."

"Do you have the security footage that gives the time stamp of when she could be seen leaving the house?"

"Yes. Here it is."

The black and white footage was grainy and it appeared to be Coco. You could barely detect the expression on her face. She looked serious. She wasn't smiling. She could be seen getting into her car and sitting for one minute. Her lips moved, but because there was no audio, no one could determine what was being said.

"Is there any additional security camera footage of the defendant in and or around the house?"

"No, there is no more footage."

"What time did the deceased pass away?"

"The coroner presented the time of death as 4:21 a.m. that Sunday morning."

Experts have determined that it would have taken less than two hours for Nathaniel to inhale the gas or the carbon monoxide that would ultimately cause his death. This leads us to believe that the gas oven may have been turned off, but it certainly must have been turned back on at some point during those early morning hours."

The entire room seemed to gasp out loud.

"Show us the floor plan of the Taylor residence please."

An overhead projector was used to show the graphics of the floor plan of Nate and Burgundy's two-story, six-thousand-square-foot house. There was an island kitchen that included the double sinks and dishwasher. Right across from it was the gas stove and oven.

"As you can see, the guest room is located only two feet from the kitchen. The bedroom door was found open. That's where Nate was located. He was unconscious at the time EMS arrived."

"Was there anyone else in the house?"

"Just the youngest daughter. But even she was found knocked out from the gas later on that Sunday. A small amount of it was found in her body."

"Where exactly was the body of Nathaniel Taylor found? And how?"

"His body was lying face down on the floor like he had collapsed. His body was headed in the direction of the kitchen."

"In other words, it looked as if he was trying to walk, or leave the bedroom, like he was trying to get out?" one of the jurors asked.

"That's how it appeared."

"How was he dressed?"

"He was wearing a cotton shirt and some dungarees."

"No pajamas?"

"No pajamas. And he was wearing Nike gym shoes. And white socks."

The jury murmured after the revelation of Nate's wardrobe.

"Did any other person come to the house that night after Coco left?"

"No."

"How about security footage of the vicinity around the house? Do you see anyone parking outside the house, walking up to the door, ringing the doorbell?"

"No. But we do have one piece of footage we want you to see."

A clerk set up some security footage that was shown of the backyard. It was dark that night. And in the twenty second video, a person, gender undetected, could be seen walking in the backyard. They walked and then disappeared out of view of the security camera parameters.

"Can you tell if it's a male or a female?"

"We cannot. But we know that the recording occurred at 9:05 p.m. Which means it happened before the defendant left the house that night."

"The grand jury may now deliberate."

An hour later, the prosecutor was presented with a written statement: No true bill.

"The grand jury has concluded there are no grounds for the indictment of Coco Chanel Reeves. Based upon the timing of the deceased's death and the timing of when the oven was presumably turned on, it would be impossible for her to have committed this crime. Case is dismissed."

Once Coco's attorney was informed of the grand jury's decision, he went to see her at the jail as soon as he could. They sat in a room and at first Coco couldn't tell what had happened.

"What?" Coco asked.

Her attorney whispered, "You are free to go. Right now."

"I-I am?"

"Yes. Just like I told you. They didn't have sufficient evidence. It's all circumstantial."

"But what about the gun?"

"They determined that although hiding a gun in a post office was a violation, the gun wasn't a murder weapon in this case. Your fingerprints were on it but so were Nate's. Circumstantial."

She felt her knees weaken.

"I'm free. I can't believe it. Thank you, sir."

"And one last thing. Never try to influence a witness. You could have gotten in a lot of trouble for that. You're lucky it worked out for your benefit though."

"My niece. I owe her. Big time."

Coco had been behind bars since November. She thought about what Alita once told her. She said that no matter how long a bird has been caged, his song always changes once he's set free.

The day that Coco set foot out of jail, it felt like she'd had a born-again experience.

She was handed her bag of personal belongings and she held onto it as if it were all she had left in the world.

She was thankful for being released, and more than ready to see what would happen in the next chapter of her life.

Chapter 15

Miracles

"Welcome Home Coco."

That was the banner that Coco saw when she pulled up in front of her house. She hadn't been home since late October. It was now mid-April and the notion of spring bringing forth new things couldn't be more perfect.

Flowers were blooming, plants were starting to grow again. Life felt different, better.

"I'm so glad to see this raggedy old house I don't know what to do." Coco was seated in the passenger seat of Elyse's car. Gamba was in the back, taking everything in. Coco glanced at the house in which she was practically raised; the house where she could resume raising her kids.

"Well, let me go on in and make myself at home." She got out the car, with Elyse and Gamba following behind.

Coco stepped inside the doorway, careful not to get in the way of the dozens of pink and purple balloons that bobbed on the floor all throughout the hallway.

She removed her shoes and cried out. "Cadee? Chloe? Chance?" The kids ran out from their bedroom, screaming and yelling. They raced straight into their mother's arms. Elyse left to go to the nursery. She brought Cypress and planted her in Coco's arms.

"How's my little baby?" All she could do was pray the girl remembered her.

Cypress was now twenty-five months old. At first she stared at the woman who was now holding her and kissing her cheeks. Then she blurted out, "Mama? Mama?"

Everyone cheered so loud that little Cypress became frightened. But the joy of the moment could not be contained.

"She does remember me."

"Of course she does," Dru told her.

"You look good, Mommy," Cadee told her. "We missed you so much. I hate you were in jail."

"Who told you that?"

Alita stepped in. "Sorry, sis, but at some point we had to explain to the kids what was going on. Don't worry, we cleaned things up real nice for you. We said you got arrested for protesting the killing of horses. Or was it blue whales? Something like that."

"You all are too much," Coco said with a chuckle. "I swear to God, there's nobody like my family."

They gave Coco all the space and time she needed to get reacquainted with her children. It felt like a family reunion. A time to celebrate the good, and to hopefully escape the bad.

In life there are many things that people want, pray for, and work toward. Dru felt she was no exception.

She went to visit her doctor and tried to explain how she'd been feeling.

"I'm probably being silly but I wanted to see you because lately it feels like I'm losing my balance every time I insert my eye drops. And sometimes I may hop up real quick from the couch, and I feel lightheaded and woozy."

"It could be a vitamin deficiency or low blood pressure. Let's check things out, Ms. Reeves," her doctor told her.

"We can go through a battery of tests. I'll get my nurse to draw a few vials of blood, let you give us a urine sample, and if necessary, we can check you for STD's."

"STD's? Are you trying to tell me something?"

"No, Ms. Reeves, I'm not trying to tell you anything. This is pretty routine, especially when taking blood tests."

In no time at all, Dru was in and out of the doctor's office. And a couple of days later, she received a cryptic voicemail asking her to come and see the doctor as soon as possible.

She'd been at work when she realized the doctor's office left her the voicemail. And as soon as she hung up from listening, she took a three mile walk over to Tyrique's office. They both worked in the Texas Medical Center but in different facilities. She wasn't on her lunch break, nor did she care that she left her job without informing anybody.

She stormed through the streets battling all sorts of thoughts. She decided to call Burgundy right before she reached Tyrique.

"I guess I have you to thank for what's happening in my life," she said in a sharp tone.

"Thank me for what?"

"For cursing my relationship. We were happy, me and Tyrique, and between you and Alita's negative male-bashing, insecure-acting ways, now I get to deal with stuff I've never dealt with when it comes to my man."

"Oh Dru." She paused, then. "You found out about the other woman?"

"What other woman, B? If you know something you need to tell me right now so I can have a solid reason to kill him."

"Dru, my God. Are you serious? Where are you? Are you at work? It sounds like you're walking. I hear footsteps. Please get a grip. This isn't like you."

"I know. And that's why you and Alita and even Coco

really get on my last nerve. You couldn't stand to see me happy so you put all kinds of miserable things in my head. That I can't trust my man, that's Alita. And they are all dickheads, that's Coco. And you. You telling me that I don't know for sure what my man is doing at any time of the day because some men are so good at lying and keeping the truth from a woman, that we don't know if we're coming or going."

"Dru, even if it was the truth, hell, I didn't make it up. Lita calls it like she sees it, so does Coco. Don't blame me or them. Blame your man if that's what he's doing behind your back."

By then Dru and Burgundy were engaged in a spirited shouting match. And Dru hated to find herself acting out in public. She quieted down and pulled her knit hat over her eyebrows. The day was brutally cold and her free hand was stuffed inside her pocket, while her other hand froze as she tried to hold the phone against her ear.

"Burgundy, put it like this. Ty and I have been exclusive for years. We don't use condoms because I trust him and he trusts me. So why did this nurse leave a message on my cell phone after I took the HIV test?"

"What?"

"Yeah. Like do I have something, like am I dying or what?"

"My baby. Dru, this is serious. Why would someone leave a personal message like that on your cell phone? She needs her license revoked, whoever she was." Burgundy paused. This development sounded serious. Dru was so young, she had so much promise, so much to live for.

"And so are you going to confront Tyrique right now?"

"Yep."

"In person?"

"Yep."

"On his job?"

"Sure am."

"No, no, no, no, Dru. Don't! Why blindside him? People don't like stuff like that."

"Why not? He blindsided me. He cheated on me. I certainly haven't stepped out on him. Not in all the years we've been dating and living together. I feel like such a fool. And now I guess I will join the Reeves Sisters club in that we all have the same fucking views about men. Except for Elyse. I guess she's the one who has lucked out and found a decent guy." Dru's voice quivered as she thought of Jerrod Dawson and the way things ended up concerning him. "I-I guess I'm just unlucky in love."

Dru told Burgundy she'd call her later. She was now standing outside the animal lab where Tyrique worked as a biomedical research specialist. She heard the screeches of the 50 or so primates that he tended to. She quickly texted him to let him know she was waiting outside the secured area. He came and let her inside and gave her a big hug and smile.

She immediately pushed Tyrique off of her.

"What's wrong, Dru. What happened?"

"What's her name?"

"Her who?"

"Oh, don't give me that." Her eyes watered. She was so in love with him. How could he betray her like this?

"The nasty bitch you slept with who gave you a disease. And she gave it to me too."

He stood with his mouth open. "Dru? I don't have any idea what you're talking about. Is this some type of joke? You're pulling my leg right? I haven't cheated on you, ever!"

"That's what they all say."

"And I know for a fact I don't have a disease," he said in anger.

"What do you mean?"

"I got my blood tests results, Dru. And I don't have no STD." He came and stood close to her with their noses almost touching. "Maybe I should be asking you the same questions. Who is he, Dru? What's his name? When did you find time to fuck around on me when you always claim to be studying, going to class, going to work, or doing stuff with your family?"

She was stunned. Was he lying to her? Dru couldn't even imagine. Tyrique was as honest and as decent as they came.

"Um, maybe there's some kind of mistake, baby." She came and tried to hug him but this time he was the one doing the resisting.

"Don't touch me. I don't know where your hands or lips have been last. I have to work. I have to think. Thanks for accidentally telling on yourself. Bye Dru."

He pushed her out into the hallway then closed and secured the lab door.

She trembled with anxiety. Confusion pounded mercilessly at her head. The floor began to spin in a wide, fast circle underneath her feet. She tried to take one wide-reaching step and knock on the lab door. Seconds later, she fell backwards. Dru's head bounced against the floor. Everything came to a standstill.

"Dru, can you hear me?"

Dru stirred as she heard Alita's voice. She woke up finding herself in a hospital bed, propped up and surrounded by white pillows. The room felt below freezing and a pair of ankle socks covered her feet.

"Why is it so cold in here," she murmured. "I need another blanket."

"Whoop, baby girl finally woke up." That was Alita. "I knew my baby sis would pull through."

Alita dutifully restrained herself and tried to act as dignified as her emotions would allow her. She wanted to crawl in the bed with Dru and squeeze her with all of her might. Her sister had been unconscious the past fourteen hours. It was the worse fourteen hours of Alita's life.

But they'd gotten through the worst of Dru's health crisis, and Alita tapped out a few brief texts to Burgundy and Elyse.

The nurses made sure to keep Dru comfortable. Alita pulled over a chair and grabbed Dru's hand, rubbing it and blowing on it.

"Tyrique should be here any second, Dru. He was so worried. That was the first time I've ever seen him cry and I've been around your man for years. If a man openly cries, hello! You know you've got a real one."

The two nurses couldn't refrain from smiling at the joy Alita displayed. At first no one had been sure she would pull through. But by the way her family and some church members showed up, surely those prayers had been answered.

"Hi, Ms. Dru. I hate to disturb you," said one nurse, "But I'm happy to see you're up and looking better. If you don't mind, we need to take your temperature and your blood pressure."

"And you might want to feed her too, you know what I mean," Alita said. "You've had that IV stuck to you for the longest, but ain't nothing like a good piece of fried chicken, black-eyed peas, corn bread, and a thick slice of Seven-Up cake."

"Alita Reeves, you need to quit. Soul food is the last thing I want. Plus, hospitals don't get down like that." Dru's voice sounded tired and croaky but it was still music to Alita's ears.

Alita went from being chatty to outright breaking

down in front of everyone in the room. Life was so uncertain and God knows she'd seen enough of death in her lifetime to appreciate the value of seeing another day.

Right then Tyrique strolled in with his hands clutching balloons and his arms wrapped around flower pots. He also had a copy of Dru's favorite book, *I Know Why the Caged Bird Sings*.

"For you," he said and set her gifts aside. He leaned over and kissed Dru on her cheek. Later on, she was strong enough to sit up in bed. She was ecstatic that so many people had come to see her but their long, chatty talks felt draining.

Alita respectfully excused herself and told Dru she'd see her soon.

After Tyrique stuck around for a while, the attending physician came in and consulted with Dru and Tyrique. His information left her in a daze. He gave her numerous instructions and told her to check back with him in one week. When the doctor left, Dru picked up the phone and called Alita.

"I finally found out what's wrong with me. I'm having a baby."

"Noooo."

"Yesss. Ty and I stopped using contraceptives because we figured I couldn't get pregnant. We had tried for more than two years. Nothing. Then I was diagnosed with polycystic ovary disorder. I cried when I found out. But then I focused on my other life goals. Once I let go, that's when it happened. I can't believe it happened, but it did."

"How far along are you?"

"Twenty-three weeks."

"Get out!"

"Yes."

"But you stopped having a period, right?"

"I've been spotting here and there. Nothing major. But

I didn't think much about it. The doctor told me I'm having what is referred to as a cryptic pregnancy. Apparently, it happens more than anyone could realize."

"And you never took a pregnancy test?"

"No. I didn't. It was the last thing on my mind. I mean I felt otherwise normal in spite of the dizziness and a little weight gain."

"All along your ass was pregnant. I'll be damned. I'm going to be an auntie, Dru Boo."

"It's unreal, isn't it?"

And out of nowhere, the life that Dru had once known was changed in an instant.

Dru and Tyrique celebrated their good news. And one month later, in the middle of May, they decided to throw a gender reveal party in the courtyard of their townhouse. They partied and ate good food. And when the giant cardboard box was opened, two dozen blue balloons floated into the sky. Everyone erupted into applause.

"A boy," Alita said. "It's about time we put some more boys in the Reeves family. You pick out a name yet, Dru?"

"Yes. His name is Asher. Which means 'blessed' or 'happy.'"

"I'm happy for you. Happy for Asher. Happy for all of us."

Dru's pregnancy sped along. But with each passing week, the mother-to-be did not grow more satisfied.

"Dru, what's wrong with you?" Burgundy asked one day. "I see you're still going to work every day, plus finishing up your thesis. And you're due to give birth in less than two months. You may want to slow your roll. Take it from me, I know about juggling a heavy schedule."

"I know. You're right. I'm thrilled but I'm also terrified."

"Why sweetie?"

"Some days I feel I can make it. My health feels good. I have an abundance of energy to handle my tasks. But at night, Burgundy, sometimes at night, I have nightmares. And I wake up drenched with sweat. My heart is beating out of my chest, sometimes so loudly that I can hear it. I even think Tyrique can hear it."

"What's going on?"

"I don't know."

"What are in your dreams? Do you recall specific images? Feelings? Sounds? Colors?"

"I see an image. Yes. A baby. A baby boy."

"And?"

"He's dead, B." It was so hard for Dru to speak those words, to release them from her mouth. She never wanted to give life to her fears. But she had to tell somebody.

"Is the face Asher's?"

"Being that I've never seen my son's face, I don't know if it's him or not."

She fell into silence. Both women did.

Then, Dru said. "I work in the medical industry. I hear people talking. I hear them say that the US is the most dangerous place in the world to give birth. Like mothers are dying right after giving birth. These deaths are preventable. And the highest rates of mortality are in Texas. And the race of these women is African-American."

Dru stared at Burgundy with large, haunted eyes that were riveted with terror.

"This may be my one and only chance to have a child. It's a pure miracle that I even got this far along. I'm very excited, but yeah, B, I'm scared too. I find myself obsessed. I study all the recent cases. I want to know the woman's health background, age, occupation, socioeconomic status. How many kids has she had before? What was her pre-pregnancy lifestyle like? Was she a smoker, a drinker, did she do drugs, did she work out on a regular basis? Did she eat McDonald's every day or salads and tomatoes?"

"Don't you think this is overdoing it, sis? The last thing you need to do is stress yourself out, Dru."

"I know. But all I can think about is the fact that I'm in Texas."

"So what?"

"Based on the black women who die giving childbirth, I wonder if I should trust the hospitals or the medical care workers."

"Dru, you don't need to trust anybody, but the Lord. He'll bless you to have this child, with no complications."

"I hope so."

"Believe it. For Asher's sake."

"Well, if push comes to shove I can take matters in to my own hands and hire a doula or a midwife. My chances may improve if I do that."

"Do what you feel is best, but ultimately you have to speak to your baby, eat healthy, and take good care of yourself. Forget that thesis. Forget running around like a crazy woman."

"I will try, thanks B, for listening. And how are you coming along with your foundation?"

"Very well. I have filed the paperwork for the non-profit. Things are looking good."

"And so your mission statement is to still help and empower women, right? Women who are down on their luck, who need a safe place."

"Yes, that hasn't changed."

"Burgundy, why have you changed?"

"What do you mean?"

"It's been months since you and Coco basically fell out."

"Oh. That."

"You basically fired her from working for you. You

seem like you'll help a woman you don't know before you would help your own sister. Why is that?"

"Hello? Have you heard all the shit that happened with Coco and Nate? What more did she expect? To welcome my scandalous sister and my husband's love child with open arms?"

"But, sweetie, it seems a bit harsh. Coco isn't perfect. You two have had it out before. She's not used to you holding a grudge."

"I'm not used to sisters sleeping with my spouse and having a kid with him either."

"Okay, that's fair, but at some point, you must let go. Just like I had to let go of freaking out because I thought I couldn't get pregnant—"

"This is a little bit different. Dru, if you found out Coco slept with Tyrique, you'd feel different. You'd feel like me."

Dru had no response. Because in all honesty, Burgundy was right. Few women had the strength to handle infidelity, secret side kids, and ultimate betrayal from other chicks, let alone from their own family members.

"My biggest issue with this whole thing, B, is that you're pouring a lot of time and money into helping other women get their lives back together again."

"And?"

"And for all you know, the woman that you will ultimately help might be a Coco. Did you ever think about that?"

"No, Dru. I didn't."

"What if it happens? What if you find out their life stories and some of them remind you of your sister? Your sister who's made a lot of bad choices during her life? Geez, B, I already know you're going to run into them. People like Coco are everywhere."

Burgundy nodded. Certainly, Dru had given her much to think about.

Chapter 16

The Money Bag Baby

Since Coco had been back home things slowly turned to normal. She resumed her relationship with her kids and tried to co-parent with Calhoun. She and Q struck up a newfound existence, with her allowing him to spend time with Chance as much as he wanted, but she had a strict no-sex rule this time around. Q agreed to go along with her wishes but it was hard. They had history and he still had feelings for her.

At the end of May, Coco was at home in the living room. She sat on the edge of her couch tightly clutching her cell phone. It was 10:07 on that Monday morning. She knew that a courier was delivering an important package to Burgundy. She checked the tracking status again. The package got accepted four minutes ago.

Her cell phone rang. She jumped up and looked at the caller ID. Unrecognizable number. Should she answer?

Coco took a chance. "Hello?"

At first, she heard nothing. Then she heard the faint sound of gasping.

"Hello?" she said again. She sat back down.

"Coco, it's me. It's Burgundy."

Coco immediately went over to the coffee table. Q's cell

phone was lying face up. He had no idea that she'd stolen it from him last night when he came to visit her.

She turned on the recorder app on his phone and placed her cell phone on speaker.

"Hey, what's up, B?" she said.

"I can't believe you."

"What are you talking about?"

"You know exactly what I'm talking about. How in the hell can you call yourself suing Nate's estate?"

"Oh that. Well, my lawyer advised me—"

"Did you say your lawyer?"

"Did I stutter, B?"

"How can you afford a lawyer?"

"That's not for you to worry about."

"Really, Coco? You could have come to me about this—"

"No, B. That's where you are wrong. I tried doing it your way. I gave you your space. And I thought you would've contacted me before now. But you never did."

"I apologize if I am not socializing with you based on your time frame. Are you serious?"

"I'm very serious."

"Coco, you're suing me? My husband? My businesses? This is a frivolous lawsuit. It's going to get thrown out of court."

"We'll see about that, B. Some of it might seem bogus to you but there are certain things that I know are legit."

"But why are you doing this, Coco?"

"B, around the other sisters you try to pretend like you've changed and matured and you're all open-minded, but you ain't like that at all. Not when it comes to me. I *had* to do it. I just had to." Coco hated to inflict pain on her sister but in her mind, this lawsuit was about Chance.

"Chance has the right to some money," she continued. "A DNA test proved that that sicko you married—"

"And a sicko that you felt was good enough to fuck."

"Anyway," Coco said. "The rich sicko has to pay up. Our baby deserves some of the money that Nate Taylor left you."

"I just can't believe this. If ain't one thing, it's another."

"Tell me about it," Coco answered. "I just want what's fair. I mean, hell, my child is growing like a weed. He needs new toys, summer clothes, and I want him to have new furniture for his bedroom. The car I'm driving needs too much work on it, so I'm thinking about buying a new one, and I want to pay cash. I don't want a car note with high interest. You already know I'm not pulling no 800 FICO score."

"I've heard enough. If I didn't know you were serious, I'd think it was a joke."

"It's no joke, B. I'm sorry about everything that happened. But now that I was found not guilty, I want a new lease on life."

"You want me to pay for that lease too. That's what it sounds like."

"Burgundy, under the law of Texas the child has the right to financial support. So that subpoena makes sure that it will happen. See you in court."

Coco ended the call. She stopped the recording on Q's phone.

And then her doorbell rang.

"Who the hell is this? I'm not expecting anybody."

Ever since she got released from jail, Coco had grown more paranoid. She made sure to make as little noise as possible as she advanced toward the front door. She looked through the peephole and couldn't see anybody.

But she heard loud banging on the lower part of the door.

"Coco, open up."

"Q? Why are you playing around?" She hesitated then

unlocked the door. Instead of letting him in, she stepped outside and folded her arms. "What's the problem?"

"Hey, sorry for popping over like this, Ma. But have you seen my phone? I can't find it."

"Oh, I'm sorry to hear that."

He gave her a desperate look. For a minute, Coco felt sympathy for Q. He wasn't a bad dude. In fact, he was one of the better ones that she had come across.

He slapped the back of his pants pockets and looked like he was desperately trying to remember what he did with his phone.

"Where'd you last see it?" she asked.

"If I could remember, would I be here with you right now?"

"Does that mean that you don't want to be around me unless there's a good reason? Is that what you're saying?"

"Look, Coco. I'm in a serious situation right now. All my contacts, passwords, websites, pay apps, everything was on that phone."

She nodded but said nothing.

"Can I come in and chill for a sec? I need to sit down and think. You got any beer?"

She knew his favorite brand of beer and would buy a few six packs for him and stock them in the fridge.

"Sure, I still have beer. But first, we need to continue our conversation from last night." She quickly thought. "See, I know you've grown very attached to Chance. And actually, the fact that you care about the boy amazes me. It says a lot about your character. But I need you to understand that I still need to do what I have to do on the legal side of things. And my way of fixing things is to first secure the bag. You know that Chance's real daddy had money. And I feel it's only right to make my son's situation better with some of that cheddar."

"I know all this Coco. That's why we argued about it at

my crib last night. Because I'm not with how you going about this. Why sue your own sister? Haven't you fucked her over enough, when you slept with old dude?"

"We don't need to talk about that anymore."

"No, we do too need to talk about it. I like to know what I'm dealing with."

"The only thing you need to know is that I'm serious about making Nate Taylor pay one way or another for the kid he helped create. I just don't get why you can't understand that."

"Look, let's calm down, drink a beer, and go have a seat on your couch. I'm tired as hell. I drove into work and snuck out early for lunch so I could try and find my phone." He checked his watch. "I only have a little bit of time left before I need to return to work. Or else I may get fired and I'll need to come stay with you." He laughed. She didn't. And she still did not want him to step foot inside her house.

"Wait right here," she said.

Coco returned inside the house and locked the door. She retrieved an ice-cold bottle of Heineken and brought it outside. She smiled sympathetically and handed it over.

"Thanks. But why can't I chill inside with you? You got some other man in there that you hiding?"

"I wish," she blurted but immediately felt regretful.

The crushed look on Q's face made her feel even worse.

"Q, I'm so sorry. I-I need to let you in on something." She opened the door and waved at him. "Come on in, Q. Make yourself at home."

She offered him a seat on the recliner and lifted the lever so he could relax. She removed Q's shoes from his feet. She handed him the remote control and surfed through the channels until she came across a sports network. He looked at her with a grateful smile, especially when Coco stood behind Q and started to gently squeeze and rub his shoulders and then his back.

He groaned in appreciation.

"How's that feel, baby?" she asked.

"Shocking. I didn't know you was still feeling me like this."

"I wanted to try something different with my new rules. But if the rules don't work, you may have to change them. Or tweak them. Am I allowed that?"

"I guess."

Sometimes you have to lie to get what you want.

"Again, how does this feel, Q?"

"It feels damned good." He let her continue to vigorously rub his skin, her fingers delicately rubbing away all the tension from his tight shoulders and lower back. Her hands started to feel heated and she reminisced about the good times they used to have . . . or at least the good times they tried to have, before everything grew complicated.

Coco's hands felt so good on his body that he actually fell asleep for a few minutes. Coco gazed at Q and liked how calm he looked right then. What if she gave him another chance? God knows there was no other man out there pulling for her the way Q did.

She whispered in his ear, "You love me, Q?" She kissed him on his cheek which caused him to stir around until he woke up.

Q gazed at Coco with a smile. The first smile she'd gotten from him in quite some time. And right then she realized how beautiful Q was. He was so fine it hurt to look at him.

"Does that make you feel better, Q? All I want to do is ease your mind a little bit."

"I love this, Ma. You making a man feel real good right about now, but I do have to get back to work."

"Call in sick. Tell 'em you have an emergency to take care of. And in a way you do."

"I wish I could."

"Just do it, Q. Please."

"How?" he asked. She walked over to the dining room table and grabbed his phone. She returned and handed it to him.

"You stole my phone?"

"No."

"No?"

"I grabbed your phone by accident. I had no idea I had your phone until I got home. And stop staring at me like you're crazy. Our phones look just alike."

He fiddled around with his device for a couple of minutes.

"Oh, and before you get mad again, Q, I broke into your phone but not to spy on you or anything like that. I needed to use your recording app. That's all, I swear to God. Here. I'll show you." She proceeded to tell him how she served papers on her sister, how it tore her up inside, but why she did it.

"I'm not trying to start trouble. I'm looking out for Chance, that's all. I feel so bad for him at times that it makes me crazy on the inside. You already know that Calhoun takes good care of Cadee, Chloe, and Cypress. I'll give that to him. But I feel like Chance is the forgotten child. And no way I can have three of my kids well taken care of and the other neglected. It's just not fair."

Her voice grew to a panicked shout. Q quickly called into his job and told them he'd be back tomorrow. That he needed to handle an unexpected emergency.

Coco cooked. They ate and sat and talked like it was old times. It felt good for Coco to release all the things she'd been holding onto inside.

"I want to put everything on the table, Q. I apologize for every stupid thing I've done or said concerning you. I feel really bad about those things. But I want to do better from now on."

"You sure about that, Coco, seeing as how you stole my phone less than twenty-four hours ago."

"Q, I wanted to let you know that I accidentally had your phone, but when I called you and your phone starting ringing in my hand, hell, what more could I do? I just waited for you to figure it out and come by."

"You're a hot mess."

"And you love this hot mess too."

He said nothing.

"Q, I'm trying my best to be straight with you. I-I know you're still feeling me and I probably don't even deserve it."

"How you know how I feel?"

"Because you're still here. After the felony charges, the questioning, and that short stint in jail, look who's here."

Coco's voice choked up as she talked. "It took me a long time to learn what love is. And loyalty. I've made some bad decisions in my first twenty-nine years of life, but I promise you the next twenty-nine will be different." She paused. "Can you stick it out with me and help me be a better woman?"

The change of events threw Q for a loop.

Love was inexplicable. It was maddening at times. But in a way her assessment was almost on point. Why else would he continue to insist on being around her after all they'd been through? Sure, once he found out some things about Coco that he didn't like, he quietly left her alone for a few months. But something compelled him to resurface. And now, whether it made sense or not, he found himself back in this woman's life.

The summer months blew in all kinds of legal situations for the Reeves sisters.

"It seems like my prayers were finally answered," Alita told Dru. It was the end of June. Her pregnant sister had six more weeks to go before Asher was scheduled to be born. And she, Dru, Gamba, and Elyse were seated in the rear of a Harris County Courtroom.

Jack Dawson sat in front of them. Elyse stared at the back of his neck. She felt zero emotions for the man.

But Jack wasn't the sisters' main concern.

The judge had just sentenced Jerrod for stalking and attempted extortion.

"Did you hear that?" Alita whispered. "Jerrod is getting thirteen years for what he did to us."

"Good," Dru said. "It's a shame. I tried to warn him."

The ladies spoke quietly until the judge asked them to refrain from speaking.

Jerrod was led out of the courtroom wearing an orange jumpsuit. But before the deputy sheriff could lead him totally out of view, he tried to run back in the opposite direction, like he wanted to race toward his dad, or perhaps even Alita. But the shackles around his feet prevented him from getting too far.

"He's crazy," Alita said. She calmly watched Jerrod get recaptured by three deputies. Then court was dismissed.

"The things people do for money," Dru said.

Jack Dawson turned around and stared at Alita then at Elyse. Jack's and Elyse's foreheads were just alike: heart-shaped, with a small widow's peak.

Alita noticed Jack's intent gaze. "What are you looking at?" she asked.

"I just wanted to get a good look at her. Since one of my kids just got taken away from me, I just wanted to see my other one."

"Sorry Jack, Elyse ain't yours." Alita's voice was emotional. "You may have been the sperm donor, but you were never her father. I raised her. My family raised her, my mama and daddy. You don't deserve the title of father."

Roro, who entered the courtroom, rolled over in her

wheelchair to where Alita was still sitting. "I guess we're even now, huh?"

"We're not even, Roro. This is a sad day for both of our families. Years ago, so many things about my role in Elyse's life were beyond my control. How she was conceived. How I had to act like she wasn't my child. I hated it. But I did the second-best thing that I could do, and that's just learn to be there for my baby, right now in the best way that I can."

"I don't blame you, Alita." Roro glanced at her lifeless legs. "But as far as my being in this wheelchair? I did blame you at first. Years ago, when I found out my daddy got twenty years I was upset. And I ran out the house, running and crying. And yeah, that's when I was blinded by my tears. Upset by my anger. I ran into the street. A car was coming. I didn't see it. It hit me in my hip. I flew up in the air, landed on the concrete, and I never knew how it felt to walk on my own two feet ever again."

"That's too bad, Roro. I'm sorry."

"Every day I wish I could turn back the hands of time," she said. "But I can't. It is what it is. I've lost my daddy and now my brother."

Everything felt so tense and awkward that Alita didn't know what else to say.

"Family is all we got." Roro looked at Alita, and Elyse and Burgundy and Gamba. "Your family seems to be doing well. It's just how it is. I hope things stay that way for y'all even though it hasn't been that way for my family. Hasn't been that good in a long time."

Roro gave them a sad look. Jack got up and wheeled Roro from the courtroom without saying another word.

That very same week, the Reeves sisters returned downtown for another court case.

They were sitting in another room waiting for the Reeves v Taylor hearing to begin. But before things could get started, Burgundy pulled Coco to the side.

"Look, we shouldn't be doing this."

"You've left me no other choice, B. What would you do if you were in my shoes?"

"I could never be in your shoes." Burgundy's voice was chilling.

"And that's why I have to sue you."

"No. You don't, Coco. Look, I was going to get around to telling you this but so much has happened. I've just set up a fund for Chance. It was so last minute that I didn't get a chance to get my attorney to cancel this court date."

"B, don't lie to me."

"No, it's the truth. I did it the day after Calhoun told me that the boy was Nate's son. I did it because I knew it was the right thing to do even though it was a hard thing to do."

"How do I know you're telling the truth?"

"Here." Burgundy reached inside her briefcase and pulled out a bank statement. "This is proof of when the savings account was opened." She handed Coco a debit card. "The pin number is 8285."

Coco's eyes widened. "Um, I don't know what to say."

"Tell her thanks," Alita said. "She's for real. She told me about this last night, Coco. She doesn't want us to fight anymore. She wants us to be united again, strong, and loving each other. Her seeing Roro in that wheelchair made her feel that giving you access to this money for Chance is the right thing to do."

"Oh wow," Coco's voice sounded humble. "I believe you. And I want to say I apologize but I know you told me to never say things like that anymore. I will say this instead. I was wrong. About everything. I was wrong to lie, to hurt you, to hurt my sisters." She sniffed. "I want to do better. And I don't want to go forward with this lawsuit. It should be dismissed."

"Are you sure you want to do this, Coco?" Alita asked.

"I'm sure," she nodded. "The amount is fair and I thank you from the bottom of my heart."

"Good," Alita said. "Hurry up and tell these greedy ass lawyers because I think court is about to start."

"Yes ma'am."

Coco and Burgundy managed to speak with their legal representation and were told how to proceed from that point forward.

They left the courtroom and gathered in the hallway of the justice building.

Alita felt relieved and elated. "I want to say that I'm so proud of you, B. So glad that you took the high road, in spite of everything that happened."

"Nothing can change what happened. Of course, I hate that things turned out like they have, and I have to deal with that, and I never believed Coco tried to kill my husband. And I didn't want her to get railroaded by the system. I believe in Coco."

"God's going to bless you for that," Alita said

Burgundy laughed. "And you don't even go to church so how would you know that?"

"I just do."

"Aw, this feels so good. Group hug," Dru said. "But don't squeeze me too tight."

They did their customary thing and squeezed each other with warm, earnest hugs.

"We're sisters," Burgundy said. "Even when it's hard we stand up for each other. That's the way it's always been and that's the way it's always going to be."

Chapter 17

Redemption

The next day, Burgundy's doorbell rang. She peered through the peephole and was surprised to find herself staring at Marty. She opened the door and said hello.

"Hey Marty. It's been a while. A good ten months since we've seen you."

"I know," he said. "And I'm sorry that I missed out on Mr. Taylor's funeral." Marty had been the landscaper for the past three years. And at the time that Nate passed away, he was on a two-week cruise, a family reunion of sorts, and he could not attend the services. While he was on the ship, he had received word that his mother had gotten sick. He'd immediately relocated to east Texas to help take care of her. Now Marty had plans to return to the Houston area.

"I know it looks bad because I've been gone so long. I lost my phone, all my contacts. It's no excuse. I've been trying to find all my former clients, drum up business. And I'm just now able to come see you and express my condolences in person." He stared at the front lawn, which looked dry and overgrown.

Burgundy saw him staring in disbelief. "Um, our grass certainly doesn't look as healthy as when you tended to it—"

"Do you still want me to do your lawn?"

She blinked. "You know I hadn't even thought about it with everything else I've been going through. Just so you know, while you were gone, the girls and I tried to plant a garden. We got mixed results. Okay, to be honest, we sucked big time at gardening."

He offered her a gentle smile. "You tried. No judgment."

"Marty, we always loved your work. And I wouldn't mind it if you could come back on a weekly basis."

"You got it. It feels good to be back."

"Great, do your thing. You can add some new stuff if you'd like. Something bright and cheery."

"No problem. I think I know something you might like."

"What's that?"

"How about some inula helenium flowers? They're leafy and yellow. They may grow between three and six feet tall. I think they'll look good against your side fencing."

"Go for it. Can't wait, Marty."

"Wow, thanks Mrs. Taylor. It's been a minute since I've been here. I'll go out to the shed and take a quick look if you don't mind."

"I don't mind at all."

Marty started to leave through the front but stopped.

"Oh, I meant to inform you that I still have a key to the shed. I'm getting old. My memory is kind of bad. I forgot to turn it in."

"It's fine. I wasn't worried. You're like family."

He smiled and told Burgundy that he'd be right back.

She continued fiddling around the house trying to finish up the laundry. Five minutes later, Marty returned to the house. He had a solemn look on his face.

"What's going on? Did you find what you were looking for?"

He clutched a piece of paper and an envelope.

"What is that?" Burgundy asked.

He cringed then handed everything to her.

The name "Marty" was handwritten across the front of the envelope. Burgundy immediately recognized Nate's writing.

With her fingers trembling, she carefully opened the envelope and retrieved a sheet of paper that was folded in half. She read the letter. Stared at Marty. And read it again:

I'm sorry. I know I did wrong. I can't live with the guilt anymore. I'm putting an end to all the pain I've caused my family.

Nate

Burgundy clapped her hand over her mouth. Then she released a heart wrenching scream. Marty attended to her then went to contact her sisters.

Within an hour, Burgundy's family arrived to check on her.

Dru and Alita were the first ones to get there.

"Let me see the letter," Alita demanded.

"No," Dru said. "This is a matter for the police."

"That's messed up. I didn't know old boy had it in him. That means he was guilty as fuck huh, but we already knew that anyway."

"Alita Washington, show some compassion," Dru told her. "May I take a quick look at the letter, B?"

By that time Burgundy was wearing some latex gloves. She handed Dru a pair of them. "I don't want any of our fingerprints on this letter. Here it is."

Dru's eyes widened as she read. "My God. I've never

seen a suicide note in real life. Burgundy, I am so very sorry. Do you think your landscaper is the only one who saw it?"

"I don't know. But I think that note has been sitting in the shed all this time. I'm trying to figure out why Nate put it there? Did he think Marty would come across it once he came back for his equipment? Did Nate want Marty to find it and tell me what he was too afraid to tell me?"

"How can you be sure?" Dru asked.

"That's it. I'm only guessing. But I know one thing. Nate knew I was traveling that weekend. And the next best person that he trusted who would come into the shed wouldn't be his own wife. I forced him to reach out to the guy who mows the fucking lawn."

"There you go again, blaming yourself," Alita told her. "If Nate really cared he would have called you, right? He would have done anything to get his wife on the phone and try to get you to talk him out of it. Your being out of town was no excuse."

"Not necessarily. Maybe he'd rather die . . . than talk to me." Alita was stunned as well as angry.

"B, you can't be serious."

"Maybe Nate finally faced his own demons and thought that I would have never forgiven him . . . never understood why he made the decisions he made. I'm assuming that's how he felt. But I really don't know." It was so hard to know, so difficult to know the entire truth. "I don't blame myself for what happened, but somehow I think I failed him too, Lita."

"Bullshit! That man failed you. You were perfect."

Burgundy was silent as she thought about how people's perceptions did not always mirror reality.

"That's the problem, Lita. You assume you know me, assume I am perfect because maybe a lot of times I did strive for perfection. I was an expert at controlling the image of having it all together, but that wasn't always the case. The exterior of who I appeared to be did not always match what was going on in the inside." Burgundy picked up a glass vase and threw it against a wall. The glass shattered and dozens of fragments spread across the floor.

"Dammit," she cried out. "If I could do it all over again, I swear things would have ended up different."

Dru stepped in. "B, please calm down, sis. You can't change past mistakes. All we have is now. All we have is each other, sweetie."

"She's right, B. Ain't no sense in going back in time because even if you started today to try and find it, you'll never find it." Alita burst into tears. She covered her face with her hands. "Take it from me, Sis, forget Nate. He raped my child and denied it. He lied to you all that time and made it seem like you were crazy. If he wanted to end his life that's a damn shame, but he had a choice. He could have gotten help or did his time like he should have done. He took the easy way out and made life much harder for his family."

"I can't argue with you, Lita," Burgundy said. "Because even when I confronted Nate about what he did to Elyse, he made excuses. He blamed her, for God's sake. He never ever took responsibility. Not even through to the very end."

"Does this mean that you don't accept his written apology on his suicide note?" Dru asked.

"I don't know. I'll have to think about it. Now that I know what happened, I'm thinking more about Elyse than anyone else." Burgundy turned to Elyse. She hugged her. Then she burst into tears, a rarity for a woman like Burgundy.

"I feel like I totally failed you, Elyse."

"No, please B. I'm good. I'm shocked. But you only did what you thought was right. I don't blame you anymore."

"Are you sure?"

"I'm positive, B. We're good. For real. I have nothing but love for you."

Love.

It was always the one thing that seemed to make rough times feel better. The entire moment overwhelmed Burgundy. Yet she felt inside her soul the sincerity of Elyse's love and forgiveness. The lady had grown from a withdrawn, moody person, to a woman of love, light, and confidence.

Burgundy continued to weep until every ounce of condemnation left. And as she quieted down, her spirit felt lighter. She knew beyond a doubt that the guilt she'd been carrying for months was now lifting from her shoulders. She felt a pureness and a liberty that was badly needed.

"Thank you, Elyse. Thank you."

Alita stood back and joyfully watched the wonderful exchange between Burgundy and Elyse.

"Love always wins," Alita said.

"Yes, it does." Dru wiped a few tears of her own.

"And guilt has to be treated like a hot potato. Drop it and forget about it," Alita remarked.

"If I can forgive B, she will one day forgive herself," Elyse added.

"I must say that I raised a hell of a woman," Alita continued. "Elyse is almost as angelic as me."

Burgundy and Elyse burst out laughing. Dru lapsed into hysterics. Then Alita joined in. All the ladies stood around joking and smiling at each other. They laughed until their stomachs hurt.

Alita proudly stared at Burgundy. The woman had endured so much in the past year or so, that it felt very good to see how far along she'd come. "I'm amazed how strong you are B, even though you say you don't want people to think you're perfect, but guess what. In a lot of ways, I think it's true—"

"Nooo. I'm not that at all. I'm only human."

"And that's what makes you so beautiful. Just like Ciara and Beyoncé."

"What? You're exaggerating, Lita."

"Maybe I am, but it's my opinion and I have a right to it! And there ain't nothing you can do about it, so let me finish."

"Alrighty then, with your crazy ass Kanye West always-interrupting-somebody self." Burgundy knew she needed to step out of her big sister's way and let her be exactly who she was.

"You may not think you're perfect but to me, you are perfectly you, Burgundy. You are true to yourself even if others don't like it or agree with it. And you took your big old life insurance money and not only did you help make sure your kids were okay, but you went a step further and helped out me and Elyse, Coco, and Chance, and you also gave money to help out total strangers through your foundation. If that ain't perfect behavior I don't know what is."

Dru agreed. "What Alita is trying to say, B, is that you are going out of your way to treat these ladies as if they are your family because you want to help women. That's all Alita wants to point out. You care about others and you come through at clutch time, whether we deserve it or not. God knows some of us, hint, hint," she said, and smiled at Alita, "Some of us sisters are more messed up than others, but still, you are right beside us to see what you can do to make the situations better."

"Oh, you guys, please hush up, you're starting to embarrass me." Burgundy felt humble and dazed at the same time. Those qualities had always been a part of her, and helping others felt natural.

"Well, thank God I'm in the position to do what I can. I

do what I do because I want all of us to take back the reins of our lives no matter what has happened. Nothing—no divorce, no rape, death, betrayal, none of it can destroy us."

Burgundy believed that her true strength came from family and their mutual support of each other. "We are sisters. We are queens. And we adjust each other's crowns."

"You got that right," Alita said as they all leaned in for a group hug.

It was a balmy July evening and Natalia announced, "I want some crab legs." Sidnee squealed "Me too." Burgundy texted Edmund then called Alita who agreed to meet them at the crab shack restaurant.

They all pulled up in the parking lot at the same time. Soon they were shown to a booth large enough to seat six. Menus were passed around the table and orders were placed.

Alita sat next to Shade and tightly clutched his arm.

Burgundy spoke up. "You two sure look cozy. I *love* how love looks on you, Lita."

"You love how love looks on me?"

"You look like you don't have a care in the world."

"Oh girl, stop."

"Go ahead and admit it. I played matchmaker last year and now you all are so tight you look just like an old—"

"Don't say it," Alita told Burgundy.

"Why shouldn't she?" Shade asked.

"'Cause I could say the same things about him and her that she's saying about me and *you*." Alita noticed the way her sister stared dreamily at Edmund as they sat hip to hip.

Burgundy laughed out loud and enjoyed the feeling of being happy and complete. They were camped out in a half circle corner booth. The men held down both ends with their women seated next to them, and the kids were safely lodged in the center.

Natalia had been listening to the adults talk all that time.

"See what you did, sweetheart?" Burgundy said to her. "This was your idea. You pulled us together."

"I did? Cool beans."

The entire table erupted in laughter.

After a while, buckets of food were brought out and everyone cheered then dug in. They had a feast of hot and spicy snow crabs for the adults, shrimp for the kids, and smoked sausage.

The music was loud and made the floor vibrate. Burgundy had to yell across the table every time she wanted to talk. But it was all in good fun. It had been far too long since she'd been able to escape from her issues and simply enjoy herself.

It was karaoke night. Quite a few restaurant patrons joined in, singing aloud to country and western songs as they stood on a tiny stage that was set up in the center of the restaurant. Neon lights flashed across the ceiling

Caught up in the middle, Edmund stood up. "Come on, Natalia."

"What?"

"I heard you love to perform. Let's do this. You and me. We're about to dance."

She glanced at her mother, then looked back at Edmund. His twinkling eyes seemed so warm and inviting. She made her decision. Burgundy moved out of the way to let Natalia out. Edmund grabbed her hand and they walked together to the stage.

"What's your favorite group or song?" Edmund asked.

She whispered in his ear.

Edmund touched the screen, performed a search, and dutifully set up a playlist.

And when Natalia's favorite song by her favorite group began to play, it all felt so magical. Her facial expression turned into sheer delight. The throbbing baseline got into her legs and her arms and her neck. She laughed and let Edmund swirl her around in a circle. But then she wanted to do her own thing, imitating The Milly Rock and The Floss. Her arms and hands swayed back and forth. The crowd cheered them along.

Burgundy wiped away tears. This entire scenario was so unexpected. She felt happy and lighthearted and didn't want anything to spoil this special moment.

Alita couldn't help herself. "Go Nat, go Nat. Go Nat. Baby girl is giving me fucking life."

Natalia turned up even more. Wagging her finger back and forth and setting her hands on her back hip. She reached back and tugged her ponytail looking like Ariana Grande.

She gestured at Edmund to follow her and he quickly did. She strutted around in a circle dancing and singing at the top of her lungs.

"B, I think you'd better go get your man before Natalia steals him."

"They're too cute. I don't want to interrupt. Considering how bumpy things have been with those two, this is like a breakthrough. Plus, she's been preparing for this moment for years. All the dancing and singing lessons."

"Ain't that something? I thought y'all had a *Mommie Dearest* type of relationship."

"Don't even try it, Alita. I've always been proud of my daughter. I know she's strong and observant. She can read people well and can spot a phony in a second, and that's what's scared me."

"You think she's sees something bad in Edmund?"

"I won't say all that. I think that she is just possessive and afraid of being abandoned. And anything that can possibly take me away from her, well, she's going to be suspicious. But the more she spends time around Edmund, I'm sure she can sense that he's a good solid man who would never hurt me. I just want to know for sure that she feels the same way I do."

"Which is?"

"I love that man. He's so perfect for us . . . an answer to prayer. He's my rock right now and I need all the help I can get, Alita. I know you can understand that." Burgundy's face lit up. The music had changed to a different song, same group. Natalia didn't look like she was ready to sit down just yet. She poked out her lips, walked up and down the floor, and rocked back and forth, but in a childlike way that was appropriate for her age. Edmund co-signed everything she did, clapping and yelling her name. They seemed like a team.

"Can you believe it? She's a little scene stealer. I love it," Burgundy said.

"Yeah, but what will Natalia do after the music stops playing, B? When they switch to a song that she doesn't like?"

"I hear what you're saying, Alita. We'll just have to find out. And I am going to hope for the best, alright?"

"Alright, Sis. I'll do the same."

Later that night after they got home, Burgundy was in her bedroom seated in a chair. She looked amused while Natalia and Sid both fought over who would roll up her hair. Burgundy had medium length hair that she liked to wear in a bob. But Natalia told her, "You need to make it prettier and wear some curls, Mommy." She proceeded to get a box filled with pink plastic rollers. Her coordination wasn't that great as she dropped a few rollers and wanted to cry as she watched them scatter to the floor.

"Natalia, you don't need to do this."

"Please Mommy. I want to do your hair."

"Okay, sweetheart."

Natalia picked up the rollers she'd dropped. She got the comb and brush and made her mother sit down. She dragged a tiny stepladder across the floor, then she climbed a couple of steps, and used the big comb to try and insert a part. She squirted setting lotion on a section of the hair then rolled it.

When she was done, she handed her mother a mirror.

Burgundy was stunned. "This looks pretty good."

"I told you I could make you look pretty."

"Are you trying to say that I'm ugly, Natalia?"

"No, you're the prettiest mommy in the world. And I love you so much." She grabbed Burgundy around the neck and planted several sweet kisses on her cheek.

Burgundy enjoyed experiencing one of the best evenings she'd had in a long time. "Thanks Nat. I love you too."

"That's why Mr. Edmund is always over here. Or why you're always leaving the house and going to Urgent Care."

"W-what?"

Natalia's face wore an innocent look. She resumed poking around in her mother's hair and singing softly to herself.

Burgundy was convinced that her daughter had no idea what she was talking about, that she just had a habit of listening in on grown folks conversations and repeating everything she heard.

Natalia ignored her mother's questioning eyes and pressed her nostrils against her mother's head. "I can tell you washed your hair. It smells good, like strawberries. Mr. Edmund will love that."

"Yes, baby, I think he will."

"Do you love him more than Daddy?"

"Natalia, I don't know what you're—"

"You love him, Mommy. I can tell. You smile when you're with him. And he loves you, too. He does a lot to show you how he feels about you. Just like you do when you show me and Sid that you love us. I like it. Love looks good on you."

"I can't believe you're saying all of this."

"I have to, Mommy. In my class, I know kids whose parents fight. They go to bed scared and they hide under the bed or under the blankets and cover their ears."

"What?"

"My friends don't always see love." Natalia stared solemnly at her mother and let the unspoken words speak to Burgundy.

"Baby girl. I am so sorry to hear that your classmates are going through this. Hopefully they can get some help."

"I am glad we have love in our house, Mommy. I think Daddy would like it too."

Burgundy wanted to blubber like a big kid.

"Well, Natalia, to answer your question about Mr. Edmund, I love him in a different type of way from your dad. Of course, I do have much love for him, Nat. I certainly don't want to lie to you about those kinds of things."

"Good." She paused. "What do you do when you go over to Mr. Edmund's house?"

"Oh, my. Um. W-we spend time together. We talk. We watch television."

"And?"

"We eat our favorite foods."

"And?"

"Um, Natalia. There are some things little kids shouldn't know. And I think you already know enough, young lady."

Natalia nodded and backed down. She then stared at Sidnee's hair and offered to comb it. Sidnee complained and squirmed, then she began to relax and let Natalia have her way.

"You girls are growing up so fast. You're taking care of

me, your sister. I am very, very proud of you, Natalia, and don't you ever forget that. You girls are my life."

"And Morning Glory."

"Yeah, that too."

"And Mr. Edmund."

Burgundy paused. It was true that he'd taken up an important space inside of her heart. And God only knew what it all would lead to, but for now, she was content. She felt stronger and steadier with each passing day.

"Natalia, I just want you to know that having love in your life is very important. For children, for parents, for everyone. Just like when a family buys a dog or a cat and they love their animals and give them a home and make the pets feel welcome and important. Everyone on earth wants and needs to experience that feeling, that loving feeling that lets them know that people are there for you and they care, and they want to be involved with all parts of your life, good or bad."

"Okay. And I'm sorry, Mommy. I'm sorry about those bad things I said to Mr. Edmund. I'm sorry but please don't put me on punishment."

Natalia unexpectedly burst into tears. She threw herself in Burgundy's arms. They cried together for a few minutes. Burgundy didn't want to break down like that in front of her kids, yet the release felt good and powerful, like a cleansing of sorts, and an unexpected doorway to new beginnings.

Sidnee stared at them and soon began to cry too. Before long, the three of them looked like drowned rats there were so many tears. Burgundy's hair suddenly knotted up and got sweaty and smelly.

"So much for that strawberry scented hair that I just had." Burgundy started cracking up. The girls quickly imitated their mom. There they were, the Taylor women, laughing until their sides hurt. By then, their clothes were damp and snot ran from their noses.

Burgundy was glad that Alita wasn't around to see them.

But she was also glad that love finally felt like it was winning.

Chapter 18

Evolution

On a quiet summer evening in July, Dru gave birth. Asher came two weeks early, which was a nice surprise. But he was healthy and Dru suffered no serious complications.

"This child is proof that if you keep the faith, sometimes, the thing that you hoping to have can actually be yours." She kissed her newborn and gratefully held Asher in her arms. Three days later, Dru and Tyrique brought home their first born.

"And now I feel complete," Dru said to Coco who had come over to help her with the baby.

"Motherhood looks good on you, sis."

Coco gave Dru a few pointers on how to nurse the baby, and some of the additional things she could do to childproof the home.

When Coco's cellphone rang, she quickly answered. "Hi Q. How is Chance?"

"He's good. We hanging today like mad crazy. Little man is wearing me out."

"I love it. But I hope you won't get too worn out by the time you bring him back home." She spoke with Q a little longer, and then hung up.

"Sorry about that. But when Q has Chance and calls me, I pick up no matter what."

"No problem," Dru told her. "How are things coming along with Calhoun?"

"I guess he's alright. I mean, as long as he does well by the girls, me and him don't have much to say to each other." Coco stared dreamily into space. "I think he's jealous because Q is now back in my life."

"That had to be hard for Calhoun to learn even though he did marry someone else."

"Why didn't me and him make it, Dru?"

"Coco, some things just aren't meant to be. Like sometimes, other people are rooting for a former couple to get back together, but what they don't realize is that the chemistry is all wrong. They don't know the details, but you must learn for yourself, Coco, that there are times when your relationship is not going to work out."

"Like what happened between you and Jerrod?"

"Exactly. When you think about it, you and I both dodged bullets. God is steadily working hard to protect us; he steers us away from the bullet, but we're chasing after it, like we want it to hit us or kill us. It's insane."

"When you put it like that, I think you're right. So now it's the era of Coco and Quantavius. Coco Chanel Mitchell. How's that sound?"

"Sounds silly if you ask me. I don't see Q as the marrying type."

"Hey," Coco said with a laugh. "If I plant that wedding bell seed inside his head, he just might up and marry me. Wouldn't that make Calhoun mad?"

"It would make him mad, but it would also make you look crazy."

"Oh Dru."

"Don't 'oh Dru' me. Please don't mess over Q like that.

I think you're feeling him or maybe you appreciate what he does for your son, but do not marry that man just for revenge. Don't use people like that."

"Dru!"

"Coco. I'm warning you. I won't be coming to your wedding so do not send me an invite. I will not stand by in silence watching you get your hooks into a man just because you want to make your ex jealous. That's wrong."

"For all you know, I'm the rebound."

"And neither of you deserves to have that title. Just think about what I'm telling you, Coco, and don't make any more stupid decisions for at least the next twenty years."

"Okay, damn, Dru."

A stand-by side chick. That's something Coco never wanted to be. The leftover meal that's eaten when there's nothing better to eat.

The woman that a man messes around with just to be doing something, but she's not his first choice.

That's how Coco had been feeling after hanging out with Q for another month. She decided to pump the brakes on her bogus relationship with Q. She told him she was no longer interested. And finally, in July, Coco's luck began to change. She met a new guy and they started to date. These dates felt different than the norm. Coco found herself being picked up by someone who owned a decent ride and who always arrived on time. This man opened her car door for her. He drove them to outings such as outdoor concerts, a few waterparks, and he even took them to a place called Tantrums. On this adventure, Coco got to let off some steam. She picked up a sledgehammer and totally destroyed a slew of old electronics, smashing up everything in sight until a timer went off. Coco never laughed so hard. She and her date enjoyed wonderful, memorable times together.

Coco didn't want to get her hopes up, but after a series of successful dates with her dream man, and as they continued to get to know each other, the goosebumps she kept feeling prevented her from keeping it in any longer.

By the end of the month, she placed a call to her sister.

"Alita," she said.

"What?"

"I got me a dude. A white dude."

"Stop lying. Noooo."

"I'm not lying, sis. Don't get me wrong. He ain't *white* white though; he's swagged out white, like Eminem. But he's still white."

Alita said, "Wow. I never could have believed it."

"I can barely believe it myself, but so far so good. We're having an amazing time hanging out, and I can tell he's feeling me. He thinks I'm fun and gorgeous. And he loves my cooking of course."

"Well a man has to eat."

"And he checks on me a lot to make sure I have everything I need."

"That's nice, but what about the other important shit, Coco?"

"Oh, he accepts all my kids."

"Coco!"

"He's just a really good dude. I'm happy. I can see myself with him. And thank God he is down with the swirl."

"What's his name?"

"Trevor."

"You went from Calhoun to Trevor? That's like chalk and cheese."

"I don't care. That's his name, whether you like it or not."

Alita burst out laughing. "As soon as you told me, I could have guessed his name. Either Trevor, or Connor, or Jacob, or Billy Bob—"

"Shut up, Lita. His name could have been Christopher Columbus, I wouldn't care as long as Chris treats me right."

"Chris Columbus won't treat you right, but I'm glad that Trevor does. Good for you, sis." Alita beamed from ear to ear. "We've got Jungle Fever, Coco's got Jungle Fever. Trevor's got Jungle Fever. They're in love."

"You're so silly."

Alita still wasn't satisfied. "I see you keep avoiding my question, I've been asking you about the most important part?"

"What Lita, what?"

"Is it true what they say about white men?"

Coco laughed. "Girl, please. Put it like this. He ain't packing a number-two pencil. His dick is as thick as a tree trunk and he knows how to put it down."

"Well, that's alright then girl, I ain't mad at you."

"And Trevor's credit score is 820."

"What the hell is he doing with you? He sounds unreal. Like you made him up."

"Lita, stop. He's as real as they come. He's single. And he's all mine."

"Coco, I gotta see this guy. When can you make that happen?"

"It'll be a long time before I let you meet my new man, Lita. A real long time. If ever."

"Why I gotta wait that long? That ain't fair."

"Let me think about it and I'll let you know when or if it's okay for you to meet my Prince Charming. You're not about to mess up my good thing, Lita. Not with your track record. No way."

The two sisters laughed and chitchatted, and for the first time in a long-time, life felt like old times.

It was late on a Friday night. Burgundy had worked her fingers to the bone that day, running back and forth from one restaurant to another trying hard to stay on top of her business.

By the time the day ended, she drove herself home, got a plate of food from the fridge that Liz had prepared for her, and then microwaved it. She brought the plate of meatloaf, mashed potatoes, and a green salad on a tray and set it on her bed. She picked up the remote control and found a romantic comedy to watch on Netflix. She scraped up some food on her fork and opened her mouth. By the time she finished eating several mouthfuls of food, Burgundy was sound asleep. The TV blared for the next few hours. When she awoke around two, her stomach felt knotted up.

She cried out in pain. Her forehead was covered in sweat. And the clothes that she was still wearing stuck to her chest. The tips of her fingers felt like ice cubes.

"I need to use the bathroom and change into my nightgown." She got up out of the bed, and fell right to the floor. She grabbed her stomach. The pain hurt so badly she wondered if she was about to die. Fear took her over. Her cell phone wasn't with reach. The girls slept upstairs. She was worried that if she called out to them they wouldn't hear her.

"Owww, my God. It hurts. God help me."

Normally, Burgundy kept her cell phone on the other side of the room. It would be charging all night long. It was actually only a few feet away but the pain was so terrible that the distance seemed like a few miles.

She got on her knees and slumped back to the floor on her belly. Her legs had no strength. So she mustered up all the power she could and began to crawl on her hands and knees. She kept going and cried as she reached over to touch her cell phone.

"Lord, please don't let me die. Please don't leave my kids without any parents." She grabbed her cell phone, clutched her stomach with one hand, and dialed Edmund with the other.

He arrived in no time at all. The alarm went off, but she had given Edmund the four-digit passcode and he turned it off as soon as he entered the house. He raced to her bedroom and held her in his arms.

"You're hot as hell. Do you have a thermometer?" he asked.

She mumbled and instructed Edmund to check the medicine cabinet.

Soon he took her temperature and whistled.

"One hundred and one. You need to go to the hospital."

"No, just pat me with some cold, wet towels. I'm scared, Edmund. Don't leave me. Don't take me to the hospital either."

"Okay, but I'm not comfortable with that," he said looking skeptical.

He got some towels, ran cold water on them and patted her head, cheeks, neck and shoulders. He removed her top and found a clean, dry shirt and helped to pull it over her head. Edmund looked down on her with tenderness and made sure she felt comfortable.

"Baby, how you feeling, describe it to me."

"It's indescribable. My head is throbbing. And it won't stop. I feel like I want to die. Like I'm about to die."

"No! No you're not!" He shouted. "Don't say that." There were circles under Edmund's eyes, and it seemed like he'd aged ten years. "Take deep breaths and picture yourself getting better. Can you do that for me?"

"Uh, I don't know. I can't picture it."

"Burgundy?"

"Okay, all right." She took a few deep breaths until her breathing felt normal. But seconds later she moaned over and over again.

"What the hell is going on?" Edmund asked, trying not to feel anxious.

She lay back on the bed then turned over and fell into the fetal position. "Everything hurts. The pain is terrible. And I'm thirsty. I feel bloated. I feel like pure shit. I can't take this."

"That's it. Let's go. Now. We're going to the emergency room."

"No, no. Last time I did that someone died. I-I don't want to die."

"I don't want you to die either." This time tears surfaced in Edmund's eyes. He couldn't imagine life without Burgundy and he did not want to lose her.

"I love you, Burgundy, you hear me? And you are going to make it. Think about your kids."

She could only moan in response.

He asked her if she had eaten. Burgundy nodded, then pointed to the plate of food that had been halfway eaten.

"Fuck," he said. He noticed the romaine lettuce that had been recalled recently. It had been on the news all day. But since she had been so busy maybe she hadn't heard.

Edmund got a spoon, then picked up Burgundy and carried her to the commode.

He made her slouch next to the toilet seat. He opened her mouth and stuck the spoon down her throat. She gagged then emptied her stomach.

Burgundy lay on the cold floor of her bathroom. When he took her temperature again, and it gave a normal reading, Edmund relaxed for the first time since she'd called him.

"I feel so much better," Burgundy told him with a grateful smile. "That was the worst pain I ever felt in my life."

"You feel better, my love?"

"Yes. Yes, I do. Thank you, sweetie."

"Damn woman, you had me going there for a second."

He lifted Burgundy up in his arms and carried her back to her bedroom then went to run a warm bath. Unbeknownst to her, Natalia had snuck into Burgundy's room. She'd hidden there on the floor on the far side of the bed. She quietly laid on her stomach watching everything that had been happening. No one had noticed Natalia. But she definitely saw them. Her eyes took in everything as she watched the tender care that Edmund supplied to her mother. Natalia heard when Edmund told Burgundy he loved her. She saw her mother's petrified look from the fear of dying and noted the loving way that Edmund eased her anxieties.

"Thank you, Daddy," she quietly said to herself as she wiped a few tears from her eyes. Then Natalia carefully made her way out of the room without anyone noticing her.

A couple of weeks later, Burgundy set up a surprise for Natalia. But she held her breath and crossed her fingers. She had no idea how everything would pan out.

She'd visited Natalia's school without her even knowing. She talked with her teachers to see how the girl was progressing since her father passed. They said that her grades had slightly dropped, and she'd become sullen and cynical in the immediate aftermath of Nate's death, but during the last couple months she'd improved in more positive ways.

"I'm very glad to hear that. At times I feel she's doing well, and other times I'm not so sure."

"We understand, Mrs. Taylor, and don't worry, everyone in the school loves Natalia. We keep her busy and she enjoys staying busy. We pick up on her moods and try not to push her too hard. I think she'll be just fine."

"Great. That's all I wanted to know."

Later that week, when Natalia was at school, Burgundy went shopping at Nordstrom, Natalia's favorite store, for the type of clothes she liked to wear.

That night she called Natalia into her bedroom and closed the door behind her.

"Nat," she said. "I wanted to ask you a question."

"Okay."

"How do you feel about going to the Father-Daughter dance?"

"I want to go, but my daddy is dead."

"Yes, he is, but you can still go if you want."

"What do you mean? Am I going to be dancing by myself? Will all my friends be with their daddy?" She looked mortified.

"No, Nat. I have a different type of plan."

"You mean you'll go and pretend like you're my father?"

"No, I won't be doing that. But someone else can."

"Who?" Realization settled into her eyes. "Oh. Him. Is that why we went to that crab restaurant?"

Natalia's voice sounded accusatory and hurt.

"No, baby. Remember you're the one who asked if we could go to that restaurant?"

"Oh. Okay. I forgot." She laughed.

Burgundy knew her daughter very well and tried a different approach. "Tell you what. Let's pretend like you wanted to go. Out of all the dresses you own, what would you want to wear?" Before Natalia could respond, Burgundy ran into her closet and pulled out a couple of dresses that were on hangers.

"Would you want this one, or this one?"

"Oh Mommy. Those are new. I've never seen them before."

"I bought them for you, Nat."

"Thank you, Mommy. I like both of them. May I have them both?"

"Absolutely. That way you could come in wearing one dress and leave the party in a whole different dress."

Her eyes lit up. "I love that plan. I don't think any other girl will be doing that. Yes. I want to go."

"Good." They hugged, and Burgundy felt relieved.

And on the day of the event, she helped Natalia to get ready. Burgundy arranged for a mobile hairstylist to come to their house. She charged eighty bucks an hour and was skilled enough to create the most beautiful set of braids a little girl could want. Feeling overjoyed, Burgundy fussed over her daughter's clothing and shoes until everything looked picture perfect.

Edmund came to pick her up dressed in his very best suit and tie.

Burgundy felt so nervous. When Natalia emerged from upstairs and walked down the staircase, she had no idea what would happen. Would Natalia flake out on her?

Edmund stared at Natalia. "My date looks very beautiful tonight, wouldn't you say so, Burgundy?"

"I know she'll be the prettiest girl on the dance floor."

Edmund drove Natalia over to the school. And Burgundy drove in a separate car, making sure not to forget her daughter's second change of clothing.

When it was time to dance Edmund and Natalia resembled a couple from *Dancing with the Stars*. They were in sync, and Natalia could tell that her dance partner had been practicing. He wasn't as stiff as he'd been in times past.

"You're making me look good, Mr. Edmund."

"Don't give me any credit. You're the pro at this thing, Nat."

She frowned, then smiled. "Only my daddy could call me Nat."

"Oops, sorry. I forgot."

"But I don't mind if you call me that. You're kind of like my daddy now anyways."

Edmund said nothing. The lump in his throat kept him from talking. Besides, he didn't want to spoil the moment by saying anything stupid. They danced for a while then smiled for the camera as Burgundy took loads of photos and videos.

Midway, Natalia changed into her second outfit.

When they began to dance, she and Edmund pretty much stole the evening. Her classmates sneered at her or ignored them altogether. And Natalia relished all the attention she was getting, positive and negative.

For the last dance, she could hardly contain her joy.

She told her mother to pay attention. The music began playing. Natalia sang along, "I want to dance with somebody . . . with somebody who loves me." She stared directly at her dance partner while singing. Then she and Edmund performed a series of pirouettes that wowed the crowd.

"Are you freaking kidding me," Burgundy murmured to herself. She proudly watched as her daughter took the lead. Soon other little girls tried to imitate Natalia and Edmund, but none looked as polished.

When it was all over, Edmund came over for a hug and a smooch. Burgundy happily kissed him. She didn't care that people looked on with disapproval. It didn't bother her when she heard murmurings of "Isn't she a widow?"

Burgundy felt free enough to live and embrace her new life. And she didn't care who disagreed with her choices.

* * *

"Can you believe it?" This was the question that Alita posed to Dru one early fall morning when they were strolling through the local mall. They entered a little boutique and browsed through what seemed like hundreds of exquisitely designed cocktail dresses. Alita snatched a handful and quickly disappeared into a dressing room. Moments later she emerged.

"How does this one look?" Alita modeled a white satin strapless dress.

"I can see you in this one. It looks beautiful, Lita. I think that's the one."

"Do you? Or are you just saying that because your little man is making you feel exhausted?"

Dru smiled at her sister then peered lovingly down at Asher who sat happily in his stroller. "He could never make me tired. As long as I waited to have my miracle child, nothing he could do can tire me out."

"Ha! Wait till he becomes a teenager."

"Alita Washington."

"Oh, my goodness. Chills just went through my spine, Dru." Alita reached out to touch her sister. "You see my arm trembling?"

"Um, no."

"Dru, just think about it. Very soon I'll be making a name change.

"Yes, girl. I'm glad you're about to finally do what makes you happy."

"Mrs. Shade Wilkins," Alita announced. "I can barely believe it and I can't wait."

"He's the final husband of Alita Reeves huh?"

"Yes indeed! No more marriages for me after that. I swear to God," Alita smiled like she was joking but she felt very serious. "We're a good match. Shade has proven himself many times that he can handle a woman like me.

Ha!" She said and rolled her eyes. "Not every man in the world can handle a woman like me."

"Ain't that the truth."

Alita went on to inform Dru that in a couple of weeks she would move out of the condo that she and Elyse shared. Shade felt they should have their own place and he found them a luxury apartment located a couple of neighborhoods from Elyse.

"My daughter is growing up, becoming her own woman. I told her as long as she doesn't move Gamba in with her I'm okay with her living in that spot. She deserves it. And Leno? Thank God, he's still staying with his dad. Did you know Leno decided to enroll in the community college? I guess that's good enough to do while he works part-time at the Nissan dealership. But he also still practices shooting the ball a lot more than he used to."

"I'm glad he hasn't given up on being a pro basketball player. Maybe he could go semi-pro or play in Europe."

Alita agreed. "That would work. I'm sorry his dreams didn't go exactly as planned, but I'm happy yours did." She waved at her nephew who stared at her from his stroller.

"I have to say I'm impressed by how you've really taken on the role of being a mommy. What part you like the most?" Alita asked.

"Everything, Alita." Dru's voice was breathless and filled with joy. "I find myself running into his room all the time. And I stand and look at him when he's sleeping in his crib. I stare at everything he does, and I listen to him yawn and make little cooing noises. And Alita, this is embarrassing and don't tell anybody . . ."

"I won't. You know me. I don't talk to nobody."

"Alita," she smiled, "I take all kinds of videos of him like a crazy celebrity but I don't post them on Snapchat every hour."

"Thank God for that."

"Basically, Alita, I love the whole thing. When I spend time with him early in the morning, I love that he's looking for me. I can tell he knows my voice and Tyrique's. He sits there and waits on us to come play with him."

Dru's voice was filled with delight and wonder. "Sometimes, Lita, I want to pinch myself. Because I never, ever thought I'd live to see the day that I would give birth to a healthy baby. Honestly, I had given up. I-I thought I would only be Auntie Dru, which would have been just as fine." She leaned over to nuzzle her son's chunky cheeks. "But I swear there is nothing like being a mommy to my own child. It is a blessing indeed. I promise to be the best mother ever."

The usual poisonous words that Alita was accustomed to saying remained buried in her head. Instead her heart filled with thankfulness and pride. It felt good to see her sisters happy and thriving for a change. And she wanted all of them to succeed.

"Well, after I buy this dress we will need to go and buy little man his tux or suit or something. My treat."

Dru laughed out loud. Alita did too. For it was rare that Alita could afford to buy a pricey item for someone else. But she'd finally obtained a decent job that paid a good enough salary so that she didn't have to take on extra jobs. Her life was transforming in more ways than one.

"My goodness, Lita. Thanks for offering to buy Asher an outfit. You don't have to do that."

"Aww, it ain't nothing. I'm glad to do it. I just don't understand why it seemed I always had to go through so much hell in my life to experience good things. But I guess as long good eventually happens, that's what really counts."

"Adversity," Dru announced. "It either makes you or it breaks you."

"Well, after it's all over with and you find yourself smashed into a dozen pieces, what does that mean?"

"It means you need to take time to regroup and pull yourself back together again."

"That's how I feel, Dru. It took a mighty long time but I feel like I've been put back together again. I feel like a whole person for a change." Alita smiled. "It feels damned good, too."

The two sisters went to the checkout line and discussed other minor details concerning Alita's upcoming nuptials. It was an exciting time and a nerve-racking time, but Alita felt she was up to the challenge.

"I'm on a new path to somewhere. Exactly where it's going, I don't know. But I want to see where it leads me."

"I feel the same way," Dru replied.

Chapter 19

Power

It was Christmas Eve, a full year after her husband had died.

Edmund was at the house warming up apple cider and preparing the fireplace to be lit even though it wasn't brutally cold outside.

The fresh smell given off by the live pine tree enhanced the holiday season and put everyone in a cheerful, lighthearted mood. Natalia placed her favorite ornaments on the branches. And Sidnee laughed in delight when her mother plugged in the holiday lights that began to flash and twinkle every few seconds.

Each of them was wearing matching family thermal pajamas that were entirely lined with red and green reindeer, snowflakes, and Christmas tree decorations. Red Santa Hats topped their heads.

"Look, Mr. Edmund, something is in your stocking." Sidnee pointed to the stocking with his name embroidered.

"Ahh, cool."

He tried to peek into the stocking but Natalia stopped him. "Excuse me. No cheating, Mr. Edmund. You gotta wait till tomorrow."

"Yes, ma'am," he told her.

When the doorbell rang, Burgundy raced to the door. She greeted two women and their kids: Amaka and Camille. They were the ladies who were benefactors from the foundation she'd established. She provided funding for women who were at-risk. And the director of her foundation placed her in touch with a couple of women who did not have families to be with around the holidays. Amaka and Camille welcomed the opportunity to go hang out with Burgundy on Christmas Eve. Amaka was tall, slender and willowy, and gave off an elegant yet fragile vibe. Camille was more robust, petite, and seemed like it hurt to laugh. She was shy yet warm.

"Alrighty, then ladies. Since you're hanging out at my house tonight, you must wear the official Taylor family holiday PJ's. Make yourself feel comfy, then proceed to our family room. There's a brand new set waiting for you, in your size."

"Are you kidding me," Camille asked. In the not so distant past, she'd suffered from an addiction. She'd had a habit of taking all the antidepressants that her body would allow. She was raised in the church and loved going whenever she could. But her husband used to brutalize her with his fists right before they went to services. He served on the deacon board and was a stickler for a wife being hidden and submissive. Camille was loving but not exactly stupid. And when she'd fight back, she'd get her head busted with an iron, or clubbed in the thighs with a Kentucky slugger. Her family would ask her what happened. She'd lie about her bruises and cover for her husband. Camille suffered in that relationship for five years before she managed to escape with just the clothes on her bloodied and swollen back.

That was three months ago; her physical scars were long gone but the emotional ones still needed to be healed.

"Camille, now, you go on and get yourself changed.

Use the guest room bathroom. Get some apple cider. There are chocolate chip cookies baked by my sister Coco. I don't know if you've met her or not. She's one of the best bakers in the city."

"I heard that," Camille said. "I love to bake too. And my son will probably eat up all the cookies so I hope y'all made a lot of them."

The ladies proceeded into the house and after a while the whole gang sat around listening to Christmas music and simply enjoying the moment for what it was.

"I love this," Amaka said. At first she'd been too shy and intimidated to really get relaxed. Her own personal story was so humiliating she thought that Burgundy would judge her like so many other people had done in the past.

"When I lost it all, I never thought I'd get back on my feet," she said in a tiny voice. "Julius, that's my ex," she explained to Edmund. "He was a good guy, but really sucked when it came to money. And I trusted him to take care of the finances and he pretty much squandered the money. It was a settlement inheritance I got when my parents got killed in a plane crash. When we first got married, we struggled a lot. So, after the money came, we kind of went nuts with lots of shopping sprees. But I calmed down and started wanting to get serious about the money and savings and investments. But Julius got caught up. And anyway, I lost it all. We lost our beautiful home. We became homeless. He wasn't working. I lost my job. I lost it all. We lived in my car. Me and my son. And Julius, for some strange reason, blamed it all on me! And he beat me up 'cause now he was homeless. Anyway, after he tried to set our car on fire, that was it for me. I had to leave. And if it wasn't for you letting us stay at the safe house, I don't know what I would have done."

"Amaka, don't give me the credit." Burgundy was serious. "I was blessed to have a vision, and fortunate enough that it came to the light of day. But honestly, God should get the glory."

"God is why I ended up on the streets," Amaka said.

"Then God must be the reason that you're now off the streets, too," Burgundy said with a smile. "Things happen, good and bad to all of us. The sun shines on all of us, Christians, atheists, and the rain falls on each of us all well. Anything can happen to anybody. It's how we respond to those things that count."

"She's right," Camille said. "We want to blame God for the bad things, and pat ourselves on the back for the good stuff. But I don't care who does what, I just like when things work out in the end. I like it when life feels right and I have a feeling that I and you are going to be alright, Amaka."

Amaka barely smiled but after staring at the beautiful house and the love shown between Burgundy, Edmund and her kids, a little bit of hope got stirred in her heart. She wanted all those things. She may have lost it all before, but surely she could gain it back too.

Everyone had a grand time during the rest of the evening. And the next morning, Burgundy woke up early and went outside the house to enjoy the peacefulness of another Christmas day. She stood in front of her house and looked up. Burgundy watched as the sun began to rise in the eastern sky. It was as if morning was waking up. Or like morning was letting go of yesterday. A bluish, yellowish, orangey color framed the heavens in a way that was absolutely breathtaking. She couldn't take her eyes off of the quiet, peaceful scene. Then an eagle flew overhead. She'd never seen one in person and she could only gasp. And in that moment she felt strengthened and filled with hope.

She felt grateful to be alive.

It was an after all is said and done moment. When you knew that you'd made it. Things may have been tough, but dammit, you made it through anyway.

Coco and Elyse were the first ones to arrive at the next Sister Day meeting. It was going to be at Elyse's condo. Alita had yet to arrive. Dru could potentially not even make it since she was tied up with Asher who'd gotten a slight cold. And Burgundy was on her way.

"We can talk, us two can," Coco said. I have some things to get off my chest. Things I should have admitted a long time ago."

Elyse swallowed the fear lodged in her throat. At this point she was becoming weary of all the confessions and spilled secrets. But since Coco wanted to come clean, she'd give her aunt a fair listen.

"What's up, Coco?"

"I still can't forget how bad I felt being locked up. Keeping my mouth closed about some things, and opening it up on other irrelevant shit."

"I'm sorry you had to go through being locked up. Remember how scared you were that it was going to happen. And it did. But now you're out. You don't have to even think about it anymore. You were found not guilty."

"Oh, but am I?"

"What are you talking about, Coco?"

"I'm talking about if Nate's death was my fault?"

"No! It wasn't. Unless you know something I don't know."

Coco's face went from angry to thoughtful. "See, it's like this. That night when we went to Nate and Burgundy's house, I did tell Natalia to turn off that oven. That's not up for debate. Because she did just as I told her. I went back into that house and I made sure that the oven was turned off. But then something else happened. Something I never wanted anyone else to know because if they knew I could go back into jail."

"Coco! What are you talking about?"

"Elyse, tell me something. Are you happy with your life?"

Elyse nodded. "Of course, I am. My man loves me and I am crazy about him. We're building a new life together. What could be better than that?"

"I'm glad to hear you say that." Coco clasped her hands behind her back. Once again she was in thinking, pacing, and talking mode.

"I'm glad you're happy and I want you to stay happy. But I gotta get something out. Something that's been eating me up inside for a long time."

"What's that?"

"Come over here," Coco demanded.

Elyse did as she was asked.

"Give me your hand," Coco said.

"Pinky swear?" Elyse asked. She did not wait for Coco to answer. Elyse lifted her hand and extended her finger. Coco curled hers around Elyse's. This time the two fingers stuck together like super glue. Tied together forever. Like a blood tie.

"I swear Coco, I swear that whatever you're about to tell me, I will never breathe a word to another soul."

"You mean it? Not even to your man?"

"No, I promise."

"And even if you two break up—"

"Coco, me and Gamba are together forever, you hear me?"

"Alright but just in case, Elyse." Coco's eyes watered. She thought of dreams, possibilities, hope and broken promises. Yeah, she knew that her road had been wrought with difficult changes and she was relieved that she had come to make peace with Calhoun. But Coco realized that

Elyse was still young. She did not yet know everything about love and how it could change you.

"Look, sis. I don't want anything bad to happen to you, I swear to God." Coco's voice broke. "And I know you're going to do better than me at everything in life. I just feel it, but even so, I need to know that you are going to take this secret to the grave, just like I plan to take my secret to the grave."

"Coco, you're scaring me."

"Just listen. I need you to know that Nate really did himself in. But it wasn't because he chose to do it on his own. I forced him to kill himself, Elyse."

"What? But how?"

"I told him to write the suicide note. Remember Burgundy's gun? When I went back in the house, I pointed the gun at him and told him what to say. I told him to turn that oven back on in a few hours. He said he wouldn't do it. But I told him if he didn't do it, his kids would suffer."

"Noooo, Coco. Please tell me you're making this all up."

"I'm not. I was in sicko mode because I did some dirty things, Elyse. I made him swear that he'd turn that oven back on. And I know that when I left him that the suicide note was in the kitchen. But after it all happened, and the suicide note couldn't be found, that's when I felt that Nate tried to screw me over. That if there was no note, then it would look like a murder and he was hoping that I would be charged for the crime. I think that's what was on his mind."

"But then the note was found in the storage facility in their backyard."

"Right. Marty ended up finding that note. It scared the shit out of me but it also vindicated me. The only thing that people don't know is that yeah, I made him write that note."

"But why?"

"Elyse, that man wanted to die. Seriously wanted out of here. I could tell. He knew that he was going to be arrested. He wanted to die but he didn't have the balls to do it on his own." Coco gasped. "I helped him to do something that he was scared to do himself."

"But Coco. What about Sid? She was in the house too. She could have died."

"I know. And I will never forgive myself for what almost happened to my niece. When Sid went into that coma, I swear to God, I wanted to kill myself too. I wanted to end it all. But I did something that no one knows about. I prayed to the Lord that he would bring that girl back to life. Elyse, I prayed harder than I ever prayed about anything. To my surprise, God brought that girl out that coma. And that's when I knew good things can happen even if it doesn't even look like they can. Even when we don't even deserve half of them."

Elyse was momentarily stunned. The magnitude of what Coco told her was more than she could have ever imagined. The truth was an ugly thing but it could also be a liberating thing as well.

"This is good news, yet terrible at the same time. I kind of hate that you told me."

"What are you saying, Elyse? I hope you don't betray me."

"I promised you I won't betray you and I meant it."

"Great. But why do you hate that I told you?"

"Because," Elyse said in a stubborn tone. "Sometimes people don't know what to do with secrets. Some keep them. Some tell them. And me, I just want to forget them. I want to forget all about the Reeves Sisters's secrets and live my life. That's the only thing I plan to do."

"I agree with you, Elyse. There are some secrets that family members have to take to the grave."

TWO YEARS LATER

Coming full circle may take a while but the journey will always be worth it. It was a beautiful Friday afternoon in Houston. Burgundy stood before a crowd of hundreds. The mayor was present, along with his staff, a couple of well-known African American senators, and other luminaries. They all stood before the gleaming newly renovated facility.

Beaming and feeling a bit nervous, Burgundy got into position as a dozen photographers walked around snapping tons of pictures.

Burgundy knew that many of the politicians were there in attendance for unscrupulous reasons. But she didn't care one bit.

She smiled and winked at Alita Wilkins and her husband Shade. She almost cried when she glanced at her sister Dru who was holding her son, Asher Reeves Evans, in her arms. By then Asher had grown nice and plump. He was a big boy, probably too big to be held at that age, but Burgundy completely understood Dru's need to hold her baby.

Elyse stood next to Gamba looking every bit like a happily married couple. Burgundy was so proud of her niece that she wanted to scream. Elyse was definitely one of the main reasons why the building was even in existence in the first place.

But even more than her family, Burgundy's eyes grew moist at all the nameless, anonymous women who stood in the crowd. They were single mothers, separated mothers, nonworking women who had fallen onto hard times. There were women in their twenties, thirties, and quite a few in their fifties and sixties. Life had beaten them down; they needed a house of refuge so they could heal and learn to love themselves, and find a reason for living.

Once the formalities were gotten out of the way with the mayor going on and on about how important it was to have the Sidnee Taylor Safe House For Women, Burgundy was handed the large pair of scissors so she could cut the ribbon.

"First of all," she said, "thanks to everyone for your support. This is a dream come true. A dream that came about because of a few nightmares, a few hardships I had to personally endure and overcome. If there's one thing the past couple of years have shown me is that all we have is what we experience, and what we leave behind. And so, let's leave behind good things, things that can help others."

"Amen, sis," Alita said.

"I went through a lot of challenges but decided I won't give up on love, life, family, and anything else that I cherish. And one thing I cherish is the ability to empower women. I want the safe house to be instrumental in building up women whose lives have been torn all the way down, like mine was." Burgundy gulped and fought back a stream of tears. Feeling embarrassed yet strengthened, Burgundy cleared her throat. "Give me a second. I need to get a hold of myself before I make a fool of myself."

"Too late, sis," Alita blurted out. Everyone chuckled. They were touched by her humility and clapped as Burgundy dabbed at a stray tear. Burgundy could only smile at the crowd for being patient and understanding. She blew a kiss at Alita and allowed her heart to love her crazy sister more than ever.

"Hey," Burgundy continued. "Rumor has it that I'm perfect. But I'm here to let you know that I'm not."

"We knew that already, sis." Alita was on a roll.

Burgundy smiled again. "And if it takes me making my own mistakes, screwing up and admitting that I was wrong, I'm willing to do that. But enough about me. This is about you, the women of our community, the ladies who will benefit from this dream. So, it gives me tremendous pleasure to cut the ribbon and officially open the doors of the Taylor Safe House for Women."

"Sidnee Taylor!" That was Sid, who was now eight years old. She knew enough to know that the building was named after her, a wondrous gesture that made her very excited.

People clapped and cheered and the photographers rushed over to take a photo of the smart, confident, stylish little girl who knew that she was doing something good even though she did not totally understand what it all meant.

Natalia ran over to hug her sister. She was ten years old and becoming a fine young girl. She wanted Sid to know that all was well and that she was happy for such a great event.

Burgundy continued. "Before we go see the facility, I have a special announcement. I've been thinking. It gives me great joy to be able to do something that empowers women, but I've decided to move forward on a project that will also empower men."

A gasp could be heard and a quiet rumble of surprise filled the air.

"Men need help just like women. They shouldn't be left out. They need to be made whole and know that they too are loved and needed." Her eyes moistened at the thought of Nate. He was no longer in her heart like he used to be and she could only wish that she'd been able to help him back when he was alive and struggling with his own dark secrets.

"No matter who we are or how we appear on the outside, we all need each other. And so I am making a decision about gutting and restoring a building that's currently unoccupied on the southwest side of town."

"Cool," Dru said. "Do you have a name for it yet?"

"Yes," Burgundy answered. "I'm thinking of calling it the Man Power Support Center."

At that point, Edmund Murray stepped up from behind Burgundy and boldly squeezed her hand. He kissed her on the cheek and whispered, "I'm so proud of you."

She nodded, closed her eyes and gave thanks, for big dreams that could become a reality.

When her speech was over, Burgundy stood around talking to a few people as they prepared to go inside the building. First she noticed that Raven had shown up at the ceremony. From the moment Burgundy first met the abused woman at Morning Glory a couple years ago, she was unable to get her out of her mind. Burgundy waved at Raven and welcomed her with a warm hug.

"I see you still have on your Morning Glory uniform," Burgundy told her. At that point, Elyse came over to join them.

"Yeah, it feels so good to have a steady job, Ms. Taylor. Working at your café has been the best five months of my life. Thank you and Elyse for welcoming me like I'm family."

"You *are* family," Elyse told her.

"That's exactly how you make me feel," Raven said in a thankful tone. "And I'm sure you've heard by now that my boyfriend—"

"Your ex boyfriend, I hope," Burgundy told her.

"Yes. He's an ex. A dead ex to be honest." Raven's face appeared unemotional yet strong. "God don't like ugly. I dumped him a few weeks ago. But he started harassing me and one day, he called himself getting angry. He was racing around in his car and he tried to cross the railroad tracks even though a train was clearly coming." She paused. "The train hit his car. He didn't make it out alive. Lord have mercy on his soul."

Burgundy felt astounded yet she wasn't surprised.

"Hatred and anger and ugliness never wins," she told Raven and Elyse. "Love always feels better. Love always wins."

"Amen," Elyse told her.

Before long, the crowd gathered together so they could march into the building. Everything inside looked pristine. It smelled of sawdust, fresh paint, oak floors, and new furnishings.

"Everyone, feel free to take a look around, but please follow me to this other very special room that is a surprise even to my sisters." Burgundy lead the group of people to a double glass door located at the far end of the hallway. A big red bow covered it so that no one could see inside.

"Welcome to the Sister Day Spa."

Burgundy pulled off the ribbon. They walked inside and found two manicure tables and three pedicure stations. Mounted on the wall was a cabinet filled with one hundred bottles of nail polish. There were nail tool kits at each station, and a large table filled with the latest fashion magazines.

"If you'll notice on the wall above each of these stations are all of our names engraved in gold plated signs: Alita, Burgundy, Coco, Dru and Elyse."

"Wow, B," Dru said. "I don't understand. What is this?"

"It was a secret room that the architect helped me to design. Basically our own Sister Day meetings inspired this vision. It reminded me of all those times when we'd go and just bond and talk and get everything out on the table and get empowered. The Sister Day spa is the place where abused women will come and get their nails and toes done and sip on non-alcoholic drinks. They'll get pampered and be made to feel beautiful and important. They can talk and relax and forget about their problems, if only for an hour or two." She paused. "It's a place of hope. A place of new beginnings. And so this spa represents the Reeves Sisters. How we started out and how we've ended up."

Alita was momentarily speechless. Never in her wildest imagination could she have dreamt of such a thing.

"All I have to say is . . . good job, B. I like it. I like it a lot. I wish Greta Reeves could see this. Our mama would be so damned proud."

A Sister's Power Theme Song
© Cydney Rax

We may fight
But I'm not worried
We're going to make up
Then everything will be alright
You're my sister
You're my family
I love you so
And that's the way that things should be
I've got your back
And I know you have mine
We are family and everything will be alright
That's our power
That's our strength
We are family
And that's the way that things should be
You've got a friend
You've got a friend
You've got a friend in me
You've got a friend in me
Alita, Burgundy, Coco, Dru and Elyse
These are the Reeves Sisters

THANK YOUS

Say *what*?

I get to shout out some folks again? Hallelujah!!!

Thank you to the readers that support the books, read them, and tell others (especially Trish Phillips). Your allegiance has helped to make my dreams come true.

Much thanks to my publisher, my editor Esi Sogah, publicist Samantha McVeigh, and the entire team that helps create my books.

I owe a ton of gratitude to the fabulous libraries across America and in other parts of the world. The collections people, the acquisitions librarians (or whatever your title is). THANK YOU for supporting my books. I love to browse your website and see what books are circulating.

To book clubs such as The Blended and the Beautiful of Kansas City, KS, Cover Girl Book Club of Memphis, and Allure Book Club of New Orleans, thank you ladies for reading and getting actively into the novels. And many thanks to supportive readers Alana Scott Matthews and Toni Howard.

To the Literary Lobbyist; thanks for your hard work on behalf of writers.

And: PopSugar.com, thank you for highlighting my novel and describing it in such a lovely way. I am indeed honored by your graciousness.

Special thanks to Deputy Jay Stewart whose knowledge about jail conditions was invaluable.

To my writer colleague Keith Lee Johnson. I owe you! Thanks so much for the help.

And to sister/friend/fellow writer Chelsia McCoy. You

are a breath of fresh air. Thanks for the laughs, the divine connection, the realness that is you.

And thanks to little Jayniah for sharing with me the inside story of her eight-year-old life.

To web supporters of literature such as The Root and SuperSelected.com. Thank you for bringing attention to all the excellent writers that have something to say, a message to share.

Hit me up via Facebook, Instagram or email (booksbycyd@aol.com) and let me know your thoughts about A SISTER'S POWER.

Cydney